TELLING TIME

TELLING TIME
A Novel

Marie Adams

SPHINX

First published in 2015 by Karnac Books.

This edition published 2018 by Sphinx, an imprint of
Aeon Books
12 New College Parade
Finchley Road
London
NW3 5EP

British Library Cataloguing in Publication Data

A C.I.P. for this book is available from the British Library

ISBN-13: 978-1-91257-328-8

Typeset by V Publishing Solutions Pvt Ltd., Chennai, India

Printed in Great Britain

www.aeonbooks.co.uk

www.sphinxbooks.co.uk

PART ONE

ONE

On the last day of my old life I closed and locked the office door behind me, handbag knocking hard against my hip while I turned the key, that one extra click to ensure it was double bolted. There was nothing out of the ordinary, nothing to indicate a breach in the predictable pattern of life except that I was in a rush, and now I don't know what for, or why. To meet someone important, or to catch a train?

I've always been good at closing doors, those invisible portals between one stage of life and another. I suppose this particular talent of mine, this ability to effect closure, at least within my own mind, is what helped me to shut the door behind me and move back into my own life at the end of every working day. Not to do so would mean drowning in the sorrows of others, and I have a horror of death. The transition isn't always easy. To sit for hours listening to patients, to witness raw grief and withstand the hot tip of molten anger are the everyday fodder of my profession. Now I know I was hiding behind their misery—behind that door again, where I could pretend they were all so much worse off than me, and where I truly believed that I could be of some use.

Hubris is simply a shield against the worst fears about ourselves, and I speak with some authority.

But back to that door, the one at the end of that particular working day. My office is on the top floor of a Victorian house which I share with two other therapists and a dentist on the ground floor. Careful down the steps, my hand running smooth along the banister, I remember registering that Daniel and Martha were still in their offices, "Do Not Disturb" signs hanging on their doors.

As I passed Keith's office door, the scent of clove oil and tooth decay wasn't so strong as on other days, but there was still the scream of the drill, a little muted through the thickness of the walls. I remember wincing at the sound. As ever, I was pleased it wasn't me in the chair.

There was nothing to mark out the day, nothing to warn of the disturbance to come. The familiar soft pad of the rubber on the stairwell, and the usual flash of irritation that the patch at the bottom had not yet been repaired. I didn't know that these were the last moments of the life I had worked so hard to build, closing door after door behind me to ensure my safety. Now I wonder which door it was that I left hanging. A Greek patient once told me she never entered a room without considering whether there was a window through which she might escape. So perhaps that's it; I never considered how pain will leak through all those unseen crevices, or secrets seep out from the smallest window I neglected to close.

Blind to what lay ahead I simply walked out into the evening, a soft spring night that might have been beautiful. I remember the cool air, and the soft thud of the front door as my life closed behind me. I remember looking over my shoulder just once, an afterthought perhaps, or the pang of a lover left behind in a moment of longing. In the nether reaches of my heart I always knew what my mind never dared to admit.

I had a life, a good life even. I walked out of one door and passed through another, time in reverse, like the joke clock I had hanging over the door in my kitchen, forever confusing. I noticed others staring at it sometimes, their eyes squinting in puzzlement. The clock threatened their order of things, demanding a new view of the world. Funny thing is, I was used to it and could tell time in a heartbeat.

"What time *is* it, exactly?" Frank asked the first time he saw it.

"Ten to eight," giving it a cursory glance. I was pouring coffee after an early dinner. We were intending to go to the movies. "Just reverse the numbers. It's easy."

"For you, maybe. Why would you have a clock like that? What's the point?" Frank shook his head. Not for the first time, I noticed how much hair he had, unusual in a man of fifty. A little bit of grey in the corners, but mostly a dull blonde where the signs of age could get lost for a while before showing their true colours.

"What do you mean, what's the point? It's a joke."

"Why not play it straight? It's unsettling, if you ask me."

"Nothing is straightforward." Handing him a cup of coffee. "Oh. Well, then …"

Who had given me the clock? It's not the sort of thing you buy yourself. I lean more towards clothes and music, a good hotel with room service. It was a gift, the parting shot of one of Frank's predecessors, a man like the others who finally grew tired of working through my past in the present.

"How is it?" this man had complained, handing me the clock wrapped up in pretty white tissue paper. "How is it, that someone who analyses every little thing can be so unreasonable? I think you need to figure a few things out," he suggested, not entirely unkindly. What had I done to cause him to say such a thing? Blast him for some minor infraction that replicated a larger injustice from my past, no doubt. He couldn't have known, but he'd given me the clock, so he'd registered something. I closed the gate behind that one, forgetting his name in no time, but I'd kept the clock, hanging it over one of my precious doors.

To Frank, so early in the game, the clock did not yet make sense—but it would soon enough. What I hadn't known then was that Frank was a stayer. He might not have grasped yet the reverse mechanisms of my life, his thinking was far too linear for that, but not understanding wouldn't be reason enough for him to leave.

I like buses, where everything is above ground, so that's where I headed when I left the office that day: to the stop at the end of the road. I probably figured it would take me where I wanted to go, and with less effort as the Underground is further away. I take the bus most days. For a woman who spends her working day tunnelling through the unconscious maze of others' experience, I am adept at avoiding my own. I take the Underground only when pressed, when there is little alternative but to head down directly. I like to sit up top on the bus, sometimes at the front like a child, facing the world head on. Down below, I usually end up on one of the "priority" seats, not because I'm old or disabled, but because it's the only one free. Already I feel cramped, pushed in on the sides of my life and forced to focus at close quarters. Up top I can breathe. Down below the air is thicker, people too weary to tackle the stairs.

The Underground always demands work. It's a fifteen minute walk down the road and I take it only when I'm forced to, when it's the only possible route to get where I'm going, for instance the furthest reaches of north London, or Dagenham, which I consider the end of the earth. Anywhere else I can skim along on the surface. Shoved onto the Tube I feel like I'm caught in the web of other people's misery. I am a psychotherapist by profession, well known in my field, but at the end of a fifty-minute appointment I am let loose. I can write my notes and re-calibrate my internal settings. On the Underground, you don't know who you might end up with, trapped in the middle of a tunnel with the lights out and no means of knowing how long you'll be there. How do you reach the air in an

6

underground tunnel, except by passing through more tunnels? The maze is endless and there is no map, just a relentless series of dark turns without a single hint of what might be ahead.

I finally entered therapy, initially for a couple of weeks, because I supposed it was only a bit of fine-tuning I needed. This was after I was given the clock, which was really the last straw. In my innocence I believed it was a few unfortunate habits I needed to break, like giving up smoking, or putting that foul tasting stuff on your fingernails to stop yourself biting them, taking away the sweet comfort of gnawing at your own flesh before the pain sets in and you're reminded how disgusting it looks.

I ditched my first therapist when she dared to suggest that I was resistant. I wanted someone to show me how to negotiate turns, and she was all for slowing down and working out the route. Couldn't she see I was terrified of the dark? Like I said, I dumped her. I wouldn't have been able to stay up top with this one. Her cultivated kindness irritated me and her empathy was unsettling. She wasn't pragmatic enough, like an inefficient sales clerk who clucks around behind the desk while you're waiting for her to serve you; such a simple transaction turned into a drama. When I told her I was leaving, she lifted her slim shoulders and shifted a bit in her chair, pushing herself forward a fraction before speaking, as if she thought I might miss the point. "Have you considered *why* you want to leave?"

I'd already prepared my answer, "Because I don't think this is helpful." Eyes popping open, she looked gratifyingly startled. I just wanted to know how to manage my anger sometimes, how to get through the day. "Maybe this is for some people, but I haven't got the time."

Lifting her hands she gripped the wooden arms of her chair either side, as if to steady herself. She didn't argue. She smiled, a tight little line that settled the deal. I was out the door within minutes, into the light.

Now, I recognise that when someone is determined to leave therapy, there's no point in arguing. You become better at knowing the difference between a threat and an intention. She was wise enough to know that argument was useless, she could only encourage me to reflect. Later I would be grateful, but in that moment I was just happy to be out of her door.

I wasn't thinking of doors, the ones I'd closed behind me, while I was waiting for the bus that evening after leaving the office. I didn't have time, as a number 87 came along pretty quickly heading towards town. It must have done because I don't remember tapping my little internal foot until I actually got on the bus. Who was it I was meeting, and why is it that I focus my impatience so often on this hole in my memory? It wasn't the main event. That night was simply the warm-up act no one recalls afterwards, unless it was truly terrible. Except I do remember the ride, like the last view of someone you love.

The bus was crowded, and like always I headed up top. There was only one seat available that I could see, somewhere in the middle on the right. "*Excuse* me," I said, clinging to the pole for balance as the bus pulled out. The seat was occupied by a bag of groceries, their owner staring out the window.

"Oh!" turning towards me in mock surprise. "Sorry." She heaved them over and onto her lap like a ten-ton sack of potatoes. A martyr, I thought, a woman to be avoided. I plopped myself down and focused on her insignificance, my usual method for annihilating the enemy.

Two stops later she got off, huffing and puffing with her big load and I wondered why on earth she hadn't remained below stairs. When she'd gone, I slid further down next to the window. Someone had left a Coke can behind and it rattled back and forth underneath the seats. Without a litter bin, where do you put such a thing? I picked it up and shoved it between the seats. Two people were talking loudly on their mobiles, having competitive one-sided conversations no one, least of all me, wanted to hear. I glared a few times and one

8

woman actually stared back, shunting her chin forward in an "I dare you!" sort of motion while her voice grew increasingly louder. The other was so self-absorbed she didn't bother to look around, head bent and phone tucked expertly between her shoulder and cheek, filing her nails as she spoke. They weren't worth my time worrying about. I turned to stare out the window, to see the familiar trace of shambolic pedestrians heading home after a day's work, the shopfronts and sooty brick buildings.

The bus rattled along the Wandsworth Road, not a pretty place at any time of the year. It always looks dusty, as if no one has bothered to clean the corners since the last bunch lived here, before the houses began to fade into disrepair and the junkies moved in. But there is always hope. From out of the window I registered the Congregational church, with its slogan outside promising salvation. I also noticed one more section along the route having a face-lift, a row of almshouses with scaffolding up and a sign to say luxury flats would soon be available. I wondered who would be the first to move in, imagining an aspiring City boy with his leather couch and a television the size of a wall.

The route was reassuringly predictable, except in pockets where the looting was a few years ago. I hated to see the boarded up shops, those small businesses that were never able to recover. What did they do afterwards, those people who had created a life in the form of a grocery store, or a hairdresser's? Some of them were refugees, survivors of other war zones. In the hard-won effort of establishing a shop, they had believed they were finally safe. I looked out the window to the other side. The thing about loss is that you can't replace it; so much trauma symbolised in those abandoned shopfronts.

Council housing runs like a ribbon on the left hand side of Wandsworth Road, while just a short distance behind the derelict buildings and the messy business of transition on the right is the stately elegance of Clapham Old Town. There are no Portuguese coffee shops here, with their twenty-four-hour football and men smoking and shouting through the open door at the television. Bakeries have turned into patisseries and the butchers are all organic.

I live between the two worlds, equidistant from the gritty, noisy road and the quiet confidence of Old Town. The bus stopped and started, with me up top heading towards— where? I passed my own stop, I remember that, and the double-decker continued on its route towards town, turning left at Vauxhall Bridge and up and along past the Tate Gallery and the House of Commons. I had a book in my handbag which I never looked at again. For weeks and months afterwards I was distracted. Instead, I watched history glide by and looked through the tourists to see if there was anyone I knew. There never was, but I always looked and I was always disappointed, as if somewhere in the crowd I should experience a flash of recognition, a resurrection of sorts where someone from my past might be pleased to see me. I sat up straighter, a child plastered against the glass to get a better view.

I must have landed somewhere near Trafalgar Square because the bus turns around at Aldwych.

The evening ends for me there. I don't remember the space between, or the journey home. It's the insignificance of the occasion that is so striking now. My life was about to tip over into my past and I can't now remember what I did the night before, like a drink too many and the hangover of regret. And no one has filled in the void, an evening too pedestrian an occasion to ever refer to again. Dinner with a friend perhaps, or a professional meeting? I have many more colleagues than I do friends, and they are easily left behind.

Somewhere between Trafalgar Square and home again I lost the last evening of my old life, and no one noticed, least of all me. Months would pass before I dared to admit it. For once, with the door wide open, I didn't think to pull it closed.

There were two more bouts of therapy following that first attempt and another few years before I dared to work below ground with Joanna, my last psychotherapist. I still played it safe, careful to measure out just how deep I was willing to go. In those easy questions like, "Tell me about your mother ..." I discovered there was an uneasy alliance between what I thought, and how I felt about her. My father too, so little known and for so short a time. I had built up a lifetime relationship with him through fantasy; he was perfect, as constant in my unconscious dreaming as he had been reportedly fickle in life. No man, certainly not the clock man, or Frank either for that matter, had any hope of living up to such perfection. No wonder I was so angry. My mother, a little wisp of a thing, clinging to her grief and disappointment like a talisman. The sorrow of her husband's death had given her definition, the pity of others a stand-in for constancy. I was the living symbol of her difficult life as a single parent whose child was doing well, my success the product of her own hard work. In those days my older brother, Tom, appeared to be running wild. If I failed too, so would she and the pity might dry up. For my mother, who depended so heavily on the attention of others, misbehaviour on my part would have killed her.

This was the grit of my therapy, unravelling truth from fiction and, like so many of my patients, the grief and anger of those early years. My story wasn't unusual, or as terrible as some I've heard over the years, but it was mine all the same, my own particular pool of pain.

I finally learned to manage, and Frank came along just as I was deciding to train as a therapist. Frank is a mathematician so we drive each other a little mad, he with his linear thinking and me with my worrisome tendency to exhume and scrutinise every little thing about the other. By the time I met Frank I had also learned to control my anger a little better, and to take a breath before holding a gun to a man for not

11

living up to the fantasy version of my father or, heaven help us, replicating some pusillanimous aspect of my mother. I resided more securely in the present, my past a labyrinth I believed I'd successfully negotiated over the years in therapy. I knew the route by then, as complicated as it sometimes was, and had learned to distinguish one path from another. I stayed above ground, closed my doors faithfully behind me, and moved on.

But I never told anyone the darkest secret, reserving it in a place in my heart no one could touch. It would take more than a good therapist to extract that nugget. To shift it loose would risk cracking the whole lot, shattering my life into a million tiny pieces of unbearable loss I knew I would never survive. Better to live a life at half mast than not to live at all, and so I never thought about it, I never dusted it off even once during those many years in therapy with Joanna. I never looked there at all.

TWO

On Tuesdays I begin seeing patients at seven, before Keith sets to work with his infernal drill. I am alone in the building until my first appointment. There are mornings I come in earlier, particularly if Frank is away and I am restless. I tell myself that this is an opportunity and I use the time to write. This day, though, I arrived at the office thirty minutes before my client, time enough for a cup of coffee and a quick piece of toast in the building's communal kitchen down the hall. I had to rub the crumbs from my fingers before going down to open the door. I am always a little anxious before meeting a new patient and all our arrangements for this session had been sorted out over the internet.

Dorothy was a blur on the other side of the bubbled glass, the angled pitch of an umbrella protecting her from the rain. I opened the door and she stared at me, eyes wide open in shock, not sure what to expect. As if wondering whether I might hit her or kiss her.

Instead, I offered her my hand, "Hello. I'm Lisa Harden."

Her responding grip was acquiescent, like holding air. There is so much to say in a handshake and I was disappointed.

I dropped her hand and it landed at her side like an empty swing, entirely without purpose. "There are a few stairs,

I'm afraid," I said, signalling that she should walk past me. Clutching her dripping umbrella she did as she was told, leaving a trail behind her. And it was the trail I noticed, in those few seconds that she walked ahead of me, rather than anything of her, as if that was the important thing; what she left behind.

"You can set it there, if you like?" pointing towards the large umbrella pot I keep by the front door of my office. There was a rattle and clunk as it landed at the bottom and Dorothy's eyes widened further, a child knocking over china. She let out a small, "Oh!" and smoothed down the front of her wet trench coat. I wondered why she didn't take it off but that might have exposed too much, too early. This young woman had lost her shell and her damp trench coat was the best she could do. Did she have any reckoning of how much she had already revealed?

I took a step forward—the better to see her—but she was too quick, stepping like a dancer away from me, a small pirouette unintentionally leading her further into the consulting room. There was nowhere else to go and having come up behind her, I was blocking the exit. Would she have run away then if she could? If only I had taken a step back, rather than forward, we would both have had a way out. Instead, in her terror she had pushed herself further into the vortex and I followed her in, never suspecting what she would come to mean to me.

Dorothy was stranded in the middle of the room. I have an image of her shaking her head, clearing away the rain, eyes swinging around the room to find a way out. In truth she was standing still, complacent now that she was truly trapped. She had, in fact, made her own way in. I wondered if this was her pattern, in her terror always racing towards the bright light of danger.

I was careful not to spook her again and, remaining for the moment in my spot by the door, I pointed towards the couch.

Dorothy sat down and I saw that her knees were bare; even in this weather she was not wearing stockings or trousers to keep her warm. She seemed to me defenceless, and yet here she was, alive and sitting in my office. She had found a way to reach out to me, a gesture of some significance and hidden strength, or desperation. There is often a confusion between the two, a case of mistaken identity. What looks like an impulsive act of bravery is really the ferocious action of the need to survive. Which one could it be with Dorothy?

There are moments, when staring straight into the heart of someone else's pain, that I experience a piercing point of pleasure. I excavate and touch in others what I dare not look at within myself and, in those moments, I am transcended. I am the coward sheltering behind my patient's despair. This is not true in all cases. I am a good psychotherapist, warm and engaging and most people feel safe with me. I have compassion. Sitting opposite Dorothy, I opened with my standard question, "How do you think I can help you?"

A first session with a new patient is always tinged with disappointment. The imperfect therapist sits facing her imperfect patient, and in the midst of the session there is the inevitable dawning that there are hard times ahead. In Dorothy's case, I think that moment had passed, perhaps for both of us. She was stranded, perched at the edge of my couch and sitting upright like a Methodist spinster whose best defence is disapproval. There was no leaning back into the cushions, or easing into whatever she had imagined therapy to be. She was damp and disconcerted and facing a stranger demanding too much from her in that first question: how can I help you?

But she seemed to relax then and I noticed for the first time that she was actually very well dressed. Her knees were bare, but her trench coat was fashionable and her shoes expensive. The small bag she unhooked from over her shoulder was a neat leather satchel of the kind I could only justify buying while on holiday, usually after a glass of wine.

I was surprised by my envy, a small tinge of wishing something of the other. How was it that I could find something to want in this sad woman who, so far, had offered up nothing of any substance except terror alternating with disapproval? I took note that it wasn't anything *of* her that I coveted, but rather something she owned. So this was her refuge, the carapace of possessions. But her knees were bare and her fear had been palpable. In her handshake she had given me nothing.

There is a powerful urge on the part of most therapists to hunt out something in the internal wasteland of another, but I resisted again the temptation to move towards her and instead pushed further back into my chair, a high-backed winged seat that exudes eminence. I also know how cultivating envy can be a tidy way of keeping people at bay. Again, I asked her, "How do you think I can help you?"

She looked at me directly, then. Having successfully trapped me within the web of her envy, she had the upper hand. How much more powerful was she now that I wanted something of hers? I noticed how her shoulders lifted a little, while I resisted the urge to slump. Clearly, I was no longer someone who had everything.

She had found a way to hold herself up, but she couldn't maintain her position for long and in her expression there was the pulse of a tremendous effort. I watched as her shoulders began to dip again under the strain. For the first time I noticed a flash of anger, a quick spark of light in her eyes that she extinguished with a sharp tap of her right hand against her thigh. Later I would come to recognise this as an habitual tic that put out every flame before it had time to take hold. She took a long breath, her lungs expanding before she plunged into the next task. "I seem to have a problem with relationships," her voice unexpectedly brackish. Red wine and cigarettes possibly, but her voice was thin, too, as if fighting to stay on the surface of things. A curious mixture, not altogether pleasant, certainly distracting. I forced myself to stay tuned to what she was saying and I must have shifted in my seat because her eyes snapped open again suddenly with the fear I had seen at the door.

"Go on," gently as I could, "can you say more about that?"

Now, for a therapist, "a problem with relationships" is a given. It is a sentence that says everything and reveals nothing. It is the "how are you, I'm fine" of the therapy world. Already with Dorothy I knew that I would need to move slowly, no quick movements into the unconscious, nothing directly to the point. Her gambit would be to find a solution without moving too closely to the heart of whatever preceded her terror. She wanted an answer, without having to ask me the question. I remember calculating that this would be long-term work, a client unlikely to emerge from her emotional bunker any time soon.

As a clinician I exercise patience, living for those small moments when there is a piercing of the heart, when in the midst of the deepest despair there appears a glimmer of hope and, for an instant, my patient understands that there can be grace in facing the pain. I have written about this: my whole career as a therapist is based on these "enlightened" reflections.

Dorothy clearly did not know how to respond, as if my question was deeply complicated which, on some level, it certainly was.

"Do you have any thoughts on why you struggle with relationships?" trying a more direct approach.

Those shoulders of hers lifted again, this time in a lopsided shrug, a curiously false note in the face of her all-too-authentic misery. "I guess I want a good relationship and it always seems to go all right for a while, before they do something and it's all over for me then—I don't know what I'm doing there and I shut them out and I can't bear to be around them." She stopped, holding her breath in mid-sentence. "Something like that …". There was the brackishness again, offensive to the senses. I resisted the urge to turn away.

"You become disappointed in them, angry sometimes?" Remembering the lightning flash moments before.

"No, not angry. Disappointed maybe."

Her hands were clenched, small tight fists resting either side of her on the seat. Shaking her hand now would produce more than just air, though she was clearly well practised at hiding her aggression from others, maybe from herself as well. Yet there it was, knotted into those clenched knuckles of hers so primed for lifting. Then she did it: unclenched her hands and tapped against her thigh—once, twice, quick and punitive. I felt my neck muscle ping, like she had hit me, though she didn't twitch, her expression completely blank. Her tap was her fix and now she felt nothing at all.

We were playing poker, therapeutic poker, and I had clocked her "tell", or one of them at least. For my own safety I would need to keep my eye on her fists. For the moment, I decided to stick with her view of things. "Disappointed?"

"Yes ... 'disappointed'," her voice dipped, no longer harsh, almost soft. The quality of the light in the room, early morning sun rising over London's rooftops, ducked behind a cloud into bleak shadows and for the next few moments I did not exist for her. I was simply not there, or she was not. Either way, I watched her vanish, a kind of internal retreat where nothing external existed for her. Where was she? In such a dissociated state she could be anywhere, and nowhere. And why was it so difficult with me that she had chosen this means of escape so soon? Dissociation was not a trick you learned in a day. Somewhere in her past she had needed a route out when there was no door or window through which she could escape. An internal withdrawal had been the best way out. Here, in the room with me, she may not have known where she was and when she looked up, her blue eyes for once locking on mine, she was clearly confused. Who was I? She tapped her hand against her thigh, a snap to attention and took a deep breath, forlorn, back in the world again.

I meant nothing to her.

There are patients for whom the attachment to their therapist is paramount, and it happens too quickly, a kind of artificial and desperate clinging to the idealised other. They are soon disappointed and can leave therapy too early, damning themselves to an endless repetition in all their relationships, particularly those they imbue with fantasies of romance.

For other patients, it is that very attachment they avoid and the work can be painfully slow. They are so broken off from dependence on anyone that in their longing for comfort they run terrified from everyone. Dorothy was one of those. Disappointment and longing appeared to coexist in equal measure, damning her to a life of avoidance of any relationship which would actually give her comfort.

These were my first thoughts, not fully formed, but building inside me like a small bird's nest. She claimed to want help, but with every word she said, with every tentative and careful movement of this young woman's body, I could see her poised for a quick, internal getaway. In order to remain she would need to learn to trust me a little, and I wasn't sure that she was capable, certainly not at the moment, if ever.

How trustworthy is any psychotherapist? Already my attention had wavered. I had experienced disappointment in our first greeting, and flinched at the sound of her voice. I was not sure whether I felt compassion or irritation towards her, or a strange mixture of both. We had barely begun and I was already punch-drunk, forcing myself to stand up to her, to withstand the punishment, and envy, for heaven's sake, and unaccountable anger. I was confused by her power, and my susceptibility, so early in the game. Usually there is a build-up, a crescendo of experience between clinician and client before the dynamic reaches such intensity. But here it was, Dorothy already laying out her choice of arms.

I looked back into those eyes of hers, or I tried to anyway. By now they were wandering around my room in a state of what could have been mistaken for indifference, but I believed was disdain. My bookshelves were untidy and Rosie the office cleaner had clearly missed the bottom shelf,

19

a cobweb lingering in the corner where a small bust of Freud nestled next to a finger puppet of Jung lying on a miniature couch. I cringed at the misfired joke, the sense of mischief that had prompted me to place it there. My desk was a landslide of books and papers, the usual muddle of what I considered my creative life. While my therapist's eye scanned and monitored my new patient's tour of my office, I squirmed and wondered why viewing the room from her perspective was so uncomfortable. I doubted I was alone—there would be others in whom she inspired self-consciousness and feelings of inadequacy. Friends and colleagues. Lovers? Had she any awareness at all how she might be projecting her own feelings into others?

There was some truth in her view of my room. My tired old joke with Freud and Jung sparring it out over the couch was probably only funny to me, and my desk was obviously untidy, but it wasn't crucial or of any real importance in the great scheme of things. An untidy desk did not make me a bad therapist, or a limp joke an inept one. But if others disappointed Dorothy I was also doomed to failure.

Through all of this we said nothing. How many minutes passed? Maybe two at the outside, each of us in our reverie, connected to one another through the critical prism of the other. Dorothy looked back at me, a small, satisfied smile lifting her out of the gloom. I *had* disappointed her. What a relief, her expression seemed to say, what a relief.

"I guess I disappoint you, too," risking everything. This was a big gun question, placing whatever happened between her and me at the forefront of the therapy.

She crossed and then uncrossed her bare knees, arms too, struggling to find comfort. I wondered if I would ever see her again. She tapped her thigh again, a light drumming of the fingers. Was something being allowed to surface? Had my gamble paid off?

"I live in a constant state of disappointment." Now we were getting somewhere. I ignored the martyred tone, the invitation to fork out pity.

"With yourself as well?" There was more being exposed here than her bare knees. I noted with surprise, and self-disgust, that I wanted to shake her. So, I concluded, she had once been bullied, driven underground and in need of constant rescue.

She nodded, "I guess so." She tried to look away, but I was quick, a therapeutic cop trying to fill in the story when all I really had at my disposal was the resulting wreckage.

"Why don't you tell me a little about your history?" I suggested, a more subtle way of asking her about her mother, that most fundamental of relationships. We would have to get to it sometime, and why not now when she needed some distracting if she was to stay in therapy at all. Too close a scrutiny of the "here and now" would certainly drive her into fleeing the scene, and I needed a break too.

"Oh, well …" she trailed off before adding, "There's not much to tell really. Mother, father, no brothers or sisters. Normal stuff."

"Not much to tell, or you don't want to tell me?" Too sharp. How could I work with someone who wouldn't tell me anything? So surprised at my petulance I nearly laughed. What was going on here?

"A little of both." An apparently honest answer, without the brackish undertone.

"Okay, what sense do you make of your relationships ending? You say people disappoint you and then you shut them out. Are you shutting me out now?" Checking the clock on the side table, relieved to see that we had just ten minutes to go. I run a tight ship and when the clock reads ten to the hour, the session is over.

I could look at my notes and tell you exactly what Dorothy said following that last question, but whatever her answer, it is completely irrelevant. What matters is what happened between us, our experience of one another. Lord knows she must have been in turmoil, even as she was gunning for me. Now I know she had more of a sense of direction than I gave her credit for at the time, while I was caught up in a maelstrom of feelings I could not account for, usually a sign of deep disturbance in the client.

I brought the session back to earth, explaining some of the rules. If she decided to continue therapy with me she should know that I would not answer the door if she arrived too early. My appointments last fifty minutes, I told her, and during that time I attend to the patient I have in the room. I was clear about the fee; if she missed a scheduled appointment, I would charge her regardless. On the other hand, if she needed to change an appointment occasionally, and I had an alternative time available, I would offer it to her. Dorothy had contacted me through my website, so I knew she was aware of some of my other professional commitments, my teaching and professional development workshops. My writing. On those occasions when I had to cancel, or I was on holiday, I would not charge her. If she decided to continue with therapy, she would be given the same appointment time every week. I judged she would benefit from meetings twice a week, but the idea would probably horrify her at this point, so I limited myself to a suggestion of weekly sessions.

Throughout my long-winded spiel, Dorothy was wide eyed, attentive, but there was also something distracted about her expression, like she'd heard it all before, and wasn't much interested. She was preoccupied, nodding in all the right places without hearing a word I said.

The session finally ended and I told her to ring me if she wanted to continue working with me. This is my usual tactic. Pinning the client down to a series of sessions on into the mists of time is counterproductive at this point. I always suggest that they go away and consider, reflect on our session, and make their decision over the next few days. I ask them to phone and let me know. Often, it is those patients most adamant during the session that they want to continue who never return. Ambivalence seems to me a pretty healthy response to a first meeting. After all, who is going to enjoy such internal excavation as I can provide, turning over the dirt where so many fertile shoots have come to nothing over the years, stomped on before being allowed to surface. The therapy I offer is not always comfortable, but a reworking of the discomfort they feel in the world outside. In the safety of my therapy room I hope we can work through this anxiety, make sense of their experience to the extent that my patients can find some kind of rapprochement with the difficulties in their lives. I don't offer the prospect of solutions so much as I hold out hope for the possibility of understanding. I am not my patient's friend, I am their confidante and even, during difficult periods, their enemy, the one who knows too much and sees through their patterns. I can be the first person who has ever loved them, and whom they have ever come to love. And to that end I hold the boundaries. They know nothing about me except what they can imagine or surmise. I do not associate with them outside the room and if I see them in the street I do not introduce them to whomever I am with. I am also a stickler for time. I hold their confidences and I am bound, as I told Dorothy, by a rigid code of ethics. There should be no conflicts of interest on my part.

Dorothy, sitting up straight at the end of the session and with her knees covered by the little leather satchel, nodded politely. There was no more tapping of her thigh and she smiled, not a beacon of light, but a small lifting at the corners. It may have been all she could manage and in my ignorance I was grateful. We all need job satisfaction, some meaning in our lives, and at the end of a first session I wish for at least some relief for my client. The hard part, I know, is yet to come.

I walked Dorothy back down the stairs. As I opened the front door for her, Keith, my dental colleague, was coming in.

By the slightly startled look in his expression I could see he thought Dorothy was attractive. He said nothing, thank goodness; he has been ordered not to acknowledge my patients in any way. In fact he has been asked countless times never to come into the building at ten to the hour when most of my clients are bound to be leaving, or at the top of the hour when they are likely to be arriving. He can't resist crashing the time, his curiosity getting the better of him, and he rarely resists openly greeting them, like it's a social visit. He puts it down to absent-mindedness, but I'm not convinced. I have suggested to him that, as his poor memory seems to interfere with his conscious intentions, he might like to make an appointment with one of my colleagues. He retaliates by cheerfully telling me that I am "controlling", a modern, self-serving buzzword intended to diminish the significance of my request. So, we continue to meet at these crucial points of the day as he comes and goes from his office.

Dorothy, though, did not seem to register him at all, which must have come as something of a disappointment. He is, as you will have already surmised, a man who likes to be noticed. I suppose peering over someone's face with a drill in your hand about to zone in on his teeth is one way of gaining attention.

I didn't shake Dorothy's hand on the way out, which after the first session with a patient I often do. Keith pushed in through the door and then she left, back out into the rain, not saying goodbye and without looking back. A few days later there was a message on my answer machine, not the internet this time, to say she would like to continue our sessions. She would see me next Tuesday at the same time, seven in the morning. As I wrote the appointment down in my book I remember my stomach churning, as if to warn me. My body already knew what my mind could not begin to imagine.

THREE

I am a therapist who prides herself on her ability to remember details. Most clinicians are good at this, but I like to think that I am particularly good at it. If I don't recall something, I need to ask myself why, what is important about this fact or bit of information that I have dismissed it out of memory and, therefore, attention? You see, I cover my back both ways. Both remembering and not remembering are crucial.

At the weekend, however, and in the evening after work, I try to let the day go, leave my patients behind and re-enter my own life. My marriage to Frank is another portal out of one room into another, and this one has light.

Frank has a great capacity for reassurance. I sometimes wonder if he has acquired this through his relationship with numbers, their very concreteness providing him with a stability I certainly don't have. I cling to Frank because he is planted firmly in the ground, a rock of rational thinking. If both of us were busy analysing the other, empathy flying back and forth in both directions, life would be insufferable. The extension of compassion is one thing, to receive it quite another. Perhaps that is why I so often write about it, my preoccupation with this therapeutic essential nothing but an effort to understand what I so abhor receiving myself. I believe I extend it towards my patients, not in a gushing sort of way, but through my very capacity to understand and perceive their pain, though with some clients it isn't so easy to identify with their distress. With my new patient this week, I had experienced such inexplicable confusion I wasn't sure I had really taken her into account at all. Too early to speculate and I pushed any thoughts of her to the back of my mind.

This was the weekend, a Saturday, and Frank was home again after his conference in Denver. I tried to imagine him there, all cowboy boots and hats, the smell of cattle in the air. I grew up in farm country and my husband is a city boy, north London stamped on his forehead with every disgusted nod towards life beyond the M25. Already he has compromised himself by moving south of the river into Clapham, which is as far as he is ever likely to go. But he must have some curiosity towards what he can't bear himself, because he married me and I am the one who loves the smell of an open pasture. No confining spaces there, the prairie as wide as the sky. I left because I could not bear so much pain, a point like the North Star where there was never any possibility of escape, no matter how open the field or deep the horizon. What provided so much freedom was also a trap.

Frank was still asleep when I woke on Saturday morning. Along with my monthly magazine column, I was also giving a speech at the end of the following week to a group of counsellors attending a conference focusing on *The Role of Empathy in Therapy*. They wouldn't like what I had to say, encouraging therapists to hold back, not to lay it on too thick. I am not averse to this "core" principle, far from it, I simply loathe sentimentality. Is it empathy we are extending, or collusion? How can we work with anyone's deep despair if we don't allow it to surface? Laying the empathy on too soon may result in an unhelpful diversion into short-term comfort. Even worse, we may never find the route back to the primary distress.

I could go on about this for hours. My column is widely read, and not always because people agree with me. I am not deliberately provocative, but I don't avoid it either. I take risks. The intention behind so public a stance is to promote self-reflection and insight. Without that, I believe, we are nothing, our lives spent in reaction to events, rather than in the creation of personal meaning.

Before training as a therapist I had worked in advertising, and I was good at it. Strategic marketing is working with mirrors, shifting them constantly for the best view. I learned early that given the right line of copy anything will sell. Coca-Cola, after all, was never the "real thing". It was simply Coke. Real enough I suppose, but the message was far greater than the product. And it worked. I did the same thing with razor blades—a television advert likening them to a cross-country ski run, a clean-shaven man cutting a track, muscular, smooth, and true. He even paused for a moment to pat his cheek. There were other products, too, such as "wholesome", prefabricated bread from Winton's Homefair bakery, and the onion chopper that saved so much time in the kitchen, probably because nobody ever used it more than once.

Turns out I am pretty adept with mirrors, as well, when it comes to my own image. My writing, my professional identity is my line of copy. I am not a lie, only inevitably rather less than my public image projects. After all a razor is a razor, bread is bread, and even the onion chopper chopped, just took rather more effort than using a knife. In my case, I am a good therapist, though not so infallible as my patients and my public persona suggest. I'm not likely to argue the point: how people perceive me brings me business and I work hard to live up to the image.

On this Saturday, I let Frank sleep. He had only been home one day, and the older we become the harder it is to recover from jet lag. The night before he was so dozy from trying to stay awake that we had hardly seen one another. If I could get my writing in early, we would have the rest of the day together.

My desk overlooks the garden. Like many Londoners, we live in a terraced house and the view from my study provides some relief from the narrow confines of the hallway and the sense that the only way out is from the front or the back. There is no sliding out sideways, flat brickwork running down the walls either way. I have become accustomed to it over the years, or at least I no longer feel trapped every minute of the day. I have found other ways to stretch myself, through work and my marriage, and we travel, mostly to Canada in recent years to visit my mother and to give my brother, Tom, some relief. He is the dutiful child, while I maintain safety at a distance.

I turned on my computer and heard it whirr into action as I headed for the kitchen. Without Frank out of bed to make me tea in the morning, I start with coffee instead. Then back at my desk, steaming mug to the side. I stared at the screen before picking up the hard copy. Empathy again, words jumping like fish and thoughts of my new patient. Hardly a sip and already fidgety. Why can't I concentrate? Put the paper down. Focus. Her name eludes me but I know she proves my point exactly; too much empathy and she will be out the door. What's her bloody name!

I am so irritated that I stomp out to the garden and even pluck a few weeds—the equivalent of distracting myself with housework, not something I am prone to do even during the worst of times. Early on in my training someone suggested that a therapist's ability to care for plants was some indication of her capacity to look after clients. I bristled at the idea, then when I returned home went round the house and gathered up all my houseplants. Most of them were already drooping, either from neglect or too much water, their leaves brown at the ends, curling like talons. Chucked them all out, even the pots.

I poured myself another cup of coffee, which only added to my restlessness. Returning to my desk, I sat for another little while staring at my computer screen. Finally I gave up and went to wake Frank. I could absolve myself from having to work by rationalising that we needed time together after his trip to America. Poking him in the arm, "Frank, wake up." He gurgled a bit the way men do, a kind of "Unh, hunh" and "where am I" sort of grunt. I jabbed him again.

"Jesus, Lisa," up on his elbows shaking his head, "a cup of tea would be nice."

"Oh, sorry."

Frank would never think to wake me up without some kind of offering, and he wouldn't prod me either. He'd sit on the edge of the bed and pat me gently, waiting until I came to. I try to justify my behaviour by pointing out that I am nice to people all week at the office and when I come home I need to relax a little.

"You might want to try relaxing another way," he suggests occasionally, when I have provoked him beyond endurance. Another time he recommended I take up squash, "a nice aggressive game". Underlying his humour I know that he is hurt and for a while I try to compensate, even to the extent I sometimes make him a cup of tea. He appreciates the effort at least.

I tried hard this morning. In the kitchen again, I was careful to put in the appropriate measure before setting the pot on the table to let it brew. Another mug for myself—I would be winging it off the walls if I wasn't careful.

Frank didn't wait for me to bring up his tea. He came down to the kitchen, his feet slipping and sliding along in his old slippers. I keep threatening to throw them out, but he refuses to let me at them. They are the first things he checks when he returns home from a trip. I'm sure he even marks them somehow, in case I've moved them. In his ordered world he needs to know how close I am to carrying out my threat. Sometimes I shove them into the back of my closet to scare him. Like the joke in my office, the only one who ever thinks it's funny is me.

Frank gave me a kiss, a "Hi, honey, I'm home," sort of kiss, a bit left of centre.

"You need a shower."

"Yes, I do," grinning. "I'll have one in a minute, after my lovely cup of tea." He sat down at the table, tipped the teapot over his cup, a balancing act with a single finger on the spout to hold it firm, "So, what's on your mind?"

And there was the girl on the other side of the glass door, umbrella in hand, just a blur, a flashing thought, literally a shot in the dark, and I moved a step towards the light—towards Frank. "Do you want some cereal, toast or something?"

"Thank you, but no. Not yet." The thing about my husband is that he gets right to the point. That's probably why I married him, that and the fact that he brings me tea in the mornings. "I know you didn't wake me up for the good of my health." He said this so good-naturedly, when if he'd woken me up in the same manner I would have been furious.

"It's been a rough week," surprising myself. Looking back it didn't seem so difficult. Except for the blur, an unpleasant note in an otherwise perfectly normal week.

"Bad enough that you need to talk to Max about it?" He took a sip, winced a little and placed the cup carefully down onto the table.

"I don't think so."

Max is my supervisor, the person I bring my clinical troubles to, and we thrash out between us what we think is going on with my patients. I love Max, in a clear-cut sort of way, without the hazards of erotic confusion. He has been my supervisor for years and we meet twice a month in his office in Islington, an inconvenient distance away, but he is worth it. I try not to disturb him out of hours—disliking it myself when patients ring me over the weekend—as I know his family life is important to him. He is on his second marriage and has found himself, in his fifties, the father of four-year-old twins. I shudder whenever I think of it, but he seems quite happy about the circumstances of his new life. Sometimes I can hear them bawling in the background and I wonder if his patients are ever disturbed. I find it difficult to believe that he would let children interfere with his work life, but I can hear them and, by logical conclusion, so must his clients.

I noticed that Frank was moving his cup in small circles on the table, "noughts" he once called them, but I know he does this when he's trying to avoid something, usually to do with me. "Frank, if you want the perfect cup, you shouldn't ask your imperfect wife to make it. Go take a shower or something."

"You're crabby," without rancour, stating a fact. "Home sweet home and it's good to be back," he walked with his cup to the counter and poured in some hot water from the kettle. "Cheers," he held it towards me in a toast. "I'll go up and take my shower now and when I come back we can start this day all over again, how about that?"

I laughed, despite myself, "Okay."

I felt a little better after my verbal tussle with Frank. Back in my study, the talk finally began to take shape. Now I needed only to fill in the blanks, sort out some of the familiar PowerPoint slides to suit this new group of people. Much of what I do is a rerun of what I've done before, a matter of re-shuffling the cards. Therapy is a bit like that, too, rerunning the old stories of our history to discover new ways of framing the details. Nothing of our past can be changed by undergoing therapy, but at the end we may emerge with a different perspective. That's the theory anyway and I've staked my life on it.

Frank came down from his shower and I was ready. I could sort out why I was restless later, if there really was any deeper meaning to my morning experience other than too much coffee. In the meantime, my husband was home, irritating or not, and I wanted to enjoy him. What was the point otherwise, of this good life we had, just the two of us? We like one another, or I like him anyway. I'm not sure I'm always so likeable, but he is consistently forgiving, and sometimes that's the best that we can ask for.

There is nothing more prosaic or comforting than going grocery shopping, particularly on Saturdays when the market is open on the Northcote Road. My office is around the corner and that can be hazardous for running into patients. Frank knows to step aside if I am stopped, though that is rare. Usually I nod if they catch my eye and keep on moving. Others want complete anonymity and nothing passes between us at all. However, I am also human and sometimes I can't help registering them in my expression, though never with anything more than a smile. Sometimes clients don't recognise me on the street. For them I exist only in my room, without any other encumbering attachments. They want exclusivity, the unconscious dream of a mother all their own surfacing in this impossible fantasy.

So, on the street, particularly in my own neighbourhood, I maintain a constant, low-level radar. I also dress for the part, though not to extremes. I always wear skirts, my weekend style a slightly toned down version of my working self where I aim for a relaxed professional, rather than a formal or intimidating business style. I have never worn jeans, not since my teenage years when I turned my back on "childish things". Adulthood is my preferred state, despite some evidence to the contrary, usually in the form of demands for attention from Frank, or the occasional flash of temper out of proportion to the actual event. This, as I point out to my patients, is a dead giveaway of something unresolved from the dregs of our personal history. How are they to know that I speak with such authority?

There were no patient sightings on this morning and, having bought fish and vegetables and a large loaf of bread in the market, we headed to our favourite pub to have lunch.

I ordered a salad and a cappuccino. After only one sip, I knew it was a bad idea. I pushed the cup to one side. My salad arrived, and so did Frank's all day breakfast. Every Saturday I turn up my nose, and every Saturday he ploughs happily through the same plate of bacon, egg, mushrooms, and baked beans. To cap it off he has two rounds of white toast with lashings of butter. Leaning over to the next table to fetch the brown sauce, he flashes me a grin as always, which I ritually try to ignore.

This was the minutiae of our life together, our family pattern. Moving through the predictable rhythms of our day, these were our little tensions and our pleasures, the little pokes of fun and our irritations. You might wonder where the drama was to knit us together, but this was our very own small play and the way we held ourselves upright against the world. In these predictable little stories I knew I had struck gold, and I felt very safe.

While Frank finished up, I watched through the window: the stalls set up outside, part of the regular market, the popular butcher's stand and a vegetable stall. Such a familiar sight and, after so many Saturdays in the same spot sitting at the same table, I almost didn't see it anymore, or not with any real definition anyway. Suddenly, from underneath the vegetable stall's shelf, on the other side with the canopy blocking my view of the body, I thought I spotted a pair of knees. High boots and a skirt landing a fraction above the knees. I raised my hand, staving off a blinding shaft of light.

"When are you planning to visit your mother?" Frank's voice brought me back into the room.

"I don't know yet, maybe in August? I'll have to sort it out with Tom. Whatever works for him. We could go up to his place in the mountains afterwards." Essential to follow the chore with something pleasant.

I pulled my chair a little closer to the table, away from the window. Frank placed his knife and fork on the empty plate and patted his tummy, a habit I find completely undignified. I know he does this to tease me. I should ignore him, only with my feverish imagination at work, I worry that he will take the joke to the next level, throwing chicken bones over his shoulder perhaps, or chewing all afternoon on a bit of gristle. This is marriage: a series of strategic manoeuvres to hold the pieces together, a variation on give and take. Now, following my compulsory expression of disapproval, comprised of a glaring look and a despairing shake of my head, Frank was satisfied and called for the bill.

As he moved towards the door, Frank switched the bag of groceries from his right to his left hand and shoved the door open with his shoulder so that I, coming out behind him, was able to lob a quick shot over my shoulder, towards the vegetable stall. Busy, bustling, but nobody familiar. I searched for Frank's hand and gave it a squeeze, "Good to have you back."

I can't remember, now, the detail of his response. My husband's hand—did he say anything back to me at all?

FOUR

pril Fool's Day again. I took an extra large gulp of
coffee and nearly choked, but it felt good, a sharp lift
to the spirits. Frank would be up to something. He
likes a practical joke. It fits his mathematical frame. A forward
planner, my husband, his pranks worked out days in advance.

I sat at the kitchen table and scanned the papers for the spoof
article, not always so easily spotted. One year I fell for the piece
claiming the arms of Venus de Milo had been found. Two perfect limbs, dredged up by a Greek farmer ploughing his field.
You can see why I am wary. I am also not fond of Sundays. The
day is too loose and I like things wrapped up and determined.
There is something about a Sunday that invites less formality
than other days, as if lying in or doing nothing is something
to be treasured, while I find the notion of so much reflective
space anathema and far too disquieting. Luckily, I usually have
deadlines to meet, though I never seem to accomplish quite as
much as I intend to and, like many other working people looking over the tip of the weekend into the prospect of Monday,
I suffer an element of pressure. A new week is about to begin,
another clean slate to be filled with creativity and meaning,
and the avoidance of failure. Failure is invariably accompanied

by paralysing feelings of shame, or at least with me it is. No wonder I work so hard.

Being surprised is a kind of failure too, not getting the joke, or seeing it coming. Every year I know Frank has something planned and every year I am caught unawares. I look in all the wrong places, always learning my lessons a little too late. The first year we were together he set all the clocks in the flat two hours ahead, which must have been pretty labour intensive, perhaps in retaliation to my insistence on keeping the one in my kitchen, still telling time in reverse. I ended up at my office at five in the morning wondering why the streets were so empty. I failed to notice the difference in light, dawn beginning to glow over the patina of London's early morning gloom. When I checked the clock in my office I thought it must be wrong. Another year he planted stalks of asparagus as if they had shot up in the night after having been planted only the day before. He knew I had been told they were fast growers. After a few stunned seconds, I actually got the joke. Perhaps the quicker I catch on the funnier I think it is.

The worst was the "free" bread, where a leaflet dropped through the door suggesting that the local bakery was celebrating a family birth and would be giving away loaves all morning. I love a bargain and shot out the door first thing. At the shop I flashed my leaflet and the poor woman behind the counter turned pale, shouting in Italian for her son, the baker, to come out quick. "You've been had, love," he said, in perfect south London. "I don't give nothin' away for nothin'," and he actually winked at me. His mother, though, hadn't yet recovered and was still chattering in anxious Italian as I slunk out the door, forgetting even to buy the loaf of bread we needed, free or otherwise. On that occasion Frank had to go to the bakery and apologise. He and the baker had a good laugh, but his mother scowled in the background and it took Frank another three weeks before he felt confident enough to return without being afraid he was going to get a bun thrown at his head.

So, what would it be this year?

Frank strolled into the kitchen, "Bloody plumbing's gone in the bathroom. You'll have to pee into a bucket until I can get hold of someone. I've left one in there for you, scrubbed clean of any floor cleaning residuals."

Agghh, another bloody thing. Why did I have to pee now!

The pail was on the floor, next to the toilet, a bright red, plastic job with a thin rim and wide enough that I was likely to sink to the bottom if I didn't manage to hold myself upright somehow. I cursed the fact that we had only one toilet in the flat. In Canada ... I thought ... but that's what always comes to mind when life narrows down in London: wide open spaces and the luxury of spacious living, including bathrooms and toilets scattered throughout. Fanciful, but also my natural source of refuge whenever I am faced with difficult aspects of day-to-day living. In reality, Canada is a daydream kept in reserve, far more uncomfortable in truth than I ever admit.

However, at the moment I was faced with the prospect of urinating into a red plastic container, probably last used to mop the kitchen floor.

Back to the kitchen, "Let's go out for breakfast." I could hold out for at least a bit longer. "Call a plumber, I don't care. Anything but the bucket." Did I detect a flicker of disappointment in my husband's eyes, the sudden withering of a barely repressed excitement? I shouted out an expletive and raced back down the hall towards the loo, Frank in hot pursuit. I leaned over that damned pail and flushed the toilet, spinning round to face him. "Hah! Can't fool me!"

"Ah, but you believed for a moment, that's the important thing. And there's always next year," Frank laughing, forever optimistic.

He would have kept the act up all morning, flushing the toilet himself at precisely noon to make his point. Using alternative means, for however long a time, would not have bothered him. What Frank didn't necessarily recognise, and I wasn't about to point out, was that all his jokes focused on some human weakness in me. Why, otherwise, would his jokes be at all funny?

A Sunday morning walk to recover, across Clapham Common towards the centre where we could sit for a while on the green and pretend this wasn't simply an island surrounded by traffic. The Common is far too busy for me, on a sunny spring day full of families otherwise trapped into flat-living or with gardens so narrow there is no room to swing a child, arms outstretched, squealing with delight. Football too, and over there a baseball game, expats playing in the park.

"What are you doing this afternoon?" Quickening my step, but tripping instead, a slightly raised paving stone catching me short. Frank grabs my arm while I reel for balance, brushing my skirt down to catch my breath. Both of us wait for a moment before continuing.

"Cricket. The whole afternoon, I hope, providing rain doesn't get in the way." A fleeting glance at the sky, though the game is elsewhere, in India, or the Caribbean, not even up north. What else was new? I couldn't remember the last time I had watched television in the middle of the day, but Frank could watch sport for hours without a twinge of guilt for wasting an afternoon. He persisted in the face of my obvious disapproval, enjoying himself even more, I suspect, as a result of my condescension. He had to make a stand somewhere, and this was innocent enough. "And you? Normally you can't stand to be out this late on a Sunday morning. You're usually itching to get to work." He took my hand.

"I'm a bit stuck with the talk, that's all. Yesterday I finally had it all worked out, now this morning I don't seem able to get going. I haven't even looked at it yet."

"Then why not sit down at your desk and try to work it out? That's what you usually do," giving my fingers a squeeze. "You seem a bit rattled to me."

I withdrew my hand, tempted to point out that numbers are equations that can be reduced to right and wrong, yes or no. Writing a serious article, or developing a presentation, is less of a concrete occupation. It demands a more circulatory kind of thinking, and a paradoxical combination of conviction and curiosity. There are no certainties in my work, only educated guesses and refined speculation, but lord knows we can all be wrong. "I'm not rattled," negotiating the path, on the lookout for more paving stones. "I'll figure it out in the end."

"Okay, have it your way," hands in his pockets.

We walked in silence for a bit, Frank watching the football while I tried to hustle him along, stepping up the pace whenever he appeared to slow down. I was about to propose we turn back when I spotted Keith heading towards us on his bicycle along the parallel path. I looked away quickly but Frank had also seen him and put a hand in the air like a traffic cop. He has always liked Keith. They play cricket together in what I call "an old timers" league, and it is through Keith's former wife that I came to know Frank.

I had met Helen while training as a counsellor, though she dropped out after a year when Keith announced he was leaving her. There had been a great deal of grief when the marriage exploded, compounded by Helen's humiliation. Despite the fact that she had been planning to leave Keith, in the end it was she who was "dumped", as she put it. It took her only six months before she linked up with someone else. For a while I trooped up to Primrose Hill where she lived in quiet splendour with an older man who once worked in the "City", the British euphemism for a career focused exclusively on the making of money. Helen never did pursue her career as a counsellor, let alone as a psychotherapist. Her days were spent in a vacuum of disappointment and visiting her was a curiously empty experience I undertook for reasons too uncomfortable to admit, perhaps to convince myself that I had chosen the better path.

"Why do you continue this friendship?" my therapist asked me one day. Was I complaining about Helen? I found it so much easier focusing on others. "Is there something of yourself you see in her?" Such a simple question but it caught me hard, a deep thud of pain in the chest I couldn't possibly articulate. I stared at Joanna. How had I been so caught off guard, and why? My head felt as if I was about to float away and I shook it to bring me back to earth. It had been years since I'd experienced such "displacement".

"You seem fascinated by her," Joanna watched me through the pebbled glass of her thick spectacles. She was unnervingly perceptive and I wasn't sure why I remained in therapy with her. Weekly sessions were part of my professional training requirement and I was forced to stick with someone. I was also frightened of her. At the end of every session I was grateful to have survived and, thankfully, her empathy was less overt than her predecessor's. Instead she poked and prodded around the details of my life until she hit a spot she recognised was tender, after which she was relentless and fierce, never letting me forget that I might have the door slammed shut, but that she knew something was in there.

In my mind Joanna had shoulders like an American football player, and I swear she widened them out with shoulder pads. Not surprisingly, I spent a lot of time with her ducking and weaving, anything to avoid a direct tackle. "You mention Helen fairly often these days and I wonder if there is something you recognise mirrored in her."

"Maybe," looking at my hands and playing with my wedding ring, "but I don't know what it could be. We're like night and day," I tried to sound breezy, but my throat was tight in that thick, airless room. I might choke if I said too much.

"Perhaps the two of you are more alike than you care to think about. You describe Helen as if she always tries to play it safe. Perhaps you do, too?"

"No! I'm out there. I do things. I take risks. I'm changing my profession and I married Frank," twisting my ring round and round, the engraving like braille, guaranteeing safety. "That's hardly hiding away." Was I shouting, hands over my ears, the sound of my voice muffled and full of echo. Joanna cocked an eyebrow and heaved those massive shoulders of hers. I swallowed and caught some air, "I wonder if we could go down to therapy every other week … I've been thinking about it for a while?"

"I'm sure you have." An eruption of laughter immediately cut short. "Are you aware, Lisa, that you often make a suggestion about withdrawing from therapy whenever we get near something you find uncomfortable?"

"No." Half lying. Clearly true. I hadn't considered it before.

"Have we touched on something now?" pushing and prodding, never letting go. "Though I don't know what it is. Do you, Lisa?"

"No, of course not." I wasn't about to offer her anything more. By this time I was slipping my ring up and down my finger, never quite taking it off before gliding it back into place. "I haven't a clue."

"Perhaps not consciously. I often feel you are hiding something, perhaps from yourself too? All your activity …"

I was in my second year of counselling training, at the beginning really. I had years to go yet, years of therapy ahead of me. I decided then and there to hunker down deeper still into my psychological trench. Even Joanna would never manage to prise me out. But she always knew I was in there, and she never did let go. In her gentle, mighty way, Joanna never did give up. Now, she leaned forward, "I wonder what so hurt you, Lisa, so frightened you that you can't bear to look at what happened?"

It was my turn to shrug my shoulders, hands quietly in my lap, wedding ring in place. Safely back in my trench, not Joanna, nor anyone else, was likely to draw me out now.

41

On the Common, Keith braked to a stop, sheepish smile on his face. This was a different bicycle, a weekend roadrunner replacing his usual collapsible steed. Beneath his helmet and Lycra togs he was an overgrown schoolboy, a dentist on day release. I stepped away to let him talk with Frank, football this time, opposing teams on opposite sides of London, comparing scores, bemoaning injuries.

"Interesting patient ..." Keith called me over. Like Frank, Keith enjoys teasing me. I think he believes I can see into his head, his best defence an unnerving refusal to take me seriously.

"What do you mean?" I looked across the green, landing on a family, another child swinging in the air, a soft blur moving across my memory, not quite tangible. I reached out for it and it was gone.

"The one I saw coming out of the building the other day. I haven't seen you since."

"Keith, you know I can't comment on my patients," turning back to face him. "You aren't supposed to be coming in and out at that point."

"But it's my building." Keith's voice is sometimes an echo of his drill, fractious and insistent, as if it's never quite broken beyond adolescence, which may account for his pointless defiance and his falling for a woman like Helen, all view and no substance.

"And as your tenant we have agreed to certain terms." Impatience hard-wired, my turn to drill down. Frank and Keith exchanged looks. Keith fiddled with his pedals, locking his right shoe into place.

"Have a good ride," Frank called after him. Keith waved, already gone.

Marching home, it was Frank who broke the silence. "I don't suppose you want to tell me what that was about?"

"My patient, the new one on Tuesday mornings. He crashed her leaving the other day. Why does he keep coming and going at precisely the times I ask him not to?"

"You can't ask him to move in and out of his own office building according to your schedule."

"Why not? A little respect, that's all I'm asking for. Nobody cares if they're seen at the dentist's, but my patients want privacy. I promise them confidentiality."

"You've been unsettled all weekend. Something about this client?" Frank was trying to make sense of things, establish what he knew in a logical frame. He wasn't far off, but there was still something nagging. "Maybe you should talk it through with Max." A statement this time, not a suggestion.

Frank can often see through me, but even with my husband I shut my doors, particularly when I don't know what might be waiting on the other side. I have very little faith in my own ability to negotiate the dark, so why would I trust anyone else to work through the gloom with me, including Frank? Better to go into lockdown. Why open up old doors when life was good enough as it was? The irony is, I never accepted that argument from any of my patients, so why did I believe it for myself? Hubris? As if I could do one better? Not likely, as it happens. Just as so many of my patients live in self-destructive "safety", deadening themselves against the terror of the unknown with drugs and sex and overwork, I was also living a deluded kind of life. The big one was tapping from the other side of the door and almost everyone could see it but me.

Once we were home I sat at my desk and read over what I had already written, unnerved a little by the thread of some thought I could not immediately grasp. It was as if in settling down to something more reflective I could not keep down some niggling worry barely below the surface of my activity. As Frank had already pointed out, I knew from experience that by focusing exclusively on the job I would eventually

43

move past the restlessness. Nothing else would exist for me, a delicious state of detachment from all life's concerns.

The speech wasn't bad, I decided. With a bit of editing I could also use it for my monthly column. I asked my audience to consider when empathy might be inappropriate? Is it ever not warranted? How deeply do we have to delve beneath the surface of appalling actions to find empathy for those we encounter? Or can we stop our efforts at anger, or hatred? When is extending empathy perhaps letting others off the hook, or sometimes a mechanism for repressing those feelings considered by most people as "negative", like fury and loathing? Empathy may sometimes be confused with love, I argued, which then leads us to embrace the world, while anger and hatred end up in expressions of destruction towards others and all too often in acts of cruelty towards ourselves. What is anorexia other than self-hatred cloaked in an effort to preserve perfection? Or even nail biting?

It's all very confusing, wheels within wheels, and sometimes in my column I rant. I suppose I'm lucky to have a vehicle for letting rip, but it is also a responsibility. People read my work as if I have all the answers. How would they know I don't always get the joke? The first time I saw myself quoted in an article by someone outside the profession I realised that my words actually arrived somewhere the other side of publication. They landed and not necessarily where, or how, I intended. A well-known, right-wing politician claimed I was advocating a tougher approach on crime, to the extent that he declared I was promoting capital punishment. He based this on my encouraging people to consider the validity of their feelings! How he managed to connect those dots, I'll never know, proof that you can rationalise anything. I was so angry I let him have it publicly on television that very week, facing him down on *Newsnight*. So furious, I forgot to be frightened, anxiety displaced by intention. All this instantly lifted my profile and during the week I paid for my public exposure. A number of patients were disturbed by evidence of the "real" me, rather than the person they believed me to be within the safety of the therapy room. The fact that I had a life beyond the office came as a shock to some of them. At least we were able to work with this. After all, whomever I had come to symbolise for them, either mother or father, or persecutory or loving sibling, that person too had certainly lived a life beyond the needs and attention of my patient. We all have a secret life.

I am not on television often, confining myself mostly to lectures and print, but whenever I am it evokes strong feelings in one or another patient. There is never indifference. For weeks afterwards I have to bear witness to hatred and grief, all stemming from my own expressions of anger in such a public forum. Those clients who come to me as a result of my public persona are also, no doubt, invariably disappointed. How could they not be? In an age when television and public success is idealised, I cannot possibly live up to their expectations. If they stick to therapy long enough, we can work through this dilemma, usually an echo of their own early relationships with the idealised parent.

All of this I considered, in one way or another, that afternoon while working on my presentation. Through the web of these thoughts I wondered who I might symbolise to my new patient. Not for a moment did I imagine whom she might symbolise for me. I didn't think about it hard, or concretely, but it was there rolling like a backdrop, informing my fingers as they tapped away developing my monthly bit of wisdom. It took some effort to stick to my task that afternoon. I don't think I was ever completely clear of some leaking anxiety from the other side of a slightly open door. I took refuge in what I knew well, the firm structure of a well-organised argument. At heart I am probably still a copywriter, wrapping up my thoughts in a tidy form of personal advertising, ensuring my self-image remains intact.

FIVE

I woke before the alarm went off at five-thirty. Frank grunted his usual early morning complaint: why the hell was he awake when he was under no pressure to rise early except to make me a cup of tea? I suspect he goes back to bed sometimes when I'm gone, recouping a few of those lost hours. His working schedule is his to set and most of his labour is in his head anyway. Frank only sits down at his desk once he's worked through one or another formulation, often refining it for weeks before beginning to scribble with his pencil, almost absentmindedly. His brain is a calculator, a big bag of numbers, but nothing tumbles out until he is ready.

That morning I was in my office by six-thirty. Before settling in I went to the kitchen, breakfasting on instant coffee and two slices of toast from last week's leftover loaf. I had a few minutes to look at my notes, focusing on my first patient of the day while I munched.

I've seen Sam, a man now in his early forties, for years. He came to me while in the throes of a cocaine habit that threatened his work and his marriage and I've never been sure which one mattered to him more. When sober he is extremely good at his job, working for a bank in the City. Despite his good fortune, he regards himself as persecuted these days because of the public perception that he makes too much money, and receives a giant bonus each year upon which he gauges his professional success. Sam is someone for whom how much money he makes is also the measure of his personal worth. Only now, after five years, are we getting down to some deeper internal work, which frightens him, so recently he has taken to skipping the occasional session. He wants solutions more than he does understanding and occasionally I wonder where, or how, our work will end. Does everyone need to understand themselves, or is it enough just to get by? Sam is proof that the question is viable, his life having improved immeasurably since he gave up drugs and partying and began to see himself as part of the general human race, albeit a segment that demands financial success. I doubt he'll ever agree with me that not being "special" is absolutely fine and that, in the end, beneath the surface of our accomplishments we are all pretty ordinary. Sam is also a charmer, so during our sessions I have to be careful not to be seduced away from the deeper material. He is a master at sidelining me, and everyone else, from any subject which might hold a greater meaning.

Oh, and Sam is rarely on time. This morning at five minutes past seven I was still sipping my coffee. In fact, I was so sure he would be late I poured myself another cup and considered our previous session. Last week Sam had mentioned that he had once had a sister. I was taken aback. Five years it took him to mention this in his therapy. Surely he had known this was important information, or had it been simmering all the while down below, beyond his reach? I had believed he was an adored only child, the one upon whom all his parents' hopes were pinned. "How old was your sister when she died?"

"A few days old, apparently. I think so, anyway."

"You're not sure?" I pushed back against the seat to prevent my moving forward. Sam never liked to stay down for very long and I knew from experience that even the most subtle movement towards him would prompt a quick lunge to the top. He would bob to the surface like a beach ball, full of nothing but hot air.

"No one talked about her much. I guess there wasn't much to talk about either. She didn't live very long."

"How old were you?" softly, softly, "How old were you when she died, Sam?"

For once he did not scrabble to escape. "Two and half, I guess. Not a baby, but pretty young. I don't remember it."

"No, but perhaps you can try to imagine, how your mother was with you afterwards?"

Startled, his dark eyes sharpened against this new light now shining in on him, not sure whether or not to continue. I remained perfectly still, not wanting to frighten him further.

"With me?" His voice turned thick, "How did my mother change with me?" Not a gesture, not a word, the slightest sound and the moment would be lost. Gradually Sam's eyes softened and then shifted to some indiscernible spot on the wall. His mother's grief would have preoccupied her, and Sam would have either been her means of distraction, or a profound interruption. Either way, he would have paid the price. She was no longer the mother she had been, exclusively his. How could she be, so racked with the loss of her second child?

Poor little Sam, so difficult to see the grief he must have experienced in the big man I saw before me, the one who clung onto his sense of self-importance like it was the last gasp in an otherwise insignificant life. I guessed that Sam had become inconsequential in light of his mother's grief: at once her only child again, but now in competition with his dead sibling over whom he could never hope to achieve victory. A dead child is always an idealised child. How desperate he must have felt as a little boy, and no wonder he worked so hard now to make himself a "player"? Who else was there to talk himself up? In the end, the patient in front of me was playing out the grief of his childhood over and over again, all his successes and financial gain simply a means of staving off his feelings of not being good enough, the impossibility of making up for the child his mother had lost.

It had taken us five years to get to this point last week when I finally learned about his sister. His dead sister.

Sam said nothing for the rest of the session. We sat in a deep, companionable silence, Sam preoccupied with his own thoughts while I moved with the tide of his mood, in and out, wondering what he might be touching on. I imagined there were no words for him wherever he was, only experience, and he was likely tipped on the very edge of pain, not yet at the heart of it. From time to time he looked at me, but it was only a passing gaze, as if to check I was still there before moving back to his spot on the wall.

Time passed quickly, as it does in such full silence, and five minutes later I had to draw the session to a close. As his therapist I may have wanted Sam to continue in this pensive current, but it is also my responsibility to stay in the world, and I had other patients to see. "I'm afraid we've come to time," my voice quiet, blasting through the silence.

Sam opened and shut his eyes, their gentle grey tones hardening into the dark shade of his adult persona. It was a quick turnaround. Too fast, indicating some sort of internal split where he could cross so easily from childhood grief to adult denial, not a soft edge in sight. He moved out of the room and down the stairs as if someone was in pursuit, opened the door and half closed it behind him by the time I caught up with him at the bottom.

"I'll see you next week, Sam", but he was already halfway down the path. Was I trying to convince myself, or him, that we would meet the following week? I could recognise terror when I saw it and Sam, I knew, was now on the run.

Still in my reverie, reflecting on last week's session, I jumped when the doorbell rang at seven-twenty, by this time convinced he wasn't going to show up.

"Hey!" as I opened the front door, "Sorry I'm late."

"Umm," giving it meaning, despite myself.

"Oh boy," bounding up the stairs. He was wearing a thick woollen overcoat, far too warm for this time of year. If it rained it would turn into a ten-ton weight. I wondered if he had put it on for this session, a modern suit of armour. Last week he had worn only a sports jacket, such a thin covering for what had transpired. Knowing Sam, he would not have questioned his motivation for donning such a thing on a warm spring morning. He left any interpretations entirely up to me.

Once in the room he dropped his leather briefcase onto the couch before plopping himself down beside it. He dug around in his jacket pocket and came out with his phone. "Sorry," he punched a few buttons with his thumbs, "I have to do this one thing …" As diversionary tactics go, this was more obvious than usual. He tapped and clicked away while I watched, resisting a temptation to yank it out of his hands. "There," he shoved the phone back where it had come from. He hadn't taken off his coat, sweating it out in the hot seat.

"Are you staying, Sam?" sarcasm leaking through.

"Not for long." He sounded so happy. "I have a quarter past eight meeting, so I have to leave in ten minutes." He checked his watch. "At 07.30 to be precise."

What could I say? Ten minutes is hardly time to make sense of anything in life, unless mulled over beforehand. Unlikely in this case. I remembered then a Jamaican colleague who told me once her clients rarely came on time. It had nearly driven her mad after working for years in London where the fifty-minute hour is sacrosanct. Following months of frustration and a building resentment she finally told herself that if her patients were only going to be there for a short time she would try to make them the best few minutes possible. I was astonished at her willingness to compromise. Registering my surprise, she let out a hefty, full bellied West Indian laugh and pointed out that I could offer patients fifty minutes, but they didn't have to take them. "You need to understand *why* they're coming late, and if you get too wound up about it you'll give yourself a heart attack." And she laughed again, thumping her chest with one hand and patting me on the shoulder like a child with the other, "You can't control everything, you know, Lisa, only how you respond. How your patients behave is their business."

"Sam, I'm interested that you are having such a short session after last week's revelation about your sister."

He stretched and lifted his arms, hands behind his head, "I guess I never thought of her before. Didn't think it was relevant." Still chirpy, almost singing, but he was also fidgety, his right knee bouncing up and down with tension.

"So, the short session?" I persisted.

"Life, I guess. Work. I didn't hear the alarm this morning, the bus was late. Whatever. And now I have this meeting," brushing me off. I felt like a speck that had inconveniently landed on his perfectly pressed trousers.

"Well, you came, so you must want something?"

"What?" arms down now, head thrust forward.

"You're here, Sam. You didn't skip the session entirely, so there must be something you want." I wasn't angry exactly, rather a curious mixture of curiosity and bewilderment. What *did* he want? Or what was it he was avoiding? Was he taking so little from me because it was a replication of what he had received from his own mother, or was he afraid of the monumental grief he was sure to feel if we revisited last week's territory, the "loss" of his mother after the death of his sister? A little of both maybe, but in truth I didn't know and it was very unlikely that Sam did either, functioning as he did most of the time above the level of reflection. This is what had created so much chaos for Sam. Over the years he had rarely understood his own motivations, or made sense of his feelings of inadequacy and failure. He responded, filling in the gaps as best he could and lifting himself out of depression with drugs and women and a terrible risk-taking that jeopardised everything.

The little reflective work he had managed over the past five years had made a difference. He now knew he suffered feelings of inferiority and he didn't much care why. His behaviour had begun to change, which was the important thing to him. Why bother pursuing the grief with his sister and mother, he seemed to be saying in his resistance to this session, and he had a point. What would he gain from working through his past now? How convinced was I that unearthing every little stone of our personal history was always a good thing?

He was sitting bolt upright in his seat, his forehead a little shiny from the heat generated within the safety of his coat. I was inexplicably exhausted, trapped in my therapist's chair, and for a moment I considered how much energy it takes to maintain safety. So much work, sweating it out every minute of every day. I took note of Sam's expression, his eyes now locked onto mine in what as children we used to call a "stare out". Who would be the first to crack? Behind the dark challenge of his glare I could see lurking a sort of pleading. Was he begging me to play his game, to let him off the hook just this once? He wanted only to be comfortable in my presence and I was making such demands of him, urging him to dig deep into his grief while he wanted only to leap across a playing field and have a bit of fun.

Sam was already a testament to my professional skills and could be regarded as a kind of therapeutic victory. He was faithful to his wife, as far as I knew, and he no longer took drugs, other than to pump up his adrenaline levels through his work and a very fast car he let loose on the motorway. I'm not sure his wife would have known quite what to do with a husband who turned reflective on her. She hadn't married a philosopher, she'd married a guy who made money and, really, that was the deal. Sam had a lot to lose through too drastic a change. Maybe it was only behavioural modification he was after, not a whole new perspective on life.

Again, I reminded myself that he had actually come to his session, if only for ten minutes. Ten minutes of what? He might be terrified of what lay ahead for him in therapy, yet he was clearly willing on some level to explore his pain. Sam at the completion of his therapy might not be at all the Sam I knew now. There would be a great deal more than air at his centre. No longer so charming, or so defensive, no longer solely defined by the measure of his financial success. Sam was taking a great risk in attending his sessions and perhaps ten minutes today was all he could manage.

How would I cope with a healthy Sam, a Sam willing to negotiate the difficult corners in his life rather than scuttling off into banal charm or a terrified corner of drugs and alcohol and generally fast living. There was a lightning bolt of pain across my chest—I caught the gasp just in time. I would lose Sam, too, as a mother does her favourite, wayward son who moves on to become someone she only distantly recognises as the child she once loved. Stranded and bereft, she is no longer needed.

How do psychotherapists cope when their clients' lives improve? In their new-found good health we also lose our patients, abandoned by them as they move into their post-therapy life without us. It is always the healthy ones for whom I feel the most grief when they leave. Like Sam's wife, I had a vested interest in his ill health—it kept him close to me. Like overprotective mothers infantilising their sons and daughters to prevent them from flying the coop, clinicians can cling to their clients too.

I crossed my arms to shut myself off, to recover before attending to Sam again. My potential loss was not my patient's responsibility, only mine to deal with. This could be my gift to him, to let him go. I pulled my arms apart and let my hands drop onto my lap, fingers loosely laced together.

Sam's eyes blinked and he let out a sigh, a huge bear of a sigh that seemed to empty him completely. He shuffled in his seat and to my astonishment I saw that he was taking off his coat. Without rising he was struggling with his arms to get loose, shaking the thing off. He left it there in an expensive heap behind him. With his elbows on his knees he held his head in his hands, the great weight of a troubled life. I was unexpectedly close to tears, a great welling up which meant I was connecting with him somewhere.

"I don't know," he muttered. "I don't know anymore," beginning to sob, big racking sobs, fists dug into the pits of his eyes. "Last week I … I don't know! … I … OH GOD!" He looked up at me. "I hate this, I don't understand it and I hate it," leaning so far forward I worried he might tip onto the floor.

"Sam?" wanting him to know I was there without intruding somehow, or diminishing his grief. He was ploughing ahead. Regardless, in this short session he was ploughing through. How brave he was.

"I could hardly work last week. And now, this morning, I have this damn meeting right after here and I don't know how I'll do it." He sounded so plaintive, so completely without. The clock was ticking, already past the time he had set himself to leave. I decided to ignore it and let him run to the end of the session. This gave us another fifteen minutes.

"Sam, it's perfectly normal to be disturbed after looking at something so difficult. And you were so young when your sister died. So young …"

"So, what's the point?" He lifted himself up from his bent position and he stared at me, daring me, "What, exactly, is the point!?"

What on earth can you say in such moments? I was connected to him in his helplessness and I could hardly see the point either. So much suffering, so much loss. There is nothing worse for a child than the loss of a mother.

Then something … abruptly, the temperature in the room seemed to change. I shivered as the cold draft of an indistinguishable shadow shunted past, and then it was gone. I heard a door squeak somewhere in the bowels of the house, perhaps Keith two storeys down, and my throat closed like a trap. I was literally speechless and, holding onto my position across from Sam, I pushed myself further into my chair. I wanted to float away, but I needed to stay put, to hold out for Sam—Sam who at least had come to his session. With a mighty internal heave I brought myself back to earth, the reassuring grounding of my professional self.

Most therapists of my ilk will tell you that it is through revisiting the pain that we can somehow find a way to symbolise it, make sense of it, place it within the context of our lives and therefore find it easier to live with. We can move on, no longer terrorised by it, no longer so traumatised that we live in the present as if it were the past, driven by our former demons. That is the point. But in the moment of the pain, there is no point. It is only raw and terrible and reasoning has nothing to do with it. Making sense of it comes later, if we're lucky, and I didn't know at this point whether Sam was one of those who would choose to stay, or to run from the prospect of so much anguish.

"What's the bloody point?" he was yelling out now.

I wasn't afraid, I was grief stricken. And helpless. I sat in my grand therapy chair and held on as hard as I could, my hands like anchors dropped to the front of my seat and clinging to the edge like ballasts. We watched one another, Sam and I, until he drooped suddenly, his head back in his hands. He was no longer crying, he was empty. More would come up, but for now he was spent. At least he had done it here, not out on the tiles with white powder up his nose or racing at a killing speed around the M25, his life turning in one more frenetic circle.

The clock had run out. I didn't need to say it this time. Sam lifted his head, checked his watch and stood up, put his coat back on and lifted his briefcase, heavy now as it hadn't been before. "I'll see you next week," his voice was soft, a little breathless. He stood still at the door like a boy, waiting for me to open it. A quiet descent, there was no racing down the stairs this time. "I'll see you next week," he repeated at the bottom and was gone.

I turned around to go back to my office. Keith was in, his drill already boring away. This time, though, I couldn't even summon up the energy to be annoyed.

Ten minutes later I still hadn't done my notes, usually an automatic function of the therapeutic hour. I write them up in the few minutes I have between sessions, but this morning I let them go, sitting instead in my chair after Sam was gone thinking of nothing. When the doorbell rang to notify me of my next client, for the second time that morning I jumped, warning myself as I got up to get a grip.

I mentally trudged through that second session of the morning, a young woman eager for self-discovery and expression. She was tedious in her own way, but at least she got on with "it", whatever that was and I needed only to listen as she groped around looking for meaning in the most mundane of life's corners, such as her pursuit for a "man who will meet my needs". She used all the therapeutic buzzwords gleaned from magazines and self-help books and she terrified me with notions of training as a counsellor, but I dutifully said nothing. It would be years, I believed, before she was truly able to ponder life and its deeper meanings, and in the meantime she was a kind of tiresome light relief. At the end of our session I was still full of the weight of Sam and his unprecedented plunge into early experience and loss. I had no trouble writing up her notes, and afterwards I left my room to find some air in the kitchen. I should have known better. There was every chance I would meet Keith or one of the other therapists. Was I desperate enough to settle for that kind of distraction?

Clutching a cup of tea in one hand and with the other holding myself intact, my arm wrapped around my stomach, I passed Martha on the stairwell on my way back to the office. My efforts to chase away that first morning session with Sam were proving pointless. I was still avoiding writing his notes.

Martha is the counsellor who works in the office on the first floor, above Keith on the main floor. There was no way I could bypass her completely. I smiled, or tried to anyway, felt my face move in a lopsided direction and widened my eyes in compensation. I know that never works when I see it in others, so why did I bother?

Martha's usually smooth brow creased into a narrow frown and her bottom lip quivered enough for me to see her confusion, "How about lunch today?" Maybe she didn't know what else to say.

We agreed to meet at the cafe around the corner. *Kisse's* it was called, a remarkable name for such a cosy cafe and considering the loaded meaning of any kind of kiss. Sitting down at the table, I moved my chair back a little so as not to be too close to her. She is a huggy sort of woman and I am forever wary, sidestepping her at every opportunity.

Martha and I function from entirely different perspectives. I try not to express a patronising tone with her, but it's so damn hard when she is so confident and with so little training. She is a nice young woman, very kind, and I am sure her clients love her but she'll never have a Sam yelling at her before eight in the morning. Only love is expressed in her counselling room, empathy dripping from the central light fixture, where hangs an arrangement of reflecting crystals. God knows it exudes from the pictures she has on the walls and little posters with aphorisms suggesting that the way to eternal and lifelong happiness is just to be "you", whoever that might be. In my experience, often there is no "you" on the other side of the "false" self, only a great, yawning emptiness that with a great deal of work may be filled, at least to some degree. There is no magic trick where you wipe away the pastiche and find an honest to goodness personality hidden underneath.

So, with Martha I tend to veer away from theoretical discussion, despite her attempts to engage me in what feels akin to religious conversion. She is evangelical about her perspective, longing to convince me that along her path lies therapeutic salvation, and those that resist are inevitably damned. She is only trying to save me. In Martha's eyes I am an infidel, while to me she is a sweet, naive woman without a theoretical bone in her body to give her structure. She is a blind believer, the worst kind.

Munching my cheese and tomato panini, I savoured the certainty that she wasn't going to like my latest column, focusing on the hazards of empathy. I was doing my best not to glower at her, to stare down her perpetually benign expression, the kind you see on ex-nuns and Jehovah's Witnesses when they interrupt in the middle of the day. Unfortunately, it only makes me want to slam the door even harder.

However, I was still drained after my session with Sam, and I knew that my appreciation of his pain had been part of what had helped him open up to such traumatic, early experience. Tomorrow I would be facing my new client. Another internal shudder, a loosening of something deep inside usually held very tight. I glanced towards Martha, who was enjoying a piece of cake, and immediately looked away again, not in the mood to witness such deep satisfaction. Today Sam's overcoat, tomorrow the terrible sight of a pair of knees ...

"You look tired, Lisa," taking another bite of her cake. Passive aggression, the British first line of defence. "Are you working too hard these days?"

I smiled at her, "No, just my regular week. And how about you, honey, very busy?" I wasn't going to have this conversation focus on me, no sir. If Martha wanted to talk, she could talk about herself for once.

"I'm fine." Martha wiped her mouth clear of a few crumbs. Was she looking at me, or somewhere behind me? It was hard to tell. Like many people who choose to investigate the lives of others, she is not good at ordinary conversation. Without something to reflect back, she is unsure of herself.

"How's Daniel? I haven't seen him for a bit?" I piped up, taking pity on her. Daniel is her partner. Another empathic reflector, I sometimes wonder how they manage to carry on a conversation if neither of them is willing to break across the path of the other's echo. Fights are probably non-existent. He conducts his practice in the room opposite Martha's, immediately below mine, though his clinical practice is small and his teaching load large. I see him so seldom I'm sure his office is only for show, which suits me fine. Daniel brings out the monster in me. His diminutive stature and his simpering expression, as if goodness can be exchanged for obsequiousness without notice, drive me to distraction. There is nothing robust about Daniel, though he is somehow impenetrable due to his wall of universal love. I'd like to give him a good old fashioned shove, break down that barrier a bit and see who is really inside. A ferret, maybe, or a weasel?

"Daniel's fine, thanks, very busy. I think he wants to ask you to talk at our next conference, sometime in September, I think, or late August."

I burst out laughing. "Why on earth would you want me to address your conference? I'll be booed off the stage, for heavens' sake … Or is that the point?" I kept my voice even, "A kind of circus act, highlighting the freak?"

Martha didn't blanch and it struck me then that she might be growing up. "It's often a good idea to expose ourselves to other perspectives, don't you think?" She looked me dead in the eye before popping another bite of cake into her mouth. Was that mischief I could see lurking behind the frankness of her expression? Well, this was a new tack.

"I couldn't agree more, but I'm still a bit surprised. Let me know the dates and I'll see if I'm free." I stood up; I would need time to think about this one. For all my public speaking, I am not fond of making a fool of myself. I prefer to stage-manage the responses and to choose my audiences, focusing particularly on those who may not necessarily agree with me all the time, but still hold me in high regard. Friday's talk was already touch and go, and any conference organised by Daniel was definitely the lion's den. "I have to head back to the office," shoving my chair back under the table. It squeaked against the floor tiles and I had to shuffle it a bit to make it fit.

Martha brushed a few last cake crumbs into the palm of her hand and scattered them onto her empty plate before smiling up at me. She crumpled her napkin and placed it delicately next to her empty plate, "Hold on, I'll join you." She stood up, too.

"Sure, all right." Sometimes there's no getting away from it, there's always someone or something running you to ground. As we climbed up the stairs to our separate offices, Martha grabbed me on the landing and slapped a kiss on one cheek, then on the other. I felt like a shaken toy. And there was the mischief again, smiling as she waved me goodbye.

"Have a good day, Lisa," her voice was an octave higher than usual. Was she trying not to laugh? "Don't work too hard."

"No, of course not," my face turning lopsided again. I nearly burst out laughing too.

Once in the office, I thought about Sam for a bit and looked at his file sitting on the desk beside the computer. I wondered how I could turn the experience of our recent work into an article. I was contemplating a longer, more academic piece. The irony that I was still avoiding writing his session notes was not completely lost on me. I could think of him more comfortably in a wider scope than I could within the minutiae of today's meeting.

Clinical notes are not only about the patient, but about the therapist's response to the client, and with Sam I hadn't quite worked that out yet. Something beyond Sam was unsettling. It was easier to think of Sam in the context of theoretical expression and professional finesse than it was to think of how, or what, he was disturbing in me. And so I gave up, folded up his file, and put it back in the locked box I keep deep in the corner and tucked neatly out of view behind the couch.

With an hour to spare, I sat down to edit Friday's speech into my regular column. There was not much left to do, thank goodness, as the task was becoming interminable. I had only to check the commas and full stops and of course the word count. I knew from painful experience that if I handed in an overly long piece, the editor would snip off the last paragraph without considering that my summing up was the point of the whole exercise.

I rocketed the article via my computer to the newspaper and felt my usual wave of relief when it was gone, followed by an immediate shiver of anxiety that I had not done something well enough. I diverted myself immediately by adding the finishing touches to Friday's PowerPoint. As always, it took me slightly longer than I anticipated, rethinking the order of things and forcing me to rework both the slides and my talk so they would match. I was still pounding away at my keys when a buzzer on my computer warned me that I had just a few minutes before my next client was scheduled. I was done, everything now in order. I had my energy back and I was on fire. When the buzzer went at five o'clock, I didn't jump this time. Professionally confident, I walked down the stairs to open the door.

SIX

I remembered Dorothy's name just as I opened my office door the next morning, half an hour before she was meant to arrive. Through the thicket of dense memory, it finally emerged. Until then I had only the vision of her bare knees in mind, and her little hand pounding against her thigh. I read her notes—one page—taken aback that I had put down so little. I knew nothing about her, not her job or where she had grown up. Was she married? Of course not, I reminded myself, she had said she struggled with relationships, though that could mean anything from the soup of friendship to the nuts of marriage or a committed relationship.

I was tired this morning following a restless night and the haunting edge of a dream I couldn't quite grasp after waking with a start around three. Must have shouted out because Frank was sitting up in bed when I shot upright and looked around the room to see where I was.

"Whoah!" I gasped.

"You were dreaming. A nightmare by the looks of things." Rubbing my shoulder, reassuring me.

I shivered. "I can't remember anything … something huge … an oversized cannon ball or boulder hurtling towards me …"

"Well, you're the therapist, but that seems pretty obvious to me."

"Why, what?"

Through the night shadows I could see Frank's brow crease. "Lisa, you've been on edge for a week now. Something's on your mind. What is it?"

"I don't honestly know." I sat back against my pillow trying to resurrect the dream. In the old days I had kept a pad by my bed to write them down, though with the end of my training I let that discipline go. I had other things to concentrate on and dreams were never my favourite "royal route into the unconscious". Joanna had once suggested that I found dreams a little too revealing for comfort. Why was I thinking of Joanna now? There was so much I hadn't told her through all those years of therapy. She constantly reminded me that whatever I kept secret from her, I was not, in therapy parlance, "working through" either, which could lead to trouble.

"Did I say anything significant?" still scrambling after the dream.

"I don't know. It was your shouting that woke me up."

It was already fading into a mushy blend of nonsensical images, though the quality of the experience, the resonance of deep terror and longing remained. Longing? Where had that come from? "Okay. Sorry for waking you up. We should try to get more sleep."

"Mmm. Good idea," He slipped down under the duvet. I slid down beside him, still restless, hunting out the nugget I knew was there in the dream and which I couldn't quite capture, like digging for gold in an old, disused mine. I was so unaccustomed to the terrain that I couldn't recognise the rich seam for what it was underneath all that black stuff, the sheets of muck and the false leads I'd laid down for myself over the years. I stared at the ceiling, then at the wall, shadows growing ever larger with the morning sun.

When the alarm sounded at five-thirty I was hugely relieved. I wanted to get out of bed and race ahead to my office where work could distract me. I then remembered I was to see Dorothy first thing and so remained in the bed for a few more minutes. I was clinging to the familiar and ignoring the underground tension, plates finally rubbing against one another, testing the ground in a last ditch effort to find a safer fit.

Dorothy pressed the buzzer at precisely seven o'clock. This time I was prepared; at the forefront of my mind her drowning image at the front door the week before, and her bare knees. Instead, she was crisp and dry today, wearing a trouser suit and high, pin-thin heels that elevated her a few centimetres above my own head height. Her light brown hair was tidied away in a neat bun at the nape of her neck, a curiously old-fashioned hairstyle which this morning looked very chic.

After a quick, perfunctory smile, Dorothy walked past me towards the stairs with brisk, determined steps, her heels like nail guns where the rubber had peeled away and the wood showed through. I trailed behind her, trying to catch up, a hand on the banister to keep my balance. She was too quick, already sitting down by the time I reached my office.

This was not the bounding enthusiasm of Sam's deflection yesterday, rather this was purposeful action, last week's tentative approach replaced by intention and an edge of aggression. I was struck again by how early in our meeting we were engaged in such overt tension. Was this the playing out of some trauma in her past? I sat down in my seat: crossed my ankles and folded my hands in my lap, facing her directly. I could see the years between us, my own youth long passed away. Feeling dowdy and elderly, I lifted a hand to pull a lock of hair out from behind my ear. I was also itchy, directly below my knee, but resisted the temptation to lean forward and give it a scratch. These moments were filled with sensation rather than thought, self-absorption devoid of reflection. Dorothy was poised, sitting quietly, elegantly, and without fidgeting, clearly waiting for me to start.

"You decided to return." I had to begin somewhere.

She nodded, but said nothing, almost regal.

"Well, before we begin I need some details from you: your address for one thing," standard routine on the second meeting, in this case also a neat diversion. I picked up a note card from the table beside me, slipping a pen from out of my diary. I was flummoxed by this new, contained presentation and I did not know how to engage her. Normally the patient begins the session and the therapist follows the trail, however for those clients who are new to the experience it can take a while to learn the conventions of therapy. Dorothy appeared to have taken the lead regardless. In her silence and her surprising self-assurance she was dominant. I was the one floundering.

She told me her address, an impressive distance to travel in order to arrive by seven in the morning. She lived in north London, near Primrose Hill, eerily close to Helen's flat. Did they pass one another sometimes, two lonely souls connected by an unknown thread to me? Travelling across town would have included both the Tube and a bus, unless she was willing to take an energetic fifteen-minute walk from the station. Probably not in those shoes.

Finished with the form I sat tall in my chair, and waited. Dorothy's eyebrows lifted in expectation and she watched me with a cool, blue-eyed gaze that dropped finally when I shuffled in my seat, an effort to dislodge another distracting itch, now at the back of my neck. Why was I so unfocused, so confounded about where to begin? There was a great deal I needed to know about this young woman. So far I had nothing, the barest details.

"I wonder if you had any thoughts after our meeting last week?" another routine question on the second session, a kind of loosener, again for my benefit rather than my client's. I needed help, and time to think.

Then I saw it, like a shaft of light beaming out from an endlessly dark space. Dorothy's nail polish, a gleaming fire engine red, was chipped, small teeth marks of imperfection just at the tips. Such a small thing, but it gave her away. She must have picked up my relief, instinctively closing both her fists and, for the first time this morning, knocked against her thighs, two gentle taps in tandem. Light warning shots, holding despair at bay.

"Last week was fine," revealing nothing at all, her voice a degree stronger than last week, a little more solid.

"I need to find out more about you," comfortable now in my seat. "You said last time you struggled with relationships but I don't know whether you are married or not, or have children? Or what you do for a living?" Too many direct questions all at once. I was so relieved at knowing at last where to aim that, like her, I was gunning from the hip. There is nothing strictly wrong with this kind of bulk querying, though you might get a more complete picture by asking one question at a time. I smiled at her. Not the lopsided variety this time, but with self-assurance and, unexpectedly, a degree of warmth.

"I'm not married, though I was once a few years ago. He left after a couple of months."

"You sound very matter of fact," maternal concern welling up, familiar to every therapist, the disconcerting invitation to *love*.

Dorothy tipped her head a little to the left and clenched her fists a little more tightly. "Maybe. I didn't like it at the time, but it's a couple of years ago now. I don't think of him anymore."

"You didn't *like* it? That seems a very small word for the end of a marriage."

She said nothing, nor did she tap. Not looking at me now either, her focus on the dusty corner of my bookshelf where last week she had found such comfort. I wasn't so disturbed this time, but reminded myself to give it a wipe myself as the cleaner clearly couldn't manage it. If Dorothy was to find some soothing in this room, I wanted it to be in the quality of our exchange rather than in a sense of superiority over me. This was well-known territory for me. Over and over again in my therapy with Joanna I had been forced to consider my own fragile self-esteem and rampaging self-doubt, which often sought shelter behind the convenient obstinacy of arrogance. I knew that Dorothy was literally tapping into a basic weakness in me, reflected in the powerful shift in confidence when either of us felt deprived of the upper hand. I had some idea of what drove me to be ahead of any game, but I did not know yet what such empty conquests meant for Dorothy.

I was itchy again, my left arm this time, a strip of skin above my watch. I gave in, rubbing the fingers of my right hand hard against it to dampen the irritation. At the same time, I leaned forward a few millimetres to draw closer to Dorothy and to bring her attention back from the cluttered corner of my bookshelf into contact with me. "And now, Dorothy? Is there anyone in your life at the moment?" Lessons learned from Joanna, persisting, persisting.

"I have friends, colleagues I see. I work pretty hard so I don't get that much time off."

"What do you do?"

"I'm a lawyer. I work for a bank in the City."

"A lawyer?"

There was something dissonant in the room, some note so off-key and sharp I nearly ducked. What had I imagined she did for a living? The truth was I hadn't considered that she did anything at all; my imagination had stonewalled in the wake of that first, disquieting session, struggling even to remember her name.

"Yes. Are you surprised?" She played out a quick rhythm with her hands against the couch. Through the thin layer of her voice I heard last week's brackishness. It seemed to rise up despite her best effort, like an unpleasant odour.

"I am a bit, though I don't know why. Should I be?"

"I suppose everybody is, me included. My dad thought the law was a good way to go. He was very encouraging."

"You have to work pretty hard to become a lawyer, particularly working in the City."

"I do work hard. I always work hard."

"Well, do you like being a lawyer? Do you enjoy your job?"

"Sometimes. Not always."

"What I mean is, do you gain satisfaction from your job? Does it feel meaningful to you?"

"I've never thought about it like that. I get satisfaction out of the fact that I'm a lawyer, which I suppose is a little different from getting it from the job itself."

I nearly cheered at that moment, Dorothy's first reflective thought. For a therapist this is like watching a child take his first step. I let her sit for a few seconds without interruption and for once the silence resonated with something more than empty preoccupation. She did not even tap.

Dorothy sighed. The moment was over.

"Can you tell me a little about your parents? Are they alive?"

"Uhnhungh." It was an unlikely sound, deep too, the hard grunt of effort.

"They're alive?" a pang of jealousy, an invitation from my client to play one parent against the other. I banished it immediately, another warning signal, straightening my back ever taller.

"Yes. All of them."

"*All* of them?" resisting the urge to laugh. "That sounds like you have more than two."

"I do. My parents are divorced and they've both remarried. I was pretty young and I don't remember when they separated. I lived with my dad most of the time."

"That's unusual."

"I know, but that's how it worked out."

"Did you see your mother? Did she live close by?" Such an easy question, containing mammoth complexities. How could it not, a mother's relationship with her child? The deprivation of a mother, a part-time mother in this case?

The reaction was immediate. Her brow furrowed and her eyes turned solid steel. It was like peering down the dark end of pistol barrels before she took aim and fired. I felt the shock of a terrible electricity charge, a direct hit to my core. Unlike with Sam the day before, I could not keep myself down. It was as if I was lifted out of my chair, my head floating somewhere above itself and I could not think. The sensation was a delirious mix of dissociation, and closer to the ecstasy of escape than any I had experienced before with a patient. Aside from the brutality of the moment and the anguish of confusion, there is also something blissful about dissociation. Even at its most distressing, at least you are not where you were, in the midst of your trauma. Spirited away above yourself, there is no capacity to think, and no emotion either, only the addictive sensation of transcendence.

I wanted to stay in this state, this ethereal sense of soaring above myself, above the world, above Dorothy, from whom I was now completely removed. In desperation I put my hands flat on the arms of the chair and put my feet squarely on the floor. Gradually, I drifted south and fell into place again: recalibrated, stunned into a new view of Dorothy as someone deeply disturbed beyond the simplicity of a few complicated relationships.

Down at last, I focused on my patient again. I needed to attend to her, and to return what she had so effectively projected into me. Had she realised my altered state? "Dorothy, how are you feeling at the moment?" My voice was dull and full of echo and my ears were plugged, just landed from a long-haul flight.

70

"Okay," her voice as if from a distance, through a time tunnel echoing, "okay okay okay …"

What was it I'd asked her? I needed to remember the question immediately before I'd floated away? This was crucial. Why else would she have sent me spiralling off into another dimension? Still struggling to clear my head, I pressed a tender spot on my neck directly below my right ear, to feel the tempo of blood thrumming through my system. I gathered my thoughts and sifted through them quickly until I landed on the moment before Dorothy had packed her charge. My question had been about her mother, about her contact with her mother. In the alchemy of therapy I was confident that she had projected into me what she could not bear herself. I had taken wing while she remained solidly on the ground, safe behind the defence of her furious denial that anything important had happened in her life at all.

"Your mother, Dorothy, did you see your mother often?" I held onto my chair. I was not going to float away this time.

She shuffled in her seat and crossed her legs, one over another in a deliberate effort to delay her answer. Her hands were solid, holding on to the edge of the couch. There was no tapping, only the slow motion rocking of her right leg, with each gentle kick the narrow point of her shoe aimed directly towards me. Then, staring at the clock on my side table, counting the minutes, she sighed again, her exasperation expressed in a short propulsion of air.

"When we lived in the same neighbourhood I saw her, but my father is a diplomat. We lived all over. My mother was in England, so in the years I was living here, at least at the beginning, I saw her pretty regularly. I came out during the summer for a month or so when we lived abroad. I saw her the same as most kids do whose parents are divorced and live in another country. Which isn't much at all."

"You sound like you think I'm stupid for asking."

Dorothy's foot stopped its rocking and she looked up quickly, her pupils again reduced to the sharp points of pencil lead. "Maybe. It all seems so obvious to me, and I don't see how telling you is going to make any difference." Her voice contained all the stubbornness of adolescence.

"Well, in that case, what do you think I *do* need to know about you?" I refused to engage in the battle. Regardless of her adolescent sulk, it was still far too early in the work to push her into corners where she did not want to go. If she stuck around long enough we would quite naturally return to discussing her mother. I wondered if the safer ground for Dorothy at this point was her father, the diplomat with enthusiasm for the law?

"I don't know. You're the expert."

"Well, that rather traps me between a rock and a hard place. You don't want me to ask you about your mother, but you won't tell me anything about your personal life either."

She uncrossed her legs and put her hands together in her lap. She was learning to contain herself here, and to read me more clearly. I doubted that her self-control had much to do with trust, so much as becoming more familiar with the rules of therapy, so far as she understood them anyway. She drifted away once more, looking around the room for something to lock onto, something other than me. I watched while she undid her hands and pressed her palms hard against her leg before clasping them together again. Only then did she return to me and I thought I saw her jump, an internal leap of surprise that I was even in the room with her. Where did she think she was? With no other way out, perhaps she was now the one dissociating.

She was in need of such soothing, a reflex in me sparked into life at the vision of her pressing so hard against her lap for comfort, gathering herself in like a child in search of a hug. "Dorothy, you seem to have difficulty concentrating. I imagine it's hard to answer my questions if you've not spoken to anyone about these kinds of things before, or not spoken about them very often?"

"Why would I tell anyone?"

My earlier irritation flashed into life. "You're answering my questions with questions of your own." My tone was sharp, almost parental. I began again, more gently this time, "Can you tell me why you don't speak to anyone about your life? Friends must ask you questions, or colleagues … or perhaps they don't?" This was an afterthought—Dorothy likely had a perspex wall around herself, a cool distance fending off every enquiry.

She avoided this tack by launching into an answer to my earlier question. Giving herself time to think, she had worked out a story.

"My mother left when I was four. She left for another man, or so my father tells me. My mother says she left me with my father because he was the better parent. She wasn't prepared for motherhood and my father could give me a better life. If there was someone else, she didn't marry him then. She married Steve a few years later, when I was about eight. I came back for the wedding."

"Where were you? Where did you come back from?"

"Ottawa. We lived in Ottawa." Dorothy moved in her chair, straightening herself up. Her eyebrows lifted and she smiled, as if I should infer something from this information.

"That's a long way for an eight year old to travel." That itch again, this time underneath my watch. I pressed it hard and shuffled it along a few centimetres in an effort to reduce the aggravation.

Dorothy moved her head from side to side, a little shake indicating I hadn't quite got the joke. For the first time I realised that on occasion I could hear a Canadian note in her speech, in the harder tone of her "r's", and the occasional flat inflection of a word scraped clean of any meaning. How did I sound to Dorothy, a more intense mirror of her own way

73

of speaking? Despite so many years in London, my voice is still broad with the patterns of my childhood, my sensibilities clearly entrenched in the prairie landscape I tried hard to leave behind. Was this what Dorothy found amusing, our geographical connection?

Nobody knows better than me that understanding often takes time in therapy. That which cannot be made sense of immediately may need time to gestate in order to come clear. I could have asked her, I suppose, pointed out her expression of expectation, but this might fit into some pattern of hers which I didn't yet understand. If I didn't play the game, I could not become hooked into the dynamic, and so I avoided it altogether. Whatever games she played with me, no doubt she played them with everyone in her life.

"My mother liked me in small doses. I spent a week with her after the wedding and then I flew home."

"To your father."

"Yes."

"How was it with your dad?"

"Easier than with my mum, but then I didn't see him so much either. I mean, I didn't see him every day, or not for long anyway. He was the deputy high commissioner and he was out a lot."

"You weren't sent to boarding school?" I had lived in the UK long enough to know that expats often sent their children "home" to be educated.

"No. He didn't believe in it. He said he'd had a horrible time as a kid and he wasn't about to send me out to the wolves before I was ready."

"The wolves?"

"He meant the world, really. He wanted to protect me." Dorothy's voice dipped into a softness I hadn't heard before. There was no sign of the brackishness now, or of detachment. I reminded myself that this was the same father who had been keen on "the law", as she put it.

74

I took a cursory look at the clock. It was nearly time for the session to end. Dorothy was quick to pick up on my diversion. "Is it time?"

"Nearly. There are a few minutes to go."

"I can't come next week. I have a work meeting early Tuesday and I can't skip it."

"I can give you an alternative appointment if you like." I nearly rolled my eyes. The "switch my appointment" defence is such a familiar one, another mechanism for control. Two sessions in and she was already at it. The giveaway was in her not asking for an alternative time. How far would she go to avoid next week's session? "I can offer you next Wednesday morning, or later in the day on Tuesday." At least I was trying.

"Sorry, it's a busy week."

"You know you will be charged?" Sometimes this works and highlights the patient's relationship with money, but the ploy had no effect on Dorothy. Not attending her therapy was clearly worth it to her.

"That's fine. I'll see you in two weeks." She was so self-assured. Despite the grinding assault of the session—at least this was my experience—there was not a hair of her elaborate chignon out of place. She stood tall again in her perfectly pressed trouser suit and her lethal high heels. It was as if I was reduced somehow, diminutive in my middle-aged role as her therapist. I had a few more details now, yet I still knew very little about her, and her elevated stature as she stood up next to me seemed proof enough of her position of power. I wanted to keep her.

She would see me in two weeks' time, and there wasn't a damn thing I could do about it.

SEVEN

I don't get nearly so nervous as I used to before giving a talk. In the old days I would vanish into the loo beforehand, letting go all my anxieties in one almighty heave. Afterwards I was lightheaded, a bit on edge and once-removed from myself. Only then could I go out in front of an audience and it was almost as if someone else was addressing the crowd; I was simply the vehicle through which the information was being served. Purging myself beforehand was the way I coped.

Frank noticed my anxiety on Friday morning before I did. I spilled coffee all over the kitchen counter. What I actually did was forget to install the pot in its slot beneath the filter and the freshly brewed coffee poured out everywhere.

I was in the bedroom, blow-drying my hair and even above the racket of the machine I heard the thump, thumping of Frank down below attempting to contain the spillage. He must have tipped the whole contraption into the sink because when I came down to see what was going on, it was lying on its side like a capsized ocean liner. Brown gunk was everywhere, seeping underneath the toaster and the cereal packets and dripping down over the counter into the barely opened cutlery drawer, overflowing onto the floor. Frank looked beside himself, clutching a roll of kitchen towel in one hand and a scrunched-up wad of paper in the other in a frantic effort to mop up the mess.

"Oh, god!" I knew immediately what I'd done. I grabbed another kitchen roll from the cupboard and began attacking the floor while Frank was still trying to hold back the deluge up top.

"Lisa," he finally said. The counter was wiped clean, the soggy cereal box in the litter bin, and the cutlery drawer dried up and firmly shut. The coffee machine, too, was back in its regal position against the wall, the pot in its slot. Frank wouldn't let me touch it, a hand in the air to warn me off. Again, "Lisa, what on earth is going on with you?" Arms crossed, paternal.

I clapped my hand over my mouth, resisting the urge to giggle, but his expression was so severe that I sobered up immediately and shoved my fists deep into my dressing gown pockets. "Frank, this is a coffee pot, not a car accident, or a …" I couldn't quite figure out where to go here, but I carried on regardless, "… or a … I don't know … a house fire … something tragic."

"Maybe it *will* be a house fire next time. How the hell should I know!" He was actually shouting, not something he does often, only when pushed beyond endurance. I was an unreliable equation at the moment, my numbers not adding up. "You aren't sleeping properly, you're jumpy and more irritable than usual, and now this absentminded incident with the coffee pot."

"What do you mean, I'm more irritable than usual?"

"Oh for heaven's sake." He dropped his arms and they hung by his sides like broken windmills. He didn't droop though, thank goodness, because I couldn't have stood that, Frank losing heart. My head felt heavy and I wrenched one hand out of my pocket to push back my hair. It was still damp. Frank was staring at me and I realised I must be a terrible sight in my white dressing gown, patched with a series of brown coffee spots and my hair awry. He raised his eyebrows, "You might not want to go out looking like that," his voice measured again, trying another approach, as he usually does when faced with an apparently incalculable problem. "If you want to finish dressing I'll bring you coffee in a minute … when it's finished brewing."

"Thank you," ignoring his sarcasm by starting towards the stairs.

"But Lisa," his voice followed me, "you do need to figure out what's going on. Something's up. Whenever you're distracted you start doing things like this."

"You mean being irritable?"

"Oh, that. You're always irritable. It's the coffee pot I'm thinking about. Next time, it might be a car accident. That's what worries me."

"I am NOT always irritable."

"See, there you are."

"Oh, for heaven's sake."

Frank never stays angry for long, but he had made me think. Forced to take my own pulse I recognised I was more nervous than usual before giving a talk. After so many years of building up my confidence I wasn't likely to head for the loo, though I did feel a bit nauseous, a touch of the old biliousness rising up in my throat. I shuddered and swallowed hard to push down the dread.

Frank came into the bedroom, placed a steaming coffee mug pointedly in front of me, then sat on the edge of the bed to wait till I'd finished drying my hair. I took a sip, stronger than I would have made it, but under the circumstances I said nothing. Leaned into the mirror to put on my make-up, I could see him in the reflection, watching me, eyebrows pinched with concern. "Frank, you've made your point, let it go. This was a stupid domestic accident. For heaven's sake, don't make things worse." I rubbed in a little foundation, smoothing out the surfaces along my cheekbones and the edge of my jaw. I hated to see women when they missed blending in their make-up, when the ridge of their face was let down by the unholy exposure of their neck.

"I'm trying to figure you out. You're very jumpy at the moment and I'm finding it a bit unnerving, to tell the truth. How can I help you if you won't tell me what's going on?"

I touched up my cheeks with a little rouge, otherwise I am pasty-faced, put on mascara, slapped a strip of lipstick across my lips and sat down beside Frank on the bed. I didn't want to talk about this, but Frank is obsessive, unlikely to let it go unless I addressed his worry directly. At the moment I was clearly a problem he couldn't quite master, the irregular fragments of recent experience not quite fitting into a cohesive pattern. I would have to oblige him on some level.

"Honestly, there's nothing actually 'going on', as you put it. I'm a bit pressed at the moment, I guess. Have a couple of difficult patients, including my new one. I see Max this week, so maybe that will help?"

Frank stood up, "That's good." He sounded so sure.

I stood up too, a kind of confrontation and an invitation for him to leave. This wasn't the morning I'd envisioned, the calm few hours I'd planned before leaving the house. It was already eight-thirty, the coffee pot disaster and the resulting debriefing having taken up at least forty-five minutes. I still needed to look at my notes and remind myself of the key points I intended to make. I was not adding up for Frank, he still hadn't fixed me in the firmament of certainty.

He smiled, a rueful blend of affection and gentle defeat. "Okay, okay. I'm going." Watching him leave, I reminded myself that he had married me precisely because I refused to remain fixed. Like an impossible theorem, I could be worked on forever, possibly without ever providing a conclusive result. I trusted that there was some pleasure for him in the predictability of the recalibrations. I never considered that sometimes even the most meaningful struggles can become tiresome.

Tipping his head towards the door, "Get ready and I'll see you before you go."

An hour later I was standing at my desk putting my notes in my briefcase when Frank stuck his head through the door. "How is it going? Everything sorted for this morning?"

"I'm not having this conversation again," I warned him, but he shook his head.

"Affectionate concern, that's all? It's been a bit of a rough morning, wouldn't you agree?"

I snapped my briefcase shut and swung it down off the desk. Frank ducked, as if I was intending to hit him.

"Don't be ridiculous."

He stood up straight, "You are a bit fierce at the moment."

All I wanted this morning was a bit of peace. I put my hand up to my forehead.

"Headache?" Frank guessed.

I nodded, "A small one so far." Barely a haze at the moment, but it would soon grow if I didn't take action.

In the early days, when I was first seeing Frank, I had been persecuted by regular headaches. They were not migraines, or so the doctors told me, and Joanna suggested that they were related to my work with her in therapy. Over time they diminished and when I stopped seeing Joanna they stopped almost entirely for a few years. More recently they visited like uninvited guests, expecting to be fed. I never knew how long they might last, and though they rarely incapacitated me anymore, they did sometimes linger, a dull throb in the background of my daily life that meant I was never entirely engaged in what I was doing. This was despite my making every effort to occupy myself so thoroughly that I could ignore them, or even drive them away. I put on my jacket, preparing to leave the house.

"Here," Frank handed me a pill and a glass of water, "Sometimes this works."

He was right, sometimes it did. I popped the capsule and took a swig of the water.

"There." I handed him the glass. We kissed lightly, "Have a good day."

"You too," he patted me gently on the arm, like a child being sent off to school. "I hope it goes well."

I heard the door click behind me as I went out, and the hard thud of the double lock as the hammers fell into place.

The venue was a new one for me, on the north side of the centre of London near King's Cross. I took the bus, sitting up top as usual. It was a two-bus run, changing at Aldwych to cut across the centre and past the London School of Economics where the pavement was busy with rushing students. Their backpacks slung over one shoulder, they used them like battering rams against the army of strolling tourists perpetually in their way. Students believe they own the world, or in my experience they do. The harsh reality of adult life, the shedding of that sense of entitlement, is sometimes brutal. I watched as a young woman tore through the pedestrian traffic like a car weaving through a series of chicanes, hair flying and feet slapping so hard against the concrete I could hear them all the way up here in the gods. The tourists she left behind reeled backwards and forwards as if on magnetic balls, bouncing back into position as she knocked against the next one, not once breaking her pace. Was she really in such a hurry, or was this her way of establishing her place in the world? I wondered what she was studying—the sciences, politics, drama? Whatever it was, she was certainly racing to get there. The bus moved past and she was gone.

London has a surprising amount of green and I distracted myself by looking up at the emerging, spring leaves of the trees, rather than continue looking down at the teaming streets of Holborn and Bloomsbury. As ever, I wished I could identify them. The one tree I could distinguish was a maple: not many of those in London. And pine trees: Canada and the scent of childhood, a vision of myself soaked in innocence and blind sentiment. I shook my head, caught up short with the pain of it. What had been a slumbering throb in the background was now molten, scorched by the track of a dreadful memory. I pushed it back so quickly it didn't have time to take form, to actually generate thought. I could no longer bear to keep my head up, had to hold it steady in my hands and close my eyes for a few minutes until I became anxious I'd miss my stop. I winced at the light and the stream of people down below. The world felt very crowded this morning.

As I stepped off the bus I was forced to find my bearings and the headache lifted for a time. The pill must have been finally taking effect. Nothing flows easily on the Euston Road. It is one of London's busiest, the roar of irritable traffic signalled through the high level of horn honking, alongside screeching police cars and ambulance sirens. The BT Tower, festooned with satellite dishes, looms like a bad omen over the area. There is a grim determination about the pedestrian traffic, most of it heading towards the train station across the road. Everyone seems to shout, perhaps to be heard above the traffic and the frenetic clattering of suitcase wheels rolling over the cracked and uneven pavement.

Zigzagging between the cars at the traffic lights I managed to cross the street in front of the station and a few minutes later I was inside the lobby of the hotel where the conference was taking place. There was a high reception desk to one side; every other wall was covered in the dull smoke of mirrored glass. Walking towards the desk I could see myself walking across the room, a shadowed reflection of someone I might be—a slender, middle-aged woman of means, a professional with something at stake, or so her expression revealed. This woman was not easy with herself, her brow a little too furrowed and her shoulders a little too stiff to give her any real elegance, though no one would know, either, that she was a woman fraught with nerves. She looked very contained.

I stopped in mid-step halfway to reception, and the woman stopped as well. We stared at one another, a squaring up of unequal parts revealing ourselves to one another across the expanse of an empty hotel lobby. I was the first to turn away, to draw a line in this field of vision. I headed across the room, my eyes on the desk. I had a talk to give, a mission to accomplish, and I refused to be sidetracked.

The reception area outside the conference room was crowded. I was immediately ushered into a corner by one of the organisers, who pointed out that I was scheduled to speak first, followed by a panel discussion that was certain to prove "very interesting". Before leaving to greet another speaker she touched my arm, a soft intimate gesture I resisted the urge to brush away. This was the crowd I was to address, a group dedicated to the proposition that "congruence" is all. Why was it that so many therapists of this type felt obliged to put such effort into their authenticity?

The din in the room was feverish, the coming together of old friends. A few stragglers at the edge of the crowd, newcomers to the community, no doubt, still finding their way. There was no uniform here, instead a riot of lively clothing and free-flowing scarves. There were random shots of unusual hair colours, green on one woman, and a purple tinge to one young man's platinum fringe. I wondered who on earth their clientele might be. Perhaps they worked in the voluntary sector. Not everyone ran to this extreme, most looked like the professionals they were, tidy and presentable with nothing to distinguish them at all but for the studied sweetness of their expressions, apparently a condition for membership of this organisation.

I spotted Martha on the other side of the room. She waved, a little circular spin of her hand as if she were washing a window. I was oddly relieved. In her determined, little kind way, I was grateful this morning for someone familiar. Small beads of perspiration on my forehead as I turned towards the wall so no one would notice me wiping my brow with a Kleenex I managed to dig out from my briefcase. For good measure I blew my nose, discretely, but the effort tapped against the edge of my headache and I shoved the tissue down deep into my jacket pocket.

When I turned around to face the room again people were taking their seats in the auditorium and I was guided up to the main stage to sit alongside my colleagues, all of whom appeared to me to be on the other side of the theoretical fence. My headache fluttered in the background and then settled down again as the chairwoman stepped up to introduce me. I was calm by then, only a small flicker of nerves apparent in my damp hands, but I knew this was a prerequisite for every public occasion. Without the push of some adrenaline I would land too softly on my audience and my intention was, really, to pack a punch. What was the point otherwise? Walking up to the podium I held onto my notes and picked up the Power-Point control. I stared out over the crowd. The auditorium was completely full. I smiled.

"Good morning," my world back in position, "I imagine you're a little startled to see me here …"

I won them over. If they did not agree with my views on empathy, my encouraging them to pull back rather than roar forward, they were not overtly hostile either. Their questions afterwards were respectful and the panel was not nearly as defensive as I'd worried it might be. I had certainly faced worse. But for the simmering heat of my headache in the background I would have said I had a good time. The earlier medicine was maintaining its holding operation and the discussion was a useful distraction.

Looking thoughtful, walking towards me with her hands placed a little below her waist and to the front of her hips, Martha came up to me at the coffee break. Before lifting her right hand to take a biscuit, she tapped her abdomen twice, very gently. My headache roared like a freight train into the foreground and I must have gasped, or grimaced, because Martha looked at me oddly.

"Lisa? Are you all right?"

"I have a headache," tried to smile, pushing past the pain. "I didn't know you would be here today?" taking refuge in small talk.

"I decided at the last minute, when I saw your name on the programme."

"You came to hear me?"

"I've actually never heard you before, and I thought it would be interesting."

"And was it?" I took a sip of my coffee but it tasted bitter. I stretched over to put my cup down on a windowsill, the closest available shelf.

"Yes, very. Even if I don't agree with you, but you know that already." She was actually smiling. "I think you make a lot of sense some of the time."

"You've changed your position?" This was a different Martha, though the old one shone through sometimes, not quite letting go of childish things. I remembered her little washcloth wave across the room.

"Not really … or maybe … I suppose that comes with experience. Anyway, I don't have to agree with you all the time in order to think some of what you have to say has value."

I nodded. Perhaps I had misjudged her all along. Certainly I had never given her the respect she was extending towards me.

"Anyway, I have to go, get back to my seat before the next bit begins." She leaned forward and kissed me. She caught my involuntary cringe and patted my arm, "Just expressing a little empathy. You might need a bit more than you think you do, Lisa. See you later."

I watched Martha walk away, elbows bent, hands back in position already giving her child comfort. I drew a quick breath at the recognition. She might only be a few weeks along, her gesture an instinctive urge to protect what was still barely there. Had she told anyone yet? Daniel of course, but no one else, not at this stage. How would she continue to work, a baby in situ? My head drummed—I hated the idea of what lay ahead for her. Was this the closest I could admit to envy? Equipped only with the burden of inexperience, how would I know what it takes to mother a child?

Throat clenched and eyes burning, flushing out the tissue from my pocket to steady myself against the windowsill. Please god, I did not want to weep here. To stem the flow I put my forehead against the cool glass of the window. I needed to leave. Everyone was back in the conference room and I was alone in the reception area, the place littered with dirty coffee cups and plates of biscuit crumbs.

I was expected to attend the rest of the morning session, my absence would be interpreted by others as rudeness. Having given my speech I wasn't willing to stay around for the aftermath to hear the other speakers, showing them due respect. They couldn't know that I had a vested interest in their perspectives. How could I argue with them if I wasn't firm in my knowledge of their points of view? But today I was reduced to inexplicable pain.

I scratched out a note for the organisers, pleading illness. Citing a headache would have sounded like an excuse, a child skipping lessons. I walked down to the lobby and through the same shimmering hall of mirrors. I didn't look this time, heading straight for the fresh air. What I got, instead, was the hard landing of the Euston Road, still roaring with traffic and howling with emergency sirens. I stuck my hand out, begging for a taxi. One by one they rolled on by, already full.

A bus came along and I climbed on board. I stayed downstairs, the effort of climbing the steps to the top too much this time. I sat towards the back and put my head down on the hard, cool metal handrail of the empty seat in front. I could not bear to look out. I did not want to see life, or hear the heartbeat of a city I could not possibly enjoy. Kept my head down even when someone took the seat, the top of my head grazing their collar. I could smell hair oil, like silt or wet mud, and hear their pulse, body heat thrumming through the back of the seat, radiating life. When they left the bus a few stops down the line, I was bereft. I wanted to chase after them. What did they look like? Was it a man or a woman? Or a child? Perhaps a teenager, the energy had felt so fierce and so full of infinite possibilities.

I lifted my head and sank back in my seat, the one in front now a vacant space. My day was done. I wanted to go home and sleep. That was the only cure, to blank out and sleep through the pain, by which time I might find some relief when I woke up, my world back in its predictable shape.

Frank is right, everything needs a shape and form, otherwise we are lost. Positively lost.

EIGHT

Martha was to be avoided, timing my comings and goings to ensure we didn't meet in the communal kitchen or anywhere else. I brought sandwiches and ate them on my own between patients, or went home for lunch. Once or twice I saw Keith, but always while greeting or escorting a patient out the door. Would he never learn? Daniel, Martha's partner and the third therapist in the building, was his usual elusive self and perhaps he didn't really exist at all, although the evidence would soon be there in Martha for everyone to see.

When did the nightmares really begin? Slowly, creeping up from behind. This time I shot bolt upright choking, the bed-clothes sodden and Frank gently clucking beside me, "Lisa, Lisa, wake up."

I could not describe the dream to Frank—it was gone the moment I opened my eyes—gradually returning over the course of the day: a mass of jelly rising up out of the earth, a skinless, translucent egg of blood and sinew that throbbed to the beat of my own heart. I ran and ran but I was powerless and, with me as its life force, it began to grow larger, finally forming a mouth out of which came nothing but a dreadful, silent scream. The nightmarish theme continued intermittently for weeks, the viscous lump of mucus small and silent, at other times actually taking wind and howling, the sound more like a screech than a cry, an accusation rather than a plea for help. Weekends were the most difficult, when I spent time with Frank going to the market and having lunch, so called relaxing. With nothing to distract me my anxiety levels skyrocketed, manifesting in the worst nightmares on Saturday and Sunday nights.

There was no longer anything comforting about the prospect of sleep so I used the time to write, often staying up way beyond midnight. I also developed early morning habits, at my desk by five-thirty, relieved to be occupied by something other than night-time terrors. But the harder I worked, the less productive I seemed to be, words piling up like rubbish. In desperation I tried writing a professional editorial, focusing on the productivity of therapists. I had strong views on the subject, questioning why some therapists refused to contribute to their profession in any practical way. Did they think they were separate from the rest of the community? We all need to take a stand, I argued, and to learn from one another. Sometimes I thought of Martha, her little heart-shaped face glowing with quiet certainty. I saw her walking away from me, her hands tapping against the sides of her swelling abdomen. How did she contribute, I wondered, or would she be reduced in the end to simple domesticity? I bristled with irritation and wrote all the more.

Frank sometimes skulked in the background, urging me to come to bed. "You'll be exhausted, Lisa. You *are* exhausted."

"I can't sleep, you know that. Anyway, I have to finish something here," resenting his intrusion when I was working so well. Instead of retreating, he took to making me cups of camomile tea, hoping they would lull me to sleep. I gave in eventually, when there were so few hours left in the night that I calculated my chance of having a nightmare was at least reduced.

During the day I took refuge in the unhappiness of others, focusing hard on my client work, particularly with Sam. We had been making great headway and I was disappointed when he showed up one morning following a mighty weekend binge. Now we were stalled, back at the crossroads of his addiction. No therapy is a linear track, yet I had wanted to write about Sam and now I would have to admit that there were blockages, tracks of time when our sessions did not go smoothly and he stubbornly refused to let go of old defences.

The first I knew of Sam dropping off his wagon was when his wife rang me late on a Saturday afternoon to ask if I had seen him. There was nothing I could say to her except "no". Under the rules of confidentiality this could be breaching the code, but she sounded so desperate that I gave in. Her dignity was already suffering and calling me was likely her last resort. After several years of sobriety, no doubt she had begun to believe in a linear track too.

Sam finally turned up home on Sunday night, burnt out and hyper with anxiety and withdrawal. Attending his session the next day, he was shaky and full of predictable self-disgust. I could hardly contain my frustration. Like his mother, I had pinned all my hopes on the idealised notion of the perfect patient, convincing myself that his good behaviour was down to my brilliant skills as a clinician. If so, the converse was also true, that his toppling back into previous habits was a reflection of my inadequacy as a therapist. I stomped my internal foot—why was he was not *letting* me be a good therapist?

I understood all these feelings, but that didn't help to diminish them. Sam and I were in the midst of a childhood re-enactment. He was playing to a weakness in me, confirmation of personal worth through my success as a therapist. Everyone needs job satisfaction. I required more—I wanted to write about Sam, to send the flag up on my success for others to see. Already committed to writing the article, perhaps I could halt the narrative just before the point when Sam gave in to temptation? Who would know that it hadn't always gone smoothly? I could stop the tape on Sam, hold it on the pause button at the moment he developed insight, rather than letting it run beyond when he fell off the edge and I would be seen as less than perfect. I had worked in advertising, after all. Sam's binge was hardly a selling point. I was like a car being hauled in for a recall. Something had gone wrong and now it was up to me to minimise the damage.

Sam looked so small sitting there, shoulders slumped and his head in his hands. While he was reduced, I had swollen up somehow, the powerful shadow over his diminutive one. I had begun to think of Sam as one of therapy's heroes, and now he was simply human, reflecting something of my own imperfections. I was hardly likely to want to publicise that. Instead, I would find a way to bring him back from the brink. As far as I was concerned, freedom of choice had nothing to do with it, not this time anyway. I was disappointed, but I was also wired and fired, ready to forge ahead.

Now, I held my disappointment in check. Why had he opted to stoke himself up with drugs over the weekend? Instead of reflecting on his past, we were now forced to focus on his current behaviour, a neat way of avoiding what he found difficult. One layer of pain to cover another, I pointed out, and which one did he find easier? I was almost beside myself with frustration. I pressed hard into the back of my seat to stop myself giving him a telling-off. Judgemental and critical, I wanted him to recognise his mistakes, as if he wasn't already aware of the havoc he'd caused. He looked terrible during that session. His face was a battlefield, with small patches where he had either missed or nicked himself while trying to shave. He was "working from home" for a few days and dressed in jeans and an old shirt, very different from the smart young man I usually saw on Monday morning, drawn up neatly in a Paul Smith suit and high-gloss shoes.

He conceded that with drugs he had a choice, some control over how he behaved and what he felt. He could predict the consequences. "At least with coke I know what's coming. I'll feel good and then I'll feel terrible, like I do now. But I'm not powerless, like I feel here. These days I never know what's going to happen, and I hate it."

"So you concede you had a choice. You didn't have to take the drugs."

He sniffled, an undignified leftover from the weekend. "My wife says she'll leave me if it happens again."

"That's not surprising, considering your history. Is losing your wife a price worth paying to avoid facing your past?"

Sam's response was to look up, eyes pleading for mercy. I imagined him as a child then, all too human in the face of his mother's expectation that he live up to the perfections of her dead child. Is that why he had binged, to test that I would still care about him despite his failure? Or would I be the therapeutic mother who replicated the sins of his own, biological mother, deserting him for the imagined ideal of the dead sibling?

There is nothing like a patient to draw out the failings of a therapist. I remembered my own mother, whose sense of worth as a parent was predicated on her children's success. I needed to succeed so she would not feel a failure. Like Sam, I was easily diminished behind the facade of my success. For a moment I faltered, a flush of hot shame rippling up from my neck. Sam couldn't fail to notice. His eyebrows twitched and furrowed before lifting in surprise. "I'm sorry," his voice quavering with guilt and regret.

"Sam ... I ..."

"It's okay. You should be angry. I didn't mean to wreck everything, I wanted a break from it, that's all."

"Of course you did."

"I guess maybe I should find another way to escape? What do you think?" he tried to joke.

"I think that's a good idea. We could talk about it here, you know."

"I tried to, but you seemed so keen. You want me to keep going, sorting out everything all at once. But it's pretty scary for me. I don't know what the hell I'm doing, and I'm having all these feelings and horrible memories and my wife says she doesn't know me these days." He was leaning forward again, not in desperation, rather to make his point more clearly, reaching out for me, begging me to listen.

Sam's pain was lodged like a hard little stone deep in my chest. He had carried that hurt for most of his life, hidden from view from everyone, most of all himself, and now it was there, relentlessly pressing immediately below his throat, so hard he could hardly breathe. No wonder he had spun out of control for a weekend. Even his therapist would not listen to his need for some kind of momentary relief. A binge was exactly the diversion he needed.

Why couldn't I tell him I was sorry, too? Because I was sorry. I couldn't move beyond my pride. I held my ground, a little more compassionate than earlier, but still on my high horse of a therapist's chair, my back pinned straight and my hands in my lap. "We need to get you through this, to understand why you slipped so spectacularly, and then maybe we can take it a bit easy for a while if you're finding it difficult."

"I've just told you I find it hard!" Flashing, furious, a last ditch effort.

"We've come to time, Sam, we need to end for this morning."

"Unngh," he groaned as he stood up. It would take him another few days to physically recover from such a binge, and probably weeks before he found a way to forgive himself.

He didn't look at me as he left the room and, at the front door, he didn't bother saying goodbye, striding out into the warmth of a lovely summer's day without a nod in my direction. Wanting to slam the door behind him, I shut it ever more quietly.

The following week Sam arrived for his session all brushed up and trim, as if the binge had never happened. He was energetic again, too, riding along the crest. I took this as a sign that we were to remain on the surface of recent events, much as we had done during the early days of our work together. Further evidence of Sam's lack of trust in me came in the form of a self-help book, *Healing the Soul, a Manifesto for Recovery*. He pulled it out of his briefcase and showed it to me. "Bloody brilliant," he said.

I kept my frustration on hold, but it was gathering wind in the background. I no longer "floated" in Sam's presence, I was now suffused with impatience. As with Dorothy, I was sometimes plagued by a series of roaming patches of discomfort; I was thirsty, and my skin was dry, like parched earth. I no sooner scratched one bit of my arm, than my leg or my wrist or the back of my neck sprang to life, small circles of hell demanding attention. It was increasingly difficult not to fidget and I tried to distract myself by focusing even harder on Sam.

"This is helpful?" I waved a dismissive hand in the general direction of the book, stabbing a little at my right wrist at the same time. "I didn't take you for a big reader, Sam."

"Mmm, I'm not," he seemed not to take notice. "But this one is good, says I just need to get to know myself." So excited, on the verge of a quick fix.

"You make it sound pretty easy." I wanted to yank it out of his hand and turf it out the window. Instead, I sat high in my chair and snubbed my nose at the book, a jealous woman disparaging the competition. I lifted my left hand and rubbed at the back of my neck, grinding my fingers in where the aggravation felt most severe. I couldn't leave it alone.

Sam heaved a sigh, "I thought you might say that. It's been at the top of the *New York Times* best-seller list for ten months!"

If only it were so easy, one book and we could all be saved. Like the Bible, promising salvation. This was the precise moment I decided to make "self-help" the subject of my next column, the imperative to fight back. I was envious, too, that someone had known to write this handy little text now making the author a fortune. I doubted it did anyone any harm, though it was clearly interfering with Sam's session today. Or was it part of his therapy? I wasn't actually sure. I was so annoyed at being temporarily dumped by my client for the wisdom of a paperback written by a man he didn't know and, more importantly, who did not know him. How could it begin to touch on Sam's experience, to see who he was and what he might need? My anger was cranking up, nearly out of control; I had to force myself to look at Sam, to hear what he was saying.

"I messed up, that's all I did. I don't have to mess up again. That's what the book says."

"I've said that, too, but it might also be important to think about why you 'messed up', to use your words."

"I get so tired of all this, Lisa." Sam put the tattered copy back into his briefcase, a deflated child whose favourite toy has been dismissed as frivolous.

I tried to retrieve the session. "What's important about the book for you, Sam, what does it mean to you?" But his spirit had gone and along with it his tiny button of hope. Now I was full of remorse. I hoped I hadn't ruined it for him entirely. I upbraided myself: why shouldn't he be allowed to find support from a self-help book?

The session ended, neither of us having found a way beyond my formidable lack of empathy. Once again, Sam walked out the door without a word, only the book in his briefcase pulsating with hope.

I didn't have lunch that day. Went straight down to the high street and bought my first load of self-help books from Waterstone's, including Sam's on healing the soul. It had been years since I had last looked at a shelf of popular psychology books, a short-lived era following on from the "clock man" and before my first bout of equally short-lived therapy. Every volume I picked up seemed to me to be weary with clichés. This was what I was up against, like being in competition with a dumb blonde; what man is likely to appreciate the steadiness of a familiar wife over the attentions of a beautiful mistress? All my learning was useless in the face of such certainties as these authors provided. They didn't seem to me thoughtful so much as confident, handing out straight and simple answers in the face of complex questions. I felt sorrowful and hopeless looking at them, but I wasn't about to give up. My mood would shift once I began to formulate my argument. These books provided the security of absolutes and a mountain of formulae for success. Happiness was forever at hand.

I wasn't interested in those with a more reflective or academic perspective, I was aiming for the ones promising salvation. There were at least ten volumes encouraging positive thinking, a whole series on relationships—finding them, keeping them, and getting out of them—and another complete section given over to Sam's favourite, beating addictions. As I rifled through them I could feel my agitation building. I was also embarrassed to be seen in that part of the bookstore I had previously nicknamed "desperation corner", as if to seek help in such a public place was somehow shameful.

I plopped more than a dozen books onto the counter at the cash desk. The clerk lifted her eyebrows in surprise. "I'm a therapist," I announced, as if that made one whit of difference.

"Well, then"—catching herself, "It clearly isn't working," is what I imagined she wanted to say. Why was I so angry? I shoved my card at her. She was a patient young woman, but I could see relief when the transaction was completed. She handed me my two carrier bags and muttered, "Enjoy."

I was overloaded, my arms nearly shifting out of their sockets. I struggled all the way back to the office. I wasn't thinking of my nightmares then, or my recent bouts of dissociation. I didn't consider why I was avoiding Martha, or that anger was coming a little too easily to me these days. I wasn't taking into account Sam, and how he had tried to tell me he needed more help than I was giving him at the moment. Loaded up with so much armoury, I was intent on what I was about to start writing. I certainly didn't think that any of these books might have something to do with me.

Keith was pulling up to the curb when I stepped around the corner to the office. "Need some help?" he offered, flipping a pedal into place on his tiny bike.

"Yes, thanks." I was actually sweating with the effort, inelegant patches of damp underneath my arms.

Keith opened the door and shifted his bike in first before taking hold of one of my bags. "Christ, haven't you got enough books?"

"Not like these. They're all self-help."

"At last!" He raised his free hand in the air, an "alleluia" sort of gesture.

"What do you mean by that?" I thumped the bag down on the step above me.

"Nothing, Lisa, it was a joke." He was quick to pull back.

"Funny, it didn't sound like one." Keith hadn't been hauling them all the way from Clapham Junction and he was already at the top of the stairs waiting outside my office. I dropped my bag down and rummaged inside my pocket for the key.

"How's business?" He picked up the second load and followed me into the room, his head swivelling this way and that. It wasn't often he came this high in the building, all his drilling taking place down below. Not since the last time when I had asked him, several years ago, now, to please repaint the room.

"Fine, thanks. Yours?"

"Going well, going well," dropping down onto the couch, bouncing a little as if to test the springs. "Is this where your patients sit?"

"You know it is." I dragged the bags along the floor to just inside the door. I would look at them more carefully later.

Keith got up and moved to my high-backed therapy chair, giving his bottom another little wiggle. "Not much give, that's for sure. Better, though, isn't it, sitting over here? Not nearly so difficult doing the staring, as opposed to being the one stared at."

"Something like that. Would you like to make an appointment?" I actually placed my hands on my hips, a termagant ready for battle.

Keith lifted his eyebrows, "Jesus, no," standing up. "Maybe I'll borrow one of your new books."

"Anytime, Keith, anytime." I dropped my hands and smiled. He made a move towards the door and then stopped, looking back at me. His expression serious, uncharacteristically hesitant.

"What is it?"

"I saw that patient of yours the other day."

"What do you mean?"

"The one with that look. You know, the early morning one."

"That look?"

"She … well … anyway … I don't know, she looks sort of …"

There was a rush of heat, a splurge of perspiration at the back of my neck. Clutching the top of my chair with one hand, I bent down and shoved the first bag of books a little further across the room. "You know I can't talk to you …"

"Yeah, yeah. I know. It's just that …"

"What?" I was still holding onto the chair. I shouldn't be hearing this, should not be asking him to tell me more.

"She was walking near your place, at the end of your road. I was driving past on my way home and she was standing there, staring down towards your house. Does she know where you live?"

I sat down, finally, to catch my breath; a flash of lightning heat and a hand flat against my heart. Slow down. Slow down.

"Lisa? Are you okay?" Keith came back into the room.

"I'm fine, I'm fine. Sorry."

"It probably doesn't matter. I don't know why I told you. I know you don't like talking to me about your patients. Or me talking about them with you is probably the better way of putting it."

Keith finally left, after I'd convinced him that this was a middle-aged moment, a flush of heat a little more severe than usual. I don't suppose he believed me, but he made his excuses—a patient waiting—and left me alone.

After he'd gone I leaned against the door, barring it shut. What had he told me? That my patient was a stalker? What could she have been doing, so far out of the way of her own neighbourhood and standing at the end of my road? Keith was imagining things, or was there something more? I was hot again, a wave of nausea rising up to catch me in the throat before I could swallow and shove it down again. Swinging the door open, I raced to the loo.

I returned to my office, shaky but intact. I had a few hours to calm down before seeing my next client. So many books to read, I would use the time to work through the pile. Gunning for the lot, I would pace my way through every page and rip the whole business apart.

NINE

The self-help books only deepened my bad mood. I shuffled though my pile. I couldn't bear to sit down and read through any of them completely. I hated the language they used, continually encouraging the reader to share, or forgive, or to move on, and they were particularly fond of closure. The notion of "controlling your feelings" was particularly distasteful, with the implication that personal salvation is a disciplinary issue, like giving up drink or drugs. It was the simplicity of it all I so disliked.

I could rant to myself all I wanted, but whenever I sat down to write on the computer my ideas inevitably dissolved into irretrievable particles.

Are you someone who wants a quick fix, are you someone who imagines there is a short and easy answer to everything, and there is a snake oil salesman somewhere who really will have the solution.

Scribbled by hand in another feeble attempt to begin, *Addiction and self-medication are a defence against pain. Are you addicted to self-help books, imagining that they can provide a solution to whatever ails you?*

Whatever happened to the long view, the idea that it takes time to accomplish anything well, and nothing worthwhile ever comes easily? Tried again, never getting beyond the first sentence.

These were cheap shots. I found it impossible to take an intellectual approach, to reason through my muddled feelings to form a coherent argument. Reading back what I had written, I sounded angry and patronising rather than thoughtful and compassionate. It was the genre I was targeting, not my readers. I wanted to *help* them, not aim for them with a mushy diatribe that insulted their intelligence, and reflected poorly on mine.

When I was a child, teachers encouraged us to look things up in books. Dictionaries and textbooks, biographies and fiction, that's where the answers were, all contained within the covers of a book. No wonder people believed in the promise of a quick fix. Self-help books promised so much, and delivered so little, but I couldn't find the words to say so in a manner that wasn't insulting. Meantime, the deadline for my next column was approaching. Somewhere in this stack there must be an answer to my writer's block. I knew my being stalled wasn't due to a lack of effort, I simply couldn't concentrate on a single theme, or get past my fury to establish a reasoned argument. Couldn't get past the clichés and false promises, or the image of Sam stuffing his book back into his briefcase, his expression full of grief and disappointment.

I wasn't about to give up. Late one afternoon, down on my hands and knees, rummaging through a messy pile in my office, I discovered a couple of titles, *Learning to Live*, and *How to be Creative*. Underneath both of them, my favourite: *Rules of Engagement: Learning How Not to Give Up on Life*. I stood up from the floor with a grunt, ashamed of myself for even trying to find an answer here.

My anger now compounded by defeat, I decided on another tack.

I ditched the idea of the self-help books and instead wrote a column summing up the themes of the last six months, synthesising my views on empathy and arguing against the current tendency towards sentimentality and idealised notions of happiness. How much better it would be to leave these fantasies behind in childhood and instead grow up to understand that happiness may simply be the absence of current tragedy, or the accommodation of loss into day to day living. No one is exempt from heartache.

For the few hours it took me to write the column, and for the first time in weeks, I was no longer anxious. I pinged it across to the paper immediately, afraid I might lose my nerve. I am never comfortable with the gap between intention and accomplishment and I was afraid they might recognise that this time I had taken the easy way out.

That night I woke up screaming and sweating from the effort of keeping myself ahead of another nightmare. This time the translucent egg had teeth, the roots of them visible up and through the gory glare of its wide-open mouth, the epiglottis swinging like a rope, pink and vibrating with every screech.

Frank reached out, gathering me in. Was it only me who was shaking? Both of us fully awake, he headed downstairs for what was becoming a regular, four-in-the morning cup of tea. I took comfort from the sound of his pottering down below and the hissing of the kettle as it peaked to boiling point, the soft clunk and fade-away as he picked it up and poured water into the pot. I lay back against the pillows and tried to pace my breathing to the familiar rhythm of this reassuring, marital ritual. Still sweating after the nightmare, I kicked the quilt to the bottom of the bed.

I snapped out of my reverie at the sound of something dropping hard onto the tiled floor, a cup or a milk jug, little jagged fragments scattering everywhere. I heard what I thought was an expletive from Frank, and then nothing further. By now, the tea was way past its brewing point.

"Frank?" Sat up and flicked on the bedside table light. No response from below.

I carefully stepped out of bed and wrapped a dressing gown around myself. Dug out my slippers from under the chest of drawers and paused in front of the mirror. A woman caught between light and dark, stripped of her mask. Another moment longer to pass a brush through her hair before slowly heading down to the kitchen.

The rough edges of the shattered porcelain scraped against the floor underneath my slippers, before I saw Frank sitting at the kitchen table. "Frank?" He was in semi-darkness, only the light from the hallway casting shadows around the room. Had he been making tea in the dark? He had one hand wrapped around his cup, moving it in noughts, his thinking circles, and with the other he was pressing his fingers hard against his forehead. He didn't even look up when I came into the room. "Why are you still down here? What's wrong?"

I pulled out a chair and sat down at the table.

He looked at me then. For the first time I saw his exhaustion, written in the deeper lines of his face, the shaded, hollowed out space around his eyes. He squinted at me—I was too close to him, and he moved his head back a few inches as if to get a better view. "I can't stand it, Lisa, I can't stand it anymore," his voice was thick, caught in the midst of grief.

"What do you mean?" I reached out a hand to take one of his. He pulled away.

"Don't, Lisa. Don't."

"Frank, I don't understand. Please, talk to me."

"I've been trying to talk to you for weeks. Why on earth would you listen to me now?" As I sat, he stood up, his chair squealing against the floor as he shoved it backwards, the screech of the mutating jelly shooting through—my nightmare—its throat quivering in terrible rage. Wanting to cover my ears; instead hands in my lap, gripped together hard.

Frank walked around the mess on the floor and poured himself another cup of tea from the pot. His hands were shaking, small tremors I had never seen in him before. He stood still for a moment, looking out the window before turning around to me again. Even in these shadows I could see he was struggling against tears, small pools reflected in the rims of his eyes.

Why had it taken me so long to notice that I was causing him distress? Did I really believe that Frank could take anything that I threw at him? I wanted him to be my self-help book, to sort out everything in my life in an instant. It finally dawned on me—this was why I found it so difficult to write about these damn books. My form and staple was Frank. He was my text.

"I'm sorry Frank … I …"

"No, Lisa, no! Listen to me. You are not well and you need to get some help, from Max, or therapy, and you certainly need to take a break. I can't help you if you won't tell me what's wrong." He took a big breath. "For god's sake, tell me what's going on. Please try to tell me."

"I don't know … Maybe my patients …?"

"Too easy. You've had complicated clients before, so why now? What are you not telling me?"

"I don't know. Honestly, I swear I don't know." That was the truth, or nearly the truth as far as I knew it, but something was hovering around the edges of my life, pestering me through nightmares and oversensitivity to particular clients.

"Well, you have to figure it out because I can't help you anymore. You aren't sleeping, neither am I, and this is way beyond what a mug of brew might provide. If you want a drink, Lisa, make it yourself this time." And he walked away, back up to the bedroom, while I stayed downstairs, clearing away the fragments of my favourite cup off the floor. In the dawning light I could see the flecks of blue and gold, shards of the handle I had picked up countless times to sip one of Frank's soothing cups of tea.

Still, I couldn't tell him, could not tell my husband the truth. Couldn't tell him because I couldn't yet tell myself what I had kept from Joanna during all those years in therapy. Picking those pieces off the floor my body was heavy, my head like a lead ball. I was dulled, beyond reason or emotion. I was dead, the only alternative to fragmentation. If I was thick enough, tough enough, hardened and solid enough, I could get through this. I would not have to crack like my little cup, into a thousand pieces of nothing.

Couldn't go back to bed, not with Frank lying awake as I knew he would be. Made myself a pot of coffee and sat at the kitchen table until the alarm went off. I didn't read and I didn't write, only sat and played with my cup, turning my own noughts for a few hours, though mine were devoid of thinking. Couldn't push past the numbness, beyond the boundary where I might make sense of myself. There was no clearing where I was, no prairie expanse where I might see the sky, or work out the terrain. I was locked in as much as Sam, or Dorothy or any of my patients who were trapped in their own troubled, internal worlds. And as fervently as they did, I wanted to remain in protective custody, safely hidden from myself.

I lacked the courage to advance into the underground vault where the real trouble lay. I wanted to keep my life, not change the world. Couldn't Frank see that I was actually trying to preserve something, not destroy it? Numb, even rage couldn't rescue me now.

Time passed, until I heard Frank in the shower.

When he came down to the kitchen he was quiet. Not sulking, just that there was nothing left to say. I wanted to reach out to him, so he would reach out to me. He didn't notice and I didn't push. He had gathered himself up into himself and he was simply not available.

Away from Frank and back in my office I gradually emerged out of my deadened state to begin thinking a little. He had said I needed a break, and suggested I return to therapy. Grumpy and defensive, I couldn't find Joanna's number in any listings. She was probably retired by now anyway.

My first patient was at nine o'clock. I took refuge in her familiar discomforts, her myriad and endless complaints. I could work almost by rote this morning, reflecting back her unhappiness without having to invest too much in the demanding business of interpretation. This morning I was even grateful for this client's enthusiastic hold on misery and sense of entitlement. No confrontation or challenge this morning. I only wanted to get through the day.

TEN

I was scheduled to see my supervisor that afternoon, though I hated the idea of seeing Max while I was feeling so raw. If Frank is my domestic anchor, Max is my professional ballast. For the first time in our history, I dreaded attending supervision.

To get to Max, I am forced to take the Underground. That afternoon I tried to lift myself out of the gloom by reading the newspaper on the train: politics and the Middle-East, issues I liked to convince myself are once removed from my life. But what is expressed externally is a reflection of our internal world and there's no getting away from war, even from a distance.

The route to his office has remained consistent, never more than a ten-minute walk from Islington station. These days Max lives in a small, terraced house into which he has squeezed both his professional and his personal life. His previous address, between marriages, was a mansion flat, which I preferred. It was quiet and there was a view from the window overlooking a small, private garden. Now, there is a dusty double pram shoved into the corner by the door and a pair of bright plastic, miniature cars. I can sometimes hear the children rattling around in them when I am in session with Max. The twins are now four, their noise levels escalating over the years rather than diminishing.

I know Max's therapy room almost as well as I know my own. His office is on the first floor, just at the top of the stairs. I can no longer see the garden; instead Max has a rather beautiful painting of a bird on the wall just above his chair. Sometimes, when he sits in a particularly upright position, it looks as if it's landed on his head. His patients and I conspire silently in keeping this information to ourselves, a bit of levity in the close space of the therapy room. Like me, I imagine they are afraid he will remove it if he knows. He sits in a comfortable leather chair with a crank on the side to lift the footrest. I have never seen him do it, but I imagine that between sessions and on Saturdays he pulls the lever and has himself a good old snooze. The client's chair is also leather, but without the mechanism. Shoved into the corner is the requisite couch, covered over with an Indian throw and a small pillow. His bookcase is less tidy than mine and recently a desk has appeared, usually littered with papers.

Max is a serious man, despite the unpredictability of his late marriage. He isn't without a sense of humour, though he usually considers it a distraction from the main work. I continue in supervision with him because I trust he has my best interests at heart. He believes in me as a therapist, despite my public persona, which I suspect he considers a frivolous distraction from my duty as a clinician. I am far better known than he is.

Walking up the road towards Max's front door I paused for a moment to lean against a neighbour's garden wall, to shove the last vestiges of cotton wool from the front to the back of my head. I literally needed to clear space, to move away from the morning's upset with Frank. I pulled out a lipstick from my handbag and gave myself a quick lift, straightened my skirt and yanked my shoulders up a little straighter. "Okay, let's go," I muttered, like before a job interview, my life depending on the approval of others.

Max buzzed me up from the front door. He was waiting in his usual perch, his feet firmly on the ground. He rarely gets up to greet me, just nods with familiar equanimity and calls, "Come in, take a seat," His voice is low and measured, a man who thinks before he speaks. The predictability of our encounter is part of the pleasure, part of the comfort and the trust I have in him.

As usual he dug around in a small drawer on the table to the right of his chair and pulled out a notebook. With his supervisees he always takes notes, while with patients he is attentive. Now he smiled and clicked his pen, ready for work. "What's on your mind today?" his usual opening. Again, with clients I know he waits until they speak first and this is one way he signals the difference. There isn't much chit-chat between us—we settle down to business pretty quickly—and today I am grateful for the focus.

There were ongoing struggles with Dorothy, I told him, a curious mixture of dedication and resistance and layers of defensive resentment. She was continuing to attend her therapy, though she regularly declared a week off due to the pressures of work. I could usually predict the week, or at least in hindsight I believed I could have done. She withdrew at the slightest indication that her defensive wall was being breached. There were also moments when she seemed to reach out, to extend herself towards me.

"Like how?" Max interrupted my flow.

I was caught off guard. "She looks at me sometimes, as if she wants something."

"Of course she does. You're her therapist."

"I don't mean it quite like that," I leaned forward. I wanted Max to understand, to comprehend what I couldn't quite grasp myself. "There's a knowingness about her, as if she's figured out some impossibly difficult formula and now she wants me to work out what it is. Like *I'm* the one who is supposed to figure something out here." I took a big breath and sat back in my seat. "As if she wants to be *my* therapist! ..." Max waited for me to carry on. "It's awfully hot in here, Max. Do you think we could open a window?"

"It is open, Lisa, wide open, with a pretty strong breeze coming through."

I couldn't feel it. I wanted to stand up, to walk around the room and get some air, but I knew that would startle Max so I stayed put in my chair and forced myself to wait until I cooled down, flapping my hand like an old lady in front of my face.

I was so sick of this patient, of her ability to batter me with physical sensation. Never any answers, only more and more questions. Looking up at Max, he was wary too.

"She wants to be my therapist," I repeated. I hadn't intended to speak out loud. "Or maybe my confessor. Whatever it is, I think she wants me to tell her something, but I haven't any idea what that is." I didn't tell him about Keith having seen her at the end of my road. This was a complication I didn't want to face today and I shut my eyes to blot out the image of her standing there, peering into my private life.

Max put down his pen, "I wonder what she wasn't told as a kid, or whether there was a family secret?" He was inviting me to think along with him, to consider the meaning behind what I was telling him. We often did this together, weaving ideas between us to determine the symbolism behind my patients' actions.

"Maybe. Her mother was usually a continent away and Dorothy certainly had an unusual life, living all over the world with her father." Why was I so breathless? "Every family has secrets."

"She wants you to tell her your secret," Max was watching me, his expression canny and tough. "Maybe you need to give her something of yourself."

"What the hell do you mean by that?"

Max frowned. He straightened up, though not high enough to invite the bird onto his head. "I don't mean giving her a

112

'literal' secret, but sometimes I suspect you hold yourself so far back in your professional chair that there's very little of you for the patient to hold onto."

Should I be taking this personally? He'd raised the issue of my "distance" as he called it intermittently over the years. "Max, it's a tenet of therapy that we don't speak to clients about our personal lives."

"You know that isn't what I'm talking about. How generous do you feel towards this client, how warm, or cold? Do you want to withdraw, or do you want to move closer? Maybe you're a bit afraid of what she might see in you? If this is about her need to hear a secret, and your reluctance to reveal anything, you are a perfect match, perhaps directly replicating something in her history and, I suspect, also repeating something in yours?" Max was watching me carefully, his eyes narrowed in concentration. I struggled not to squirm in the chair. "I don't know much about your background, Lisa. I'm your supervisor, not your therapist, but I do know that you find it easier to keep a distance with people. We've settled down into a nice pattern over the years, and we're both comfortable with it. Sometimes that's good, and sometimes maybe not. It's what we're used to. Do you know you've been bringing this patient to supervision almost every session? No one else, except Sam these days, gets a look in." He flipped back a few pages in his notebook, checking I supposed.

"Is that true?" Max had me cornered. I had a full load of patients, after all, at least six a day, four days a week. Some clients I saw twice a week.

"I think you need two things. You could do with a break, and you may want to think about therapy again. Get back to some personal work for a while, eh?"

"You've not taken any notes." Shoving the focus back onto Max.

"I don't with patients. Which is why I'm urging you to go back into therapy." It wasn't often that Max told me off. "First and foremost, my responsibility is to your patients. My job, if you like, is to ensure that you are working ethically and with due care and compassion towards your patients. It's my job to ask you the difficult questions. What do you think is going on? Why these two clients every week, but particularly Dorothy?"

I was bruised, shame rising again to the surface in another hot surge. Pressed a hand against my forehead, a small pasture of damp. How to win back Max's goodwill? "I suppose their presentation is a little more florid at the moment. Certainly Sam has been struggling recently and there's been disturbance in his personal life, too. He went on a bender a couple of weeks after mentioning his sister in therapy. He didn't skip any sessions, but barely made it a few times. Sometimes therapy with him feels a little like speed dating, trying to get in as much as possible in a very short time."

Max did smile then.

"He's calmed down now, though," such an effort to keep my voice level, "accepting that a relapse isn't the end of everything. He may be developing some insight into cause and effect, so when he's tempted to get loaded, tomcat around town, or tear down the highway, he's actually trying to stave off anxiety." I didn't mention the self-help book, or Sam's terrible disappointment in me.

"Do Dorothy and Sam have anything in common?"

A few moments silence, while I considered. I scratched an itchy patch above my watch, nails digging in hard. "Not that I can think of. They both work in the City, that's about it."

"We've talked about Dorothy, but what do you think Sam is evoking in you?" Max wasn't letting go.

"Evoking in me?" The only possible escape here was delay.

"Yes, you. Of course you!" Max shook his head, shiny where his hair was receding.

"Isn't that a therapy question? You've just pointed out that you are not my therapist?" Why couldn't I control my irritation, or at least the expression of it? It was a perfectly reasonable question—Max often asked it in relation to clients.

"Because it is a therapy issue! You bring both these patients week after week but whenever I suggest that there may be unconscious processes at work, you become defensive, defiant at times. You appear to want to discuss them separately, as if they have nothing to do with you. Judging by your reactions, I'd say they have everything to do with you."

I was rescued from this exchange by a light tap on the door and a small voice pleading, "Daddy, Daddy?" Both of us started, Max's notebook dropping to the floor as he got up, rushing to the door.

The children of therapists have a bit of a rough ride. They know from a very young age that mummy or daddy is working and must not be disturbed. Work with patients is sacrosanct and I had never known Max's children, despite the sounds of their bawling or laughing in the background, to directly interrupt a session. "Sweetheart, what's wrong?" on his knees in front of his daughter. The little girl was crying so hard she could barely splutter.

"Mummy. Mummy. She's hurt herself."

"Where is she? Where is she, darling?" Comforting her all the while, little soft strokes up and down her arm.

"In the kitchen," whimpering between two giant sobs.

"Stay with Lisa. Stay here and I'll go find Mummy." I stood, staring at the weeping child while Max tore down the stairs two at a time. I hadn't known he had it in him.

"What's your name?" I'm not so good with real children, as opposed to those patients like Sam who still carry with them all the despair and chaos of their early years, perpetual Peter Pans who have never grown up. But the little girl stopped in mid sob and gulped, "Melissa." Giving her head a little shake, "Melissa," she repeated.

"Why don't we go find your Daddy?" How was I to manage this child? Melissa ignored my outstretched hand. Walking

115

down the steps ahead of me she negotiated them with great care. I could hear commotion in the kitchen, and another child crying. I had never heard Max's voice so deep in his chest, nor so reassuring, "It's going to be all right. That's a good girl. Give Daddy the cloth."

Nadine, Max's wife, was sitting in a chair, slumped forward, Pre-Raphaelite hair clasped tight in a bundle at the nape of her neck. A few strands had fallen loose and they were tucked behind her ear. Her face was ashen while Max carefully wrapped her outstretched and bloody hand in a dishcloth. A near replica of the child I had followed down the stairs was standing trembling just to the side of her mother. With a jolt I recognised that they were not identical twins, and were likely the product of fertilisation. These children had taken effort. No middle-aged accident, they had been *longed* for. Was this Max's secret, his private life exposed through the physical evidence of two little girls?

There was blood on the counter and, on the floor, a lump of flesh in the largest pool just by the chopping board to the left of the sink.

Max helped his wife to her feet, "I'm taking her to the hospital, quicker than calling an ambulance. Stay with the children." An order, not a request.

The door closed behind them. The twins stood staring at me, whimpering a little, sniffling. I did not know what to do with them. "Of course you're scared about your Mummy …" They looked at me with blank eyes before launching into another bout of sobbing. Was I supposed to hold them, or stroke them as their father had done? I bent down on my knees and tried a few feeble pats before they both turned away and walked towards the television. They knew better than I did how to calm themselves down.

I sat at the dining room table, viewing the twins from behind. They were watching cartoons, not the delicate and enterprising Caspar, or Tom and Jerry from my childhood, but a quizzical creature called Spongebob Squarepants. Both of them clutched stuffed toys, Melissa had a koala bear she rocked gently on her lap and Jessica a small, white seal clasped tightly against her chest. Aside from slight facial differences, I could tell the girls apart by their clothes, Melissa in a pink flowery dress, Jessica in overalls with a little checked shirt to match. Was this their future mapped out, the little farmer staying behind with her mother, while the less capable one ran to fetch help? Proving my point, Jessica picked up the control and flipped to another station, landing on Thomas the Tank Engine, disaster and rescue all mapped out in relentless, ten minute chunks. I wished they would turn the volume down. The entire scene was turning into a nightmare.

I distracted myself by looking further into the living room area, full of the detritus of family living: laundry basket by the couch piled high with neatly folded clothes, a storage box full of toys tidied away against the wall, crayons and a colouring book open on the floor, and a doll was parked like an afterthought in the corner of an otherwise empty, plastic Wendy house. The furniture wasn't faded so much as showing signs of periodic scrubbing where stains had been removed. People yearning for children never anticipate the *mess* that follows.

I had never visited this part of the house before, or the personal quarters in any of Max's homes. Through his two marriages and the space between I had never been invited beyond his office. And yet, I had always known him. He was generous with himself, something true shining through in his work with me, despite my knowing so little beyond the bare bones of his circumstances.

Max wasn't the first to accuse me of maintaining secrets—my therapist had suspected I was holding back, too. More than other people? Surely we are allowed to keep a few, though Joanna had often argued the difference between privacy and secrecy.

117

"She wants you to tell her your secret," Max had said in our session, as if he knew I had one. In a sudden, suffocating gasp I realised the connection between Sam and Dorothy. It was what I felt towards them. They both roused in me a passion I found monstrous and thrilling, like mother love. My feelings towards Dorothy, though, were further compounded by alternating bouts of aversion and dislike, a wish to destroy her in order to preserve myself, not something I experienced towards Sam, for whom my negative feelings never stretched beyond annoyance. With Dorothy, the feelings were deeper, harder, and less manageable.

There was a terrible racket coming from the television, small animated animals singing in speeded up harmony, like the singing chipmunks. The children were laughing—I thought of my recent nightmares, that repulsive mass of jelly and its shriek in the wind as I tried to flee.

It was only then that I considered clearing the kitchen. There was paper towelling on a roll by the door and for the second time that day I went down on my knees to clean up a mess. I wiped the blood from the floor and the kitchen counter, including the piece I had imagined was part of a finger, actually a bit of onion. All I had seen was the blood and the lump. I scrubbed hard, rubbing away the memory.

I used a larger sponge I found underneath the sink for the final wash up. I did not want a single trace to remain. I threw it into the garbage with the bloody towelling and tied up the refuse bag ready to put outside. Nadine was the sort of mother who had life organised and I found another black bag in a storage cupboard by the back door that I placed neatly in the now empty bin. Done at last. It was then I remembered to ring Frank and tell him I would be late.

He was polite, not effusive, didn't offer to join, or fetch me. "If you want a cup of tea, Lisa, make it yourself," he had said to me that morning. This was not his mess, and he wasn't about to clear it up either.

When Max and Nadine returned home after eight in the evening, her hand sewn up and properly bandaged, the children were in bed. At least I could claim to have fed them—frozen pizza warmed in the oven—and helped them on with their pyjamas. They declined my offer to read them a story. I managed to sooth them, at last, by promising them a good-night kiss when their parents returned.

Max thanked me and patted me lightly on the shoulder. Nadine tried to smile, a brave effort to move beyond her pain and exhaustion. I did not want to leave but Max was guiding me towards the front door. I stepped out into the night, bleak and empty. Even after the accident, the glow of family life remained. I rattled all the way home on the Tube, staring straight ahead.

In the years to come, the twins would remember their mother's accident perhaps, but they would retain nothing of me, a strange woman who by the end of the evening they virtually ignored. I was an adult of insignificance. In order to be kept in mind, deeply remembered, I would have needed to give these children something of myself.

Secrets. In an effort to maintain just one, I'd closed the door on so much more.

ELEVEN

Frank and I walked around one another for the next few days. It wasn't that he was ignoring me, or that I was shutting him out, but rather that for the first time in our marriage we did not know how to speak to one another. We were both locked into our own turmoil, unsure how to find a way out. For the first time, too, I wondered if Frank regretted marrying me. It wasn't so much what he said, but rather what he didn't say, and the silence was like a boom call, resonating throughout the house whenever we were both at home, which was as little as possible. There were no more early cups of tea, instead I subsisted on coffee. I took to switching on BBC's Radio 4, to hear another voice in the kitchen, and we ducked into our individual studies for relief, emerging for breaks at alternate times. All weekend I listened for his footfall on the stairs or in the hallway, but it never stopped outside my door.

On the Monday, Frank went to Scotland for a few days to lecture and I was relieved. I did not have to lie beside him in bed, terrified that nightmare furies would give me away. I needn't have been afraid. Though I lay awake for hours, the little sleep I had was blessedly dreamless. Instead, the demon surfaced during the day, a hovering shadow that hurtled towards me at the squeak of a door opening or closing, or the sound of a car horn from the street below my office window. The bubble of translucent horror rose on the tail of a gust of wind as I walked by the pond at Clapham Common. I staggered towards one of the benches on the other side of the park to stop myself from fainting. This was exhaustion; no avoiding it now. By the time Frank came back from Glasgow I had a plan, in part helped by a phone call from my brother, Tom, in Canada. He'd joined the bandwagon, encouraging me to get away.

"Did Frank put you up to this?" I barked over the phone.

"Nope, I did it all myself. Anyway, he's never going to suggest a holiday to visit your mother."

"That's not exactly true." I was at my desk, my diary open in front of me. "Which dates are you planning to go?"

Every six weeks, like clockwork, Tom climbed into his truck and drove fifteen hours all night from the mountains and across the lonely prairie to see my mother, and then they both slept in their chairs while I, when I was there on a visit, held vigil with a small computer or a textbook. Twice a year I clambered onto a plane and headed out to the open sky. It wasn't enough, but by showing up at six monthly intervals I convinced myself that I was supporting Tom in a task I imagined was pretty onerous. Most of the time my mother did not know who we were, not that she ever had, but now that familiar lack of recognition was literal, rather than merely symbolic.

Tom also looked after her accounts and all her other concerns. Not a surprise as he first trained as a lawyer. He was systematically sorting through a small mountain of boxes full of old letters and documents he had stacked neatly against his basement wall, out of sight of his daily life. "I can stand it for a couple of hours a week, and that's about it," he told me when I had last visited. "There's something kind of creepy about sorting through your mother's private things."

I could appreciate the struggle, but I didn't offer to help. I knew as much about my mother as I wanted to know and I am selfish enough that I'd prefer to let Tom do the dirty work, god willing. We agreed to meet in Winnipeg in two weeks' time. No, I told him, I didn't think Frank would be coming with me. I'd let him know. Tom was uncharacteristically silent at the other end of the phone. "Everything okay?" he finally asked.

"Work's a little rough right now. I've been pretty busy, that's all."

I could have told Tom. He is my brother, but also safely tidied away in Canada, like those toys in the corner of Max's living room. Instead I said nothing, waiting for him to fill the gap, as I knew he would do.

"I'll see you in a couple of weeks. There's a bunch of stuff we need to talk about."

"What do you mean?" I didn't intend to sound panicked.

"Mom's stuff. Some papers you might want to look through, or we can go through them together. There's a box with your name on it and I don't want to throw out anything you might think is important."

"With my name on it?"

"Yeah. And there's a box with my name on it, too, if that makes you feel any better."

"It does." I put my hand flat over my diary, covering the page where I'd marked my arrival date.

"Well, good," he laughed, "I'll see you in a couple of weeks."

There was a roar in my ears, like a giant wave rushing in on the tide. This can't be … I'm imagining things. How could I possibly open that box? I couldn't open it with Tom, but I knew I couldn't open it alone either. I'd convinced myself it was lost, gone forever, kicked away and hidden behind the couch of my mother's life. She had never mentioned it, and I had never asked. I had flown the coop as fast as I possibly could afterwards, all that had happened then driving me like a tailwind across the ocean and to another life where I would never have to open the box again. Now Tom had it, propped like any other file against his basement wall. Gripped at the heart, I forced myself to stand up, then lurched towards the back door, opened it quickly, and took in great gulps of air. After all these years, and so much determined silence, my mother could be about to give my deepest secret away.

Everyone and everything was heaping up on me at once. But I had faced hard times before, my survival a tribute to the value of hard work, and I knuckled down this time, too, spending most of my time at the office. As a concession to my unsettling encounters with Max, his family, and with Frank, I began a desultory search for a therapist. I began by flicking down a few webpage directories to see if there was anyone in town worth visiting. Such a relief not to find Joanna's name, she who had regularly pointed out my tendency to "hold back" in therapy, warning that it would cause me grief in the end. I would hate her to be proven right.

"Why are you here?" she had asked me once, sensible shoes planted on the floor. She looked poised to stand up, but there was another thirty-five minutes to go. Was she itching to get away? "You're so careful not to reveal anything of real importance. So careful," shaking her head.

Joanna made all the right efforts. She was cautiously empathic, she interpreted as much as she could with the information she had connecting a few of my archaic dots, most of them centring around my mother, but none of these came close, and she knew it. Finally she named my "holding back", suggesting that I kept secrets, from myself, too. "You're training as a therapist. Undoubtedly, you will hope that your patients reveal more to you than you are prepared to reveal to me. You will want them to show themselves as vulnerable, believing that somehow there is grace in facing the worst of your demons. I assume you believe this, though I could be wrong. Perhaps you think because you are training and steeped in the theory you can do the work on your own, bypassing me altogether. You have the information, so why not? You attend therapy with me because you have to, not because you want to, or because you think you will learn anything."

I let her run on, uninterrupted. After she'd finished her lecture I was silent until the end of the session, furious with her assumptions. How dare she! In the face of my sulk she was placid, standing up at the end of fifty minutes and opening the door to let me out. I'm sure she knew I wouldn't turn up for my next appointment. After that onslaught I might even skip a few. She was right. If I hadn't been forced to return for the sake of my training, I would never have crossed her threshold again. I nearly changed therapists, except I knew I would have to go through the motions all over again with someone else. At the bottom of it all, as I believed Max did, Joanna had my best interests at heart.

"I'm afraid for you, Lisa," she had said another time, "you put so much pressure on yourself. Running so hard to avoid yourself, it may catch up with you one day." If I hadn't known her better, I'd have said she was close to tears. These days I wasn't sure I could stomach an "I told you so", the embarrassment of having to witness her self-satisfaction that I had been forced back into therapy. I didn't consider that she might feel compassion.

London is full of therapists. I didn't want to work with anyone I knew, at the same time didn't want to see anyone with whom I was unfamiliar. I could ask around. Who could I trust to be discreet? Martha might help, but she would refer me to some soft and woolly creature, providing simpering empathy without any real exploratory rigour. My reputation would also get in the way of my working with most clinicians. I was likely to intimidate them, hook into all their narcissistic worries concerning effectiveness and competence. There had to be another way to find relief other than by returning to therapy, particularly if Joanna was unavailable. Max and Frank were insisting on therapy because they weren't sure how to help me themselves.

I closed down the internet with its infernal lists of therapists and went to my email instead, deciding to put one thing into effect. I messaged my editor at the paper to say I would be taking a break from my column for the next few months. This would give me time to work out something more intellectually stimulating than my latest output, reduced to a summing up of previous columns. I remembered the *Dear Abby* newspaper column when I was a teenager, my daily window into other people's lives, and how let down I was when periodically she published a rehash of old letters on a particular theme. Maybe by then she was tuckered out, exhausted by the daily grind of churning out other people's misfortunes. Couldn't be bothered to stump up anything new. Whatever it was, I wasn't going to repeat her mistake.

I could write a book instead. People had been encouraging me to do this for years, why on earth had I not done it before? A perfect answer to my recent troubles. A book would occupy *all* my free time. Nine to ten months ought to do it, and for the duration I could lose myself in hard work. Ten minutes after formalising my break from the paper I began pounding out a proposal. Kicked into life like a hard drive, whirring to get my ideas down, I returned to my idea of self-help with new vigour. This would not be a popular psychology book in the usual form, but rather a documentation of the value of struggle and hard work, an opus dedicated to the symphony of accomplishment.

For the first time in months I pumped with creative energy, all my recent anxieties honing in on the task of conceptualising the book, formulating ideas, sorting out themes and delineating chapters.

How many people deprive themselves of the pleasure of accomplishment by never tackling anything at which they aren't instantly good? I wrote, gathering momentum. *We delude ourselves that we should be proficient from the beginning, rather than understand that expertise is the product of hard work and simple practice*, slipstreaming into the obsessive bliss of mania.

After pounding out the proposal and emailing it immediately to a publisher I knew who was interested in my work, I was exhilarated. Spontaneous for once, this time it seemed worth it. Tipped my chair back onto its hind legs and heaved a great sigh of satisfaction, swung my arms over my head and stretched, touched the wall and pressed my fingers against it hard. This felt *good*. Or it did until I slumped again a few hours later, full of regret that I had sent the proposal off so quickly, without a day's breath to take a second look and ensure it actually made sense. Didn't dare look at it again in case it read like gobbledygook. Could I get it back, fish it out of the ether if no one had read it yet? I Googled: *"Can you retrieve a sent email?"* Apparently you could, providing it hadn't been officially "received" or opened. By the time I followed the instructions it was too late. Where was inefficiency when you wanted it? I nearly burst into tears. Instead I comforted myself that it was a proposal, not the book itself and no one except a rejecting editor was likely to see it.

My impulsivity inevitably led to a heightened degree of tension, currents of guilt and shame shorting through my system in lightning flashes of stomach cramp. The heat rose up over and over again, menopausal bursts of distress breaking through the wall of my composure. On my way out of the building, still damp and shivering now, I caught sight of Martha below me on the stairs. She was in the prime of her pregnancy, a little plumper these days but beyond the stage of nausea, before the sleeplessness, the discomfort, and the backbreaking toll of it all finally settled in. I ducked out of the way, turning as if heading for the kitchen. She didn't follow me, sang out a happy hello instead before vanishing into her office on the back of a wave and a promise to "Catch up later". Since our lunch and meeting at the conference, she thought we were friends.

Frank came home from Scotland on the Friday. He was still aloof but there were signs that he was less sure of himself: still avoiding eye contact, he planted a kiss on my cheek, "How have you been?" Like a child, he did not seem quite certain how to make his way back to me after such a bleak experience as we'd had the week before. I wasn't sure how we could make our way back either, but I knew it was up to me to make the first move.

I pointed a mean finger at a chair, suggesting he sit down. Frank hesitated before placing the overnight bag he was still carrying down on the floor. He pulled out the chair a little further from the table and sat down. I'm not sure I would have done, preferring some verbal begging followed by expressions of remorse before accepting to be stage-managed. But Frank is Frank and, though reluctant at first, he was his usual obliging self, thank goodness.

We began our way back at the same kitchen table where the marriage, a short week ago now, had cracked wide open.

"Tom rang. He wants me to come over."

Frank said nothing at first, picking up the salt shaker from the middle of the table. In the absence of a cup, he began turning it in circles. I watched, mesmerised. The fingers of his hand moved slightly, his wrist not at all, yet the shaker still turned round and round. "Do you want me to come with you?" finally pausing in mid loop.

"I think I do," wanting to put my hand over his, to hold it there before he began driving the circle again. My turn not to look at him, afraid of what he might see. Instead the window, an open view of the sky.

"That doesn't sound absolutely convincing." He was sharp, unwilling any longer to always give way. He put down the salt shaker, placing it neatly in the centre again, beside its mate.

"Tom is going through my mother's papers. He wants me to help him sort out some stuff, a box he wants me to look through. I would like you there for support." I was almost ashamed.

"That's fine, then. I'll come." He stood up, heading for the reassurance of the kettle.

"Not right away," I blurted. "Come a week later, or a few days later, after I've had a day or two to find out what it is he wants me to look at." Maybe I wouldn't need Frank after all, or not as I feared I might. Maybe there was nothing in the box, or old pictures of me as a kid: Tom like a flagpole at my side outside the house, or in front of the Christmas tree, school pictures and graduation photos, my history encapsulated through my scholastic success. My mother couldn't endure failure.

"Lisa!" It was a warning. "Either you want me there or you don't. You can't have it both ways," facing up to me directly, without the buffer of humour, but he was distressed, too, his face a series of exhausted angles, eyes hollow with misery.

Why couldn't I help my husband? All he wanted was to put his ducks in a row. I remembered Max, stroking his little girl to give her comfort and I tried to make it easier for Frank. Explanation, I knew, was the way forward and I was edging towards the truth, though it was still hiding in the murky shadow of my nightmare, and perhaps more tangibly in the bottom of my mother's box. If only I could grasp hold of it, force it to remain still, the truth in the end might not be necessary and we could go on as we always had done. "I don't know what's in her papers. Maybe nothing. Probably nothing," correcting myself. "I'll want to go through them myself first of all, and you'd be hanging around with nothing to do."

"I've hung around before, though I'm not sure you've always noticed."

I blanched at the bite of last week's encounter, the nasty teeth of Frank's frustration. Sat up straighter and leaned forward, elbows on the table. Still couldn't look at him directly. Held both my hands straight out and sliced the air in his direction. "You know what I mean. Look, I'm trying, okay. Do want you there, but don't want to worry about you while I'm preoccupied with sorting out some dreary papers."

"A bit of boring paperwork? Is that what you've convinced yourself, or are you afraid of something else? I think you are, you see. I think this is what all this secrecy's about, all these nightmares, all this recent tension. Have you done anything about therapy, about taking a break?"

"What do you think I'm talking about? I'm going across the great big sea to visit my brother and mother. That's a break. That's what you want me to do, isn't it? I've also pulled back from the paper for a couple of months." I didn't tell him about the listless search for a therapist, or the frenetic firing off of a book proposal.

"I'm not sure a visit with your mother was what I had in mind." He placed a cup of tea in front of me, the first in over a week. I sipped it with relish. At this high noon point of our marriage, it tasted very good.

"That's what Tom said you'd say."

"Smart man. I've always liked him."

"Yes, well …"

"Even so, if this is going to help sort out what's been bothering you, I'm all for it."

"I didn't say it would. I said it was a break and it's something I clearly need to do."

"All right, we'll compromise. I'll give you a few days' head start, but that's it. We're in this together, Lisa, you have to open up. There's something at the bottom of this Pandora's Box of yours. Whatever's inside, you need to tell me."

I didn't mean to gasp. I stood up quick to catch it, but it cracked like gunshot in the space between us. Frank shot forward, his arms outstretched to break my fall. I held my breath tight, holding back the tears, warding off the nightmare.

"Breathe, Lisa, breathe. For heaven's sake, breathe." He rose, too, and steadied me back onto the chair.

"Hope," I told Frank, "That's what's at the bottom of my mother's box."

"I don't understand," he held up the cup.

"That's the scariest thing of all," crying between slurps, words lost in the gurgle of thick sobs. "Hope. I never wanted to have to hope."

Frank sat down, confused again.

"I'm sorry, Frank. I'm so sorry."

"Well," my affable husband drew his chair a little closer, "That's a start, at least."

TWELVE

I used the weekend to recover and Frank was solicitous. He had made his point, not pushing it further, particularly as I collapsed, spending most of the two days in bed with a headache. The lightest pressure, a stray hair, or a cool cloth was all the same, adding to the pain. Stomach cramps, too, as if going into labour. Frank was careful to see that I drank plenty of liquids and ate something light, crumpets or toast. He comforted me: "There's a summer 'bug' going around." How else was he to make sense of this?

By the time Monday morning rolled around, the pressure had eased and, while still physically shaky, I was grateful to get back to work despite dreading the task ahead. Two weeks was very short notice to give clients of an impending break. Normally I gave them a few months' warning. A psychotherapist's work life is planned out as far as is possible in advance, sometimes a full year ahead. The nature of the job is to provide a "container", to give safety and predictability, consistency if you like. Within that consistency the unpredictability of life can be absorbed, such as illness or an unexpected death in the family. That's the theory anyway. I had certainly provided reliability, not having taken any time out in months, not since Easter, and before taking Dorothy on as a client.

The first thing I did that Monday morning was look through my clinical notes of the previous week, all my "working" files, with each patient's records held together inside a tidy plastic sleeve. Instead of sitting in my usual chair, I sat on the sofa. It wasn't often I took up this position, a corner of my own therapy couch. I picked up the folder with all my notes and weighed it in my hands before opening it, lifting it up and down a few times as if on a set of scales. It was heavy. The substance of its contents seemed to add to its weight.

Sam's notes first. I turned the top page back and forth a few times as if something might magically appear, other clients' reports from last week, too, and finally, Dorothy's notes. They might as well have been blank sheets—I had registered almost nothing in every case. Instead of describing my reactions as I usually did, elaborating on the underlying currents within the room as I perceived them, I had written nothing beyond a cryptic sentence for every patient, a series of bullet points.

- *Focus on mother* (Sam).
- *Skipping next week's session* (Dorothy).

Nothing in these notes suggested the distress of my patients, the possible reasons why, consciously or unconsciously, Sam might have been discussing his mother or in what manner, or what was transpiring in the session with Dorothy that she would choose to avoid her next appointment, the session in which I would have told her of my upcoming break. Not a word written concerning the complexity of my emotions, my increasing affection for her when she appeared so vulnerable, nor my dread, even hatred at times, when she appeared to gun for me, when sometimes I believed she wished me dead. All in all, there was nothing in these "notes" to suggest my responses to my patients, or how I had felt in the room with any of them. I was the "absent" therapeutic mother to my patients that week, absorbed as I was by my own concerns, the disturbance with Frank, and the confrontation with Max. I put the notes back in the larger folder, crossed my arms over my legs and leaned forward, dropping my head onto my lap. My whole body ached: my back, my legs, the joints in my knees and elbows.

Was this self-pity? I ratcheted back upright, jiggling my legs and arms to loosen them, bending and stretching to keep me straight. Punched the cushions on the couch a few times to give them shape before walking to my usual chair and sitting down. Sheltered between its wings, I felt immediately better.

My folder was still on the couch. Stood up again, crossed the short divide and grabbed it, as if it might otherwise be snatched from me, or lost down the back of the seat. I was never going to sit *there* again. Back in my chair with its elevated dimensions, I hugged the notes to my chest and dozed a few moments before the doorbell snapped me into life. Scrambling, I shoved the folder into the box file out of view behind my desk before brushing my skirt down and riffling my fingers through my hair to lift it a little. Then ran down the stairs, nearly tripping at the bottom on the loose bit of rubber. By the time I reached the front door Keith's dental drill was humming. Cursed him under my breath, pasting a smile on my face with a twist of lipstick I had tucked in my pocket for such emergencies. By the time I opened the door I was a picture of containment, solid and professional, completely trustworthy. As I walked up the stairs behind my client, Lucy, the drill was a drone in the background, hardly discernible. I was determined—this week I intended to write a lot more than bullet points.

A supervisor early in my career, and long before Max, had suggested that I learn to "detoxify" breaks, not feel so guilty about leaving my patients behind. This had been helpful advice and gradually I had become more confident about informing my clients that I was taking time off. Now I was feeling guilty again, this time not so much about going away, but because I was giving such short notice. Lucy illustrated what I was up against.

"You took August off last year, and I took it for granted you would be doing it again this year," a dissonant chirpiness behind her complaint. Lucy's relentless good nature was a reliable counterpoint to what I suspected was a pervasive underlayer of self-pity.

"But I hadn't given you notice that I was taking a break?"

"I know, but last year ... in fact I've booked to go away because I thought you would be gone too," her voice an octave higher, still chipper and out of tune.

"Well ..."

"I would have ended up paying for sessions." This didn't please her nearly so well.

"Yes, but ..."

"I don't go away anymore except when you do. Why would I want to pay for sessions when I'm not here?"

"Lucy, I am taking a break and you aren't going to have to pay," highlighting the difference between reality and fantasy, always difficult with this patient.

"But I would have done!"

"No, you aren't going to have to now," I insisted again, before seeing the light and enquiring what this meant for her, the possibility that she had nearly ended up paying for missed sessions. I knew from experience that this was a much better tack, letting her work through her own obstinacy.

"Oh, you mean ... how does this connect with my past?" Lucy sparkled, always pleased to be involved in the hunt for significance.

I nodded, curious to see where this would lead.

Lucy had wispy, ash blonde hair with a pencil line of mousy brown along the crease. Her face was round and pleasant with a superficially perfect complexion. What lay beneath the patina of her foundation cream was anyone's guess. She had dark eyes like small, protruding buttons and her pupils floated on the surface of her expression, dull except for the occasional flash of irritability. Despite her enthusiasm for psychological foraging the exercise was purely cerebral, without troubling her too much beneath the wheels of cognition and memory. Lucy could link up the facts of her life, string out the dots between the events of her early history and her current behaviour, yet they appeared, in her presentation of them, not to relate to any depth of feeling.

Irritation, in my view, is a surface animal, the visceral expression of a more complex experience, anger for instance, or grief. Lucy resided in the sorrowful nexus of annoyance and forced good cheer, beyond which I hadn't made much headway in the eighteen months we had been working together, though I didn't discount the value of her learning to make connections. One step at a time, I told myself, you have to learn to walk first of all. Unlike Dorothy, I hardly thought of her between sessions. If Lucy ceased attending her sessions at this stage she was likely to slip through the cracks of my memory without a trace. Her pale, cute presentation and the dullness of her expression suggested stupidity, but I suspected there was much more to her than that, if only she could connect her dots one link closer to actual experience, her mother's fiery rages for instance, and her father's insistence on feminine perfection.

Men, I knew, liked Lucy for about five minutes before the tedium of her two expression existence and the relentless adoration of her attentions drove them into more exciting areas of pursuit. She was thirty-two years of age and headed for the shelf. At this rate she was destined to remain a teenager into great old age. However, Lucy had also proven herself smart enough to seek out help, and these past few months were a start. I had faith that she would eventually begin stretching her insight a little more deeply into the murky water of feelings. In the meantime, I was forced to settle for the details, except when she was irritated. As a case study she held very little interest for me, sometimes driving me into a bored, fugue state of almost total intellectual paralysis. This morning, though, we had a focus, which meant I could remain attentive.

"I guess it didn't matter much what I did, my mother always made me pay 'something' for how she was feeling. I mean, no matter how well I cleaned the kitchen, it wasn't ever quite clean enough. Or if I went to the shop, I never bought quite the right thing, the right sized oranges or solid enough apples. Sometimes she would tell me I was stupid, or she wouldn't speak to me for a while, she was that angry."

"You couldn't get anything right, not in her eyes, anyway."

"No," Lucy shook her head and looked away out the window, avoiding my eyes. Quiet for a bit and I let the silence run, until it was empty. "You can see the Wheel from your window," she piped. Like Sam in his earlier days, Lucy was a master at moving quickly from reflection into distraction.

"The Wheel?" No one had ever mentioned this before. The London Eye was a couple of miles away, with a lot of urban sprawl in-between.

"Yes, the tip of it, over the edge of that church roof."

I nearly stood to see, catching myself on the brink, "Did it feel like being on a wheel with your mother at times? There was no getting off."

"Gosh!" she burst out. Her eyes actually flickered with life for a second. Sam would have rolled his eyes and groaned, but Lucy seemed willing to run with it, "I guess that's true. My dad was easier, as long as I looked pretty and stayed sweet."

"That can be pretty hard work." We were inching closer to her underlying struggle today and I was excited.

"Sometimes, but I got used to it."

"You're still good at it."

"What do you mean?" Perfectly sculpted eyebrows crunching in confusion. She brushed a hand up and down her upper arm, bending her elbow a few times to test the muscle.

"You still work to look perfect. Or your dad's idea of womanly perfection, perhaps?"

"My mother always looked tired. I used to hate it when she wore old clothes, or didn't bother doing her hair nicely. And

138

she was always complaining to my dad that he wasn't paying her enough attention. It wasn't hard to figure out why."

"But he paid attention to you."

"Yes." She looked out the window again, linking her dots away from the indignity of my prying eyes. Turning back to face me, "You always look nice."

I was taken aback. Thanking her for the compliment was completely inappropriate. This wasn't about me, but about whom I symbolised. Connecting her dots, I was the therapeutic mother who did make an effort.

"Is that why you decided to work with me, because of the way I look?" If I had appeared tired on that first appointment nearly two years ago, mismatched or in need of a haircut, she might never have crossed the threshold again.

Lucy bobbed her head a few times sideways, not quite willing to concede the truth, "Maybe. I don't know."

"Your father seems to have conveyed the message that looks are everything."

"He would have paid my mother attention if she'd made some sort of effort, that's true."

"Why do you think she didn't?" I kept my voice quiet, encouraging her.

Lucy's eyes withdrew inwardly, a shadow of internal disquiet appearing for a moment to replace the prevailing dullness. "Maybe she believed she couldn't get it right. No matter what she did, he was always going to want something else."

"Like the wrong sized oranges, or the not solid enough apples?"

"Something like that." For once she didn't look out the window. She smiled, a sad hopeless smile and her eyes welled up, too.

"You look like you might want to cry."

"No!" a quick retreat, "I don't think so. Is it time?"

"Nearly. We have a couple of minutes left."

"So, next week's our last one for a while?"

"Yes."

"I didn't get it right, did I?"

"Is that how you think about it?"

"I guess so. I didn't get the right sized oranges, did I, booking my holiday before you told me?"

"Maybe not, but that's not so bad is it? The world doesn't fall apart as a result."

"That's not how it feels."

"No, I don't suppose it does. You sound as if it was a matter of life and death with your parents, always having to get it right."

"You can't, can you? Always get it right?"

"No, no you can't." Remembering my own mother and the relentless, demanding quality of her misery. I stood up to indicate the session was over. "It's impossible to get it right all of the time."

Lucy stood up, too. "Maybe that's a kind of relief. Maybe I don't have to try so hard, with you or anybody else." She walked down the stairs in silence.

I closed the door behind her, standing for a moment looking up the stairwell towards my office. Keith's drill was blessedly silent. In my sessions, too, Lucy had been trying for perfection. I was a hard taskmaster, wanting her to reach beyond what she had already achieved in making connections. I wanted her to crack the high dive, when she was only now learning to swim, urging her to delve below the surface to explore her repressed feelings. So, I was a demanding therapeutic mother, too, and she could never quite get it right.

The drill started up again, yanking me out of my reverie. I frowned towards Keith's door and headed back up to my office, taking care this time not to trip on that loose bit of rubber at the bottom. In fact, I tore off a chunk. I may have tripped up once, and I was damned if I was going to do it again. I marched back up the stairs like a tiger mother, ready to hone in on what there was to learn.

No wonder therapists take the month of August off—there's no one left in town to attend therapy. When I looked at my diary more closely I saw gaps where patients had already given me notice they would be away. For those clients who do remain behind it can be quite difficult, with very few therapists still working to take up the slack in case of an emergency.

"You're just like her," Sam barked, referring to his mother. "All you think about is yourself, and now you're taking a break just when I need you most. This therapy stuff is absolute shit!" spitting it out and leaning forward, pupils huge, eyes roasting with heat. Had he taken something? "Absolute shit!"

"This is difficult for you." Love gone angry, abandonment at its heart.

"Well, that's pretty fucking obvious, isn't it!"

"I suppose it is."

It was a hot morning, one of those July days full of false promise. Sam was wearing short sleeves, his skin a smooth, tawny brown. Instead of binging on drugs he was now spending hours at the gym. His shoulders and neck were bulked out and his jawbone had tightened. There was power now behind his anger, the potential for physical force. I was never afraid of Sam, but it was important for him to have some control over events. At heart I believed he was gentle, his newly developed physique compensation for his recently discovered vulnerability.

"You feel I'm deserting you like your mother did, escaping into depression after your sister's death."

"You keep saying that. What does it actually mean?" Sam's hands were locked into fists. A boxer in the ring, he rolled his shoulders a few times and swivelled his neck.

Holding my corner, I didn't respond. Sam was punching the air, much as he had as a child. There was absolutely nothing he could do about his mother's grief, about her abandonment of him during those terrible days and months, perhaps years, when she imagined her lost, perfect child.

"You could have at least have given me better warning," he finally conceded. He let go his hands and sat back in his chair. His physical strength couldn't save him from this loss, any more than his actual presence had been able to rescue him with his mother.

"Yes, and I'm sorry. I hadn't planned on taking a break now."

"You did last year, so why didn't you know this time?"

"I'm sorry, Sam." I repeated, palms upwards, pleading with him.

"Don't give me that," snarling in disgust. "I'm not going to feel sorry for you."

I said nothing, feeling empty suddenly, like a great hole had opened up in me and I was about to drop through it. Sam was watching me, baffled by my abrupt withdrawal. He was naturally attuned to this, an echo of his experience with mother. He was sensitive to any holding back, the diversion of attention from him to another, and worse, into nothing-ness. His mother's abandonment had not been from him to *something* else, but rather into the hollow of grief.

I registered this, even while I was myself capsizing back-wards into the vacuum. I forced myself forward, much as his mother must have done at times, making myself attend to my client as she had done with her very alive child. A terrible effort, duty rather than love, responsibility without pleasure.

"I'll see you next week, Sam." I tried hard not to sound relieved. My hands flat on the arms of my chair I pushed myself upright and walked slowly towards the door, groping my way back into the world.

Sam went out quietly, taking as much care as Max's daughter had done walking down the stairs. At the bottom, where I had torn the rubber patch off, he hesitated for a second before stepping over it like a puddle. I was a shadow behind him, hardly there at all.

THIRTEEN

The following Tuesday, as I sat in my office and waited for Dorothy to arrive, I was as restless as a woman in love with the wrong man, distracted in equal measure by a cocktail of both longing and dread. I moved from office to kitchen and back again refilling too many cups of coffee. Why had I arrived so early? I put it down to Frank having left the flat before me. The truth was I had been anticipating this meeting with Dorothy for over a week and I had no idea how the session would go. How could I? Dorothy was as unpredictable as the sensations she evoked in me, both exciting and terrifying, sometimes completely disabling.

I had been let off easy over the past week, most of my clients fairly sanguine about my taking a break. For some patients there might be a delayed reaction, those with unpredictable abandonment in their histories, for instance, who thought nothing of my absence beforehand, yet in retrospect might find it difficult. Sam had been the exception, his reaction resounding deeply with my own archaic guilt. Hadn't I been the abandoner once, leaving my country and what remained of my family to find a new and easier life abroad? I couldn't remember feeling remorse at the time, only enormous relief and an uplifting, internal tension focusing on what lay ahead, the promise of infinite possibilities. I could fashion myself any way I chose, without the detritus of recent events to pull me down. No one knew me in England and so I was relieved of the pressure of having to reveal myself. The old me, that young woman stranded between youth and maturity, she had hit a wall too big to find a way through. I had to leave her behind. Relief and determination moulded together to forge the new presentation of me. No wonder advertising had suited me so well. For years I had been nothing but a flesh and blood hoarding, a bundle of secrets exposing only those bits of myself I wanted the world to see.

I hadn't said goodbye to anyone, not even my brother, Tom. After spending five months in Ottawa, I had refused to return home to Winnipeg before flying to Britain. My mother saw me off, chugging along in the bus to the airport to help me with my baggage. She would return home later that day while I was on a connecting flight to London through Toronto. Did she have any regrets? My mother's determination appeared to override any sorrow at my departure. I had complied with all her wishes up to that point and she might have recognised that I was past my limit.

Didn't kiss her goodbye, my hug at the departure gate perfunctory. I could hardly bear to look at her. Had she any second thoughts? I was twenty years of age, heading off to live in a country visited solely in my imagination. My mother gave me some money, British sterling folded up neatly in a white envelope like a wedding gift. She shoved it into my hand immediately before I was about to board the plane. "Enough to get yourself settled," she said, enough to carry me through at least a few months until I found a job. She knew I wasn't a spendthrift and that the money would last. When I told her I would pay her back, her expression creased in pain as if I had slapped her. I turned away, heading through the departure tunnel towards the plane.

"Be careful!" she shouted after me.

Shrugged my shoulders and kept on walking. There was no turning back. Even then I knew we are defined by our actions, by the choices we make. After the last few months in Ottawa and following all the decisions I had allowed others to make, getting on that plane, however it turned out, was my choice alone.

Three years later I returned for a visit, confident that I had a life in London worth returning for and beyond the reach of my mother's persistent neediness. After that trip home, and every visit to Canada since, I have returned to the UK experiencing that same confounding tension between despair and hope, regret and profound relief, reminiscent of what I felt flying to Britain that first time.

Now, in preparing to leave for Canada, the emotional matrix of excitement and dread had shifted a little. After so many years, I am convinced that the Prodigal's return was good for the first few moments, at best, before the familiar familial tensions set in. I had abandoned my mother to Tom, his generosity on every visit reminding me of the selfishness of my actions. When it came time to repay my mother her money, she had refused, keeping me forever in her debt.

Except for a few bits of laundry and my make-up, my bags were already packed. I had many more patients to see between this Tuesday morning and the end of Thursday, but it was Dorothy whom I really dreaded meeting. Having skipped her last session, she still wasn't aware of my upcoming break. She was so unpredictable. From one week to the next she could be the petulant or terrified child, or the powerful sorceress. On some occasions she appeared entirely without substance, ethereal and dissociated, a million miles from anywhere. It was particularly during those sessions that I had come to feel affection towards her, as if in the search for her centre I had picked up the trail of someone neglected and worth caring about, a child to rouse my spirits into a vocation. I wanted to make peace with her and, by this means, I hoped, she could begin to make peace with herself. But I had come to hate her, too, to be wary of her attacks and her petulance, the frustration she so easily evoked in me. I had never felt so useless as a therapist as I did with Dorothy, so utterly incapable, at times, of reaching her. No matter how hard I tried, I kept tripping up, missing something fundamental.

At this stage of my work with her she was often unknowable, closed off and defended, beyond my reach. I sat in my office chair that Tuesday morning contemplating how I would tell her, as if it should in some way differ from how I had told everyone else. From behind the sudden pressure of an emerging headache, I at last recognised that it was Dorothy I really did not want to leave that summer. I stood up, as if on command, and looked out the window to see if what Lucy had said the week before was true, that you could see the Eye from this position.

From a distance the London Eye looks like a Ferris wheel, the sort I sat on as a child, rocking back and forth to scare my brother, Tom. The one who rocks the seat always feels more powerful, and poor Tom would grip the bar in a useless effort to steady things. It was Dorothy rocking the cart now, with her unpredictability and her apparent intention to make me sweat through every session with her. I could see the wheel over the head of the church steeple, the tip of it with a single pod, moving in such slow motion that it did not seem to move at all. There was sunlight again this morning. The bit of the rim that I could see glinted like a blazing star before settling into a rich glow over the London roofscape. Why had I not noticed this before? Perhaps a tree had been cut down, or a crane or building removed to make way for a clear view. I watched, transfixed, as one pod slowly vanished and another drifted into view, like a Canadian sun dog, halos of light moving across the sky. I was still standing at the window when she rang the bell.

Heading down the stairs, I heard the door open and Keith clattering in with his bicycle making small talk with Dorothy, a tired old joke about "age before beauty". Had he planned this encounter? I bristled with irritation and a proprietorial gust of jealousy. How *dare* he speak to one of my patients?

I heard Dorothy laugh, as if she had never heard the joke before, the sound of the bike clicking closed and the jangle of a couple of loose keys as Keith let himself into his office. I was on the landing at the top, Dorothy three-quarters of the way up the stairs before she saw me. She had been smiling to herself, but her expression dropped immediately. I felt huge suddenly, involuntarily lifting my arms, as if manifesting a massive span of black wings. Dorothy lurched back in terror. I reached out to grab her before she could fall and we were both frozen for an instant by the contact. Her arm was thin, soft boned like a baby. I let go of her immediately while she steadied herself on the stair rail instead.

"You startled me," catching her breath.

"I didn't mean to. I'm sorry."

"Jesus!" She brushed passed me, taking the lead again and I imagined her resisting the impulse to poke me with her elbow. I would surely have fallen.

She sat down. Her knees below her skirt were bare this week, too, but in the heat of the summer their exposure felt far less cruel. She tapped at her thigh a few times, though the movement was definitive rather than frenetic, ready to speak. I pressed back into the wall of the chair and waited to hear what she had to say.

"I have a new job. I won't be able to come to therapy on Tuesday mornings anymore."

Forceful, challenging, once again I was confounded by this patient. Flushing, I resisted the temptation to wipe my forehead. "We'll have to sort out another time then? Is that what you're asking for?"

"I haven't asked you for anything." Sulking, perhaps still smarting from our encounter on the stairs.

"No, not yet, or not overtly, but I am assuming you want to change your time if you can't make Tuesday mornings."

"You shouldn't *assume* anything about me."

"That's true." I left it there. Dorothy's hands were safely out of tapping reach, nesting neatly in her lap. I hadn't yet mentioned my break.

Following an indecent stretch of petulant silence, "Aren't you going to ask me what the job is?" Her hands might be still, but her voice was scratchy, deeply unpleasant.

"Would you like to tell me?" My hands, like Dorothy's, were in my lap. Unlike Dorothy's my fingers were clenched in preparation to ward off further attack, as if I could possibly hold out against her. I continued to watch as she veered off into the familiar, critical assessment of my room, her roving eye taking in every stain and scuff mark, each untidy section of the bookcase or stack of cluttered papers on my desk. I doubted she identified any of this with creativity, but rather with *mess*, further indication of her therapist's disorder.

When she had seen all there was to see she said, "I have a job in New York, at the UN where my father is now. My office is moving me for at least six months, maybe longer."

I never ceased to be confounded at Dorothy's profession, at her obvious competence, though I also wondered how easy she was to have around. Were they shoving her off the London grid and over to New York for a period of respite? Surely her colleagues did not see her as I did, so consistently unpredictable. As a lawyer she needed to conform to a particular process, to hold true to established principles of jurisprudence. I was witness to this clarity when she was angry, or determined, during those sessions when was set on obtaining something from me, that unknown factor which I couldn't quite fathom.

"When do you go? Are you pleased?" Blinking, my vision blurred, a surge of grief at the prospect of losing her, choking back unexpected tears.

Dorothy saw. "You're *sad* at losing me?" she sneered, shocking me into silence again. "How dare you!" She stood up, the delicacy of her skirt rustling like fine paper. "How bloody dare you!"

I was stunned into position, unable to move let alone stand up. Now it was Dorothy looming over me with dark wings. She hovered for a moment and I was mesmerised by the soft whoosh and thud of her fury as she prepared to take flight.

"How is it you know where I live?" I fought back, the question shot out with such force that it nearly lifted me out of my seat. Shaking, with all the strength I could muster I pressed against the back of my chair. I had avoided addressing the subject and now it blasted out of me in a moment of desperate self-defence.

Dorothy halted in mid take-off, retreated a few steps and, still facing me, dropped back down onto the couch. "How do you know that I know where you live? I might not." Her voice was small and defensive but, like a flirtatious teenager, she was teasing, too. She swivelled her head this way and that before plucking a cushion from the seat beside her and hugging it to her chest. I considered the weight of a bulletproof vest, far heavier than anyone imagines. It had been several weeks since Keith had suggested she might be "stalking" me, when he saw her at the end of my road. I had not wanted to believe him, and so I had ignored the information, skirting around it in the sessions and never mentioning it at all.

I had no idea what to do next. Every session with Dorothy was a high wire act, a death-defying experience I failed to understand. Max had spotted it and so had Frank. With all of my other patients there was a trajectory towards insight, towards some scintilla of change, however small. With Dorothy

I was often confused, compounded by an unnerving demand that I understand something which she appeared to be holding out towards me, and that I failed to grasp every single time. She was trying everything: each of her various forms of presentation were an effort to get me to *see*. At least I understood that, but it didn't bring me any further towards the light. Her leaving for New York might be another desperate attempt to inspire enlightenment, her own version of abandonment. In the instant of my blasting at her, I also realised that she had not been stalking me at all. Standing at the end of my road was likely a desperate attempt to have me see. If she could stand there long enough, and stare hard enough, she might be able to drill some tangible truth into me and I might finally begin to understand. I imagined her glowering towards my house, her arms straight and her hands formed into fists, head and body slightly pointed as if leaning into the wind. How long had she stood there, desperate and angry, fruitlessly longing for contact? Now she was leaving for New York. Was this because she believed I was hopeless, that she knew I would never get the macabre joke underlying all of her desperate actions?

Poor woman, she had tried everything.

Dorothy continued to sit on the couch, hugging her pillow. My head was empty and my body had gone numb too, closed down like a series of blown fuses in order to spare me too big an explosion of feeling. I didn't look at the clock, nor did I care. We were in the thick of it here and I had to recapture my ground, the child clutching her comfort pillow on my couch was making that clear. With great effort I pulled my body forward from its defensive position against the back of my seat, sat up tall, and drew my hands together slowly onto my lap.

Dorothy was rocking now, back and forth from her waist. Her head buried in the cushion, all I could see was the top of her head. There was no sound and I did not know whether she was rocking in fury or in sorrow.

"Dorothy?" Silence. "Dorothy?"

I wanted to reach out. There was nothing I could do—the prohibitions of my profession prevented me from gathering her up like a baby to give her comfort. I was like a mother spent after battle with her child, consumed with guilt for having struck a blow back at her teenage daughter, at the same time also grateful for having survived the encounter. There was some satisfaction and relief, too, that Dorothy was no longer hiding behind her anger and was showing something of what resided behind it.

She still had her head buried in the pillow. Her shoulders were shaking now and through the muffle of the cushion I could hear her sobbing. I leaned forward and stretched out a hand. It hovered just above one of her bare knees.

Did she sense it, feel the heat of my palm as I came forward to meet her? She lifted her head a little so I could see her eyes, soft in the wash of tears, before I reared back in shock when I saw that she was laughing. Her head was out of the protective custody of the cushion now and she could not hold it back any longer. She threw her head back and let out a ripple of laughter before tidying her face into a more contained expression, but her eyes were still lively and she blinked a few times to keep her laughter in check. "Boy! That was something, wasn't it? What *happened*?"

I wanted to shove her, to push her out the door and never see her again.

"What's wrong? What did I say?"

Was she really confused? I certainly was.

"Dorothy, I'm not going to be here next week. I'm off for a few weeks. I'm sorry it's such short notice."

"Oh! I didn't know." She tapped her thigh, two quick little taps that might have hurt.

"Short notice, I'm sorry." How rehearsed this must have sounded. "I would have told you last week, but you weren't here." The truth, also retaliation. I couldn't hold it back, despite myself.

151

Dorothy had recovered. Sitting up straight, eyes no longer floating in the wash, instead granite hard, facing a hostile witness. "I'm leaving for New York next month. I'll give you the date when you return, or email you? How's that? I'll be there for a few weeks sorting out accommodation and then I'll be back in London for another month before moving."

"That's fine." I handed her one of my cards with the dates of my break written on the back. The session was over. I was tempted to leave her to make her own way down the stairs, but consistency is important. My professional self, going through the motions. But I had nearly touched her. I had reached out and nearly touched her!

I followed her down the stairs. A little more of the rubber was torn at the bottom, something to trip over. Dorothy did not seem to notice. I imagined both of us falling hard against the floor. There was nothing beyond that first step to cling to for support, to stop the inevitability of a terrible crash.

I opened the door to let Dorothy out. She turned and smiled at me, the first time she had ever done so, only I could not move past the deep humiliation of our session. Instead, I closed the door firmly behind her. Through the pebbled glass I saw that she did not immediately walk away. Was she staring at me as I was at her, through the undefined blur of the window? Both of us were perfectly still on either side of the divide before she appeared to turn and gradually make her way down the walk, beyond reach, beyond any kind of recognition.

As soon as she was out of view I turned and walked back up to my office, every step another beat of my heart. I avoided the loose rubber patch at the bottom altogether, sidestepping it along the far edge of the step. I hadn't the energy to rip another bit off.

At the top I turned and looked back down, visualising Dorothy as she had stood on her way up to see me, when I had reached out to prevent her from falling. I imagined myself in her position, but with no one there to catch me. This was how

152

I felt now, as if I was cascading backwards down those stairs, backwards in time, back before I had ever developed a defensive carapace, when I was raw and terrified, completely bereft.

There had been no one to catch me then, either.

The box. I was already rifling through my mother's box.

I slammed the lid shut on Dorothy and entered my office. After shoving the cushion into its customary position in the corner, I flung open the window to let in some fresh early morning air. I didn't bother to check out the Wheel. Despite a free hour before my next patient arrived I decided to postpone writing Dorothy's notes until later in the day, telling myself I needed to consider the session from a more objective distance. In the meantime I could get down to working on my book.

I had no more need to think of Dorothy for at least a few weeks and after that she might be gone forever. When she was far away in New York, I would have no need to look for her in every crowd ever again. She would be gratefully confined to a forgettable corner of my past, a clinical footnote in my professional history. Until I gained some understanding, I was unlikely to write about her, as the confusion she evoked in me was too great. All of what I made public was geared towards gaining clarity. She was a therapeutic disaster and I her failed therapist. It was best we either terminated or, if she returned, that I refer her on to someone else, someone better equipped to manage her unpredictable shifts of mood and personality, the quality and precision of her attacks. A clinician who was less likely to take her so *personally*.

My laptop now open in my lap, I wasn't writing much down. My mind kept floating back to Dorothy, the rustle of her skirt above her knees, the pain of her laughter when I had believed she was distraught. How could I get it so wrong? I stood up and went to my desk. I opened the top drawer and pulled out an old address book. If I had wanted to see Joanna earlier, I could have easily checked here. She was listed, as I had always known she would be. I flipped open my mobile phone and dialled the familiar number. She answered at once, almost as if she had been waiting for my call.

"Joanna, this is Lisa Harden speaking."

"Hello, Lisa, how are you." The voice was warm.

"Are you still working?" Cutting straight to the point.

"For you, yes, I'm still working."

Gripped at the throat, eyes burning, I was struck mute.

Joanna picked up the slack. "I am away during August, as usual. In fact, I'm leaving tomorrow, back the first week of September. Would that be soon enough, or do you need to see me today?"

I could breathe now, at least. "September is fine. I'm also away, from Friday."

I wrote down the details of our appointment in my diary. She was no longer working from the old house, so there was a new address to register. I didn't know whether to look forward to seeing Joanna again, or to anticipate our meeting with dread. Regardless, like my mother's box, there was no avoiding it now.

PART TWO

FOURTEEN

Returning home after seeing Dorothy, I was still unsettled, despite having seen five more clients that day, all of whom seemed to appreciate my presence, particularly Lucy, who was fierce in her newfound insight concerning perfection. I was on comfortable, familiar ground there, and could honestly say that we were working well together.

That evening Frank and I had a barbecue on the patio, where I was always careful to keep my voice down because of the neighbours, particularly when speaking about my work. I told him something about my difficult session with Dorothy, without mentioning her name or revealing any of the details: that I found her a difficult patient and was relieved that she might be leaving to live abroad. I didn't admit to my raging sense of loss at the prospect of her leaving for New York, or to my intense shame at my equally powerful feelings of dislike towards her. How could I begin to describe the complexity of my feelings for this new patient, the warring conflict of emotions she provoked? Why did I still refer to her as my "new patient", though she had long passed that stage and I had taken on at least three people since first seeing her in March?

Frank's broad shoulders were bent over the barbecue, an area of expertise he had never quite mastered. Taking it up like an unfamiliar sport when he married me, he none the less enjoyed it, certainly more than he did cooking over a hot stove. Despite the unpredictability of the outcome, Frank's variously underdone or overdone hamburgers and steaks always tasted good. As he strenuously pointed out, I hadn't yet refused to eat one, even those covered in a remarkably thick layer of char. Now the burgers were sizzling as Frank sliced off a piece of cheese to melt over the top of mine. With as much insouciance as I could muster, I told him that I had contacted my former therapist, Joanna.

He didn't turn around. Instead, he scraped his spatula along a strip of the grill, as if to clean it and clanged it twice against the edge of the barbecue to shake off the grunge before scooping up a patty and placing it between the folds of a warmed-up bun. Finally, he turned to face me, placing the hamburger on my plate like a communion offering. I hoped it was at least tender on the inside. Anyway, I'm a big fan of mayonnaise and hot mustard. I could cover up most culinary offences with some sort of sauce. Frank sat down opposite, mischief in his expression I hadn't seen in weeks, daring me to take a bite. It was surprisingly good, though with a little more seasoning than usual. I nodded my approval.

"You've contacted Joanna." He took a bite of his own hamburger, slightly blacker than mine. I could hear the crunch, like a hard bit of crackling. He continued chewing, as if it was the best he'd ever tasted. "Mmm mm," bouncing his head up and down a couple of times. He licked his lips.

"Okay, okay. I get it. The hamburger is very good."

"Better than good. Excellent in fact," though I noticed he was taking a little longer to swallow than usual. I helped myself to more salad, sticking a few leaves and a slice of tomato between my patty and the bun.

"You've made an appointment with Joanna," he tried again, "What happened today that you finally picked up the phone?"

158

"The session was so hard, a little too confusing for me, I guess. I see your point."

"Which is?"

"That I am troubled by this client and I need some help to understand what's going on with her. A little more help than Max can offer ... Something about her needling me." I couldn't tell him to what extent I was troubled. Frank equated all my recent anxiety to this patient. If Frank couldn't figure out what was upsetting me about her, he had hoped that Max, and now Joanna could source the answer. Max was doing the same, passing me on to Joanna. A ripple of resentment ran through me, other people handing me over because they believed I was too much for them. I took another bite of my hamburger.

Didn't want to think about Dorothy, or of returning to Joanna. Not now. Wouldn't be seeing either of them for at least a month. I could leave them both behind and focus on my book instead. Could almost look forward to Canada, or at least to seeing Tom, now that I had a large project to tackle. Maybe my mother's box wouldn't be so daunting after all ...

I must have looked a bit dreamy because Frank cut in, "Lisa, where are you?"

"Thinking ... Sorry ... My book ..." shoving my half-empty plate further down the table. I hadn't the stomach for anything more.

Frank, eating his hamburger, sounded like he was munching carrots. I winced at the noise, like an invasion of privacy. Frank caught the look and swung it right back at me. "I can expect at least a year of you drifting off, then?"

"Maybe. Haven't tackled such a big project before." Cringing inwardly as I remembered blasting off the book proposal. Moments of spontaneity can sometimes take a lifetime to repair.

He nodded, scrunched up his napkin and dropped it down on his empty plate, a habit I considered particularly unattractive. Why turn your plate into a dump?

"Are we good now, Frank?" I burst out. "Are we back to normal?" Like with Joanna earlier that morning, I was instantly flummoxed by the threat of tears, my heart nearly drumming out of my chest. Pressed a hand hard against my breastplate, forcing it back into place.

He didn't speak for a moment, his face creasing into gravity and the shadow of his impending old age. He'd lost a bit of weight recently, and there was such fatigue in his clear effort to remain upbeat this evening. "Frank?" I reached out, refusing to hold back anymore, or at least not anymore than I needed to.

He took my hand and rubbed it a few times with his thumb, pressing it hard. "Not good, but better." He let go of my hand. "I wish you would let me come with you to Canada."

"A couple of days on my own, that's all, Frank."

He stood up, ready to clear the table. "You always want to do things on your own. What makes you think others can't be trusted to support you? Was it really so terrible when you were a kid that you had to do everything on your own?"

I didn't bother responding. He knew my mother had been a one-way sponge, always sucking it up, never letting anything go. And Tom was still a kid then, too, managing his life as best he could. How could I have relied on him?

I didn't want an argument this evening. I wanted a smooth running marital machine to tide me over the ocean and the difficult few days ahead. It was going to take courage to look in the box, not something I was so sure I could produce on command. I would also have to work out a cohesive story by the time Frank arrived, four days later. He had conceded another two days after I expressly told him it would take that long for me to recover from jet lag, visit my mother and then finally rummage through that damn box. One thing at a time.

Not looking at one another, we carried our dirty dishes into the kitchen. I rinsed the plates and slotted them into the dishwasher. We were always careful not to interfere with one another's system, resulting in a rather odd formulation of plates and cups. A dishwasher in a marriage is like driving a car; each participant has a particular technique. Allowing the other to manoeuvre without criticism is a concession made possible only through an effort of will. Both of us were trying hard.

Having filled the dishwasher, closed down the barbecue and scraped away the remaining gunk on the grills, all within the frame of a long, sad silence, we weren't quite sure what to do next. It was still warm outside, so I sat down on one of the garden chairs and Frank followed suit. He may have lost weight, but his body seemed heavier somehow as he sank into the seat slowly, using both hands to stabilise himself. There was nothing between us now but what we chose to hold back and our chairs were so close our knees were nearly touching. In the silence I could hear the distant roar of cars along the main road and the rumble and hoot of a train hurtling towards the junction.

Frank finally spoke. "I can't say everything is going to turn out fine, because I don't know. It's up to both of us. You have to do your bit, and I have to learn not to let you get the better of me at times. I'm too soft on you, you know, Lisa. Sometimes I need to stand up to you more."

"No, you don't."

At least Frank laughed at that, though I knew he was right, and I was frightened by what it might mean.

"We'll see. I can make a stab at it anyway. I won't put up with you shutting me out any longer. You can take your time, but then you could risk the marriage. I can't help you unless you let me in on your secrets." He didn't quite point at me, tapping four fingers against the metal arm of his seat. The whole chair clacked in response.

Marital conversations, they so often move in circles and I was very tired of this one. "Is there anything left to say about this?"

161

"Of course there is. You find the subject uncomfortable, and it's only recently that I think you've taken any notice of my complaint, and look what I had to do to get your attention." He stopped abruptly. "I'm becoming frustrated talking about it now as well. How about we go to bed and resume at a later date?"

"Why don't we put it away altogether? I promise to try harder."

"That's the point, Lisa, trying hard this time isn't going to be enough. You are actually going to have to *do*."

"I get it! I get it! Honestly." And for the first time I think I did. I also knew I had to tackle the next part of this alone, without a background concern for my husband or my marriage, for that matter. I needed the ground firmly beneath my feet, and for that I was willing to risk a few more days of Frank's ire.

We did go to bed soon after, talked out and drained. His body was warm and, despite the too hot night I was comforted by it, the assured pulse of his heartbeat so close to mine.

At two in the morning I rocketed awake. It had been weeks since my last nightmare. In this dream I was not being pursued, this time I was raging with a wild, murderous fury directed at the smallest of creatures, another pulsating egg with the thinnest of membranes through which I could see every organ and beat of its miniature, defenceless heart. I wanted to kill it, stomp out its life—it contained a threat far greater than its tiny size. I was deluded, and knew it, but that did not prevent me from wanting to commit murder. My nightmare: choosing to pursue self-deception over truth.

I reached out to touch Frank's shoulder, a wholly different sensation of vibrating warmth. He was still asleep and I did not want to wake him. I curled up close, shutting my eyes to the horror of the nightmare, digging my forehead into my husband's back, taking refuge in the solidity of his presence. Wherever that fury had come from, I needed to leave it behind—face up to what waited for me in Canada without the intimidation of murderous rage marching through my sleep.

Three days later Frank drove me to the airport. At my insistence he dropped me off in front of the terminal, rather than tag behind while I passed through check-in and security. Our parting was tinged with all the strain and sadness of recent weeks. I held onto him hard at the kerbside, full of regret and longing. I wanted him to push through my resistance to say he would join me on the trip now. How could I have been so foolish? I always needed Frank in my worst moments. He was the one who could sort through the chaos to make sense of things.

He patted my arm, gently detaching himself, "I'll see you in a few days." He didn't want to linger, the mood between us a vortex of unexpressed sorrow. Frank was so tired, the lines in his face this morning accentuated by the shadow of his unshaven beard. At this early hour, and in the moment of parting, it was harder to maintain our cover. I distracted myself with organising my luggage, a single, large suitcase and a leather computer bag that doubled as a backpack. Frank heaved it up and held it like a child's cardigan for me to put my arms through. "See you on Tuesday." He moved his head up and down a few times, like he was agreeing with something I'd said.

"I'll be there, I promise," I waved my travel documents in the air. "See you then."

I was doomed to a few loose hours in the departure lounge, this time without the energy to visit the shops. Not that I ever bought anything beyond a newspaper or make-up, but I usually enjoyed looking, defining myself by the luxury I imagined I might someday be able to afford. Not today. I flipped open my laptop and worked on a possible introduction to my book until my flight and the departure gate flashed on the screen. I purchased one more giant coffee and marched my way down the long passageway to the far end of the terminal where Air Canada was invariably parked.

On the flight I hardly looked out the window, continuing to work. The middle-aged man beside me said not a word and I did not interrupt his silence, having learned years ago that once conversation is struck up with a passenger on a long haul flight, it is very difficult to put out.

I punched out sentence after sentence, preoccupying myself with industry. I reiterated the message of my proposal, that hard work is the beginning of a sense of accomplishment and the development of expertise built over an extended period of time. I was making a noble effort to keep my mind from straying but, occasionally during a pause to collect my thoughts or formulate a sentence, an image of a patient during the last few weeks would flicker to the surface through a crack in the wall of my concentration. Sam and his rage reared up, with his insistence that my desertion was too sudden, and Dorothy with her sham of good intentions and her laughter at my expense. I was grateful when someone like Lucy surfaced, her anodyne good nature and enthusiasm for insight like a salve against the provoking and humiliating memory of Dorothy's attacks.

I was writing about the value of hard work, focusing on therapy, yet I felt more like a failure than I had in years, unprotected and vulnerable as I headed for the wide-open prairie and the visit with my mother.

Halfway through the flight I closed the computer and put on my headphones instead, comforting myself with a Sandra Bullock movie, a guilty pleasure on nearly every long haul flight where no one could see me. Who, after all, would know that I had once dreamed of another life, of the handsome prince and an escape into a world of privilege? Heading back to where I'd left such fantasies behind, a film with a Cinderella theme was a salve, though it hadn't finished by the time we landed in Toronto, depriving me of a last rush of pleasure.

As usual, I had to spend a few hours in Toronto waiting for my connecting flight. Having refused food on the overseas crossing, I passed the time by having a late lunch. This was part of my re-entry pattern, gulping down a cup of Tim Horton's coffee, accompanied by a double-glazed doughnut. Those few hours in Toronto were always a transition period for me. Like astronauts returning into the earth's atmosphere, I needed to decompress and find my legs again. My accent, instead of helping me to stand out, now forced me to blend in. I was nothing except another one of the mass of Canadians milling about in the airport, nothing to distinguish me at all. After so many years living abroad, this always took a little time to get used to.

I sipped my coffee and ate my overly sweet bun and told myself that I had already proven that I could manage my life, that there was nothing I need fear. When my connecting flight was called, I stood in the line to board the plane. As proof of my identity, like all the other passengers, I held out my Canadian passport. No one looked at it twice.

I was home.

FIFTEEN

In Winnipeg there is a new airport, slicker than the old one: souvenir shops and restaurants, with high tech ordering on tablets. My hometown has grown up, expanded in my absence. I am a stranger again, until I hit Portage, the long avenue of my youth opening up into six lanes all the way to town. This road, in either direction, if I stay on it long enough, will take me to the coast—Highway No. 1, an asphalt thread linking the country from one end to the other, a means of escape I failed to recognise as a young woman. Instead the city was like four walls without a door, until disaster struck and they all came tumbling down.

The rental car is smooth. Automatic, it starts at the push of a button, the air conditioner purring. I clutch the steering wheel with both hands and aim straight for my mother's nursing home. On this road, along this track, I float above myself, watching the young woman below. She is the one driving the car: another era, another time zone. She knows the terrain, the map of the city, with her childhood articulated through the indelible actions of muscle memory. She knows when to turn and when not to, recognises hotels and businesses along the strip leading away from the airport. Names have changed over the years, yet this is such familiar territory. The Institute for the

Blind on the left, the big electronics store to the right, fast food chains and the Richardson Building up ahead, tumblers falling into place. Where the roller rink used to be, now an imposing university building, the periodic table embossed in its facings. She blinks away the changes. A sudden chill in the air and the new hockey arena looms, monument to the prodigal Jets. She remembers the old one: bright lights and the smell of hot dogs, the sweet yeasty scent of spilt beer, and the slap of the puck against the boards. Blades scraping the ice, the roar of the crowd as another one lands in the net. The sound of the organ slugging out yet another tune: new for old, Eaton's department store gone and a rip in her chest, a streak of pain like fabric tearing across the grain. The car veers for a second into another lane and a truck honks behind her. Hard and angry, too long a scream. A shout like a roar and the car is back on track.

She creeps to a standstill at the traffic lights; the man in the car alongside glares. Lifting her hand, she smiles in grim apology. What does he know? This young woman trekked this quarter mile stretch between Eaton's and the Hudson's Bay Company a thousand times. An Eaton's girl, taking refuge behind the counter in the book department after school and between classes while at the university. Now a tired acre of thrift shops and the grey, sloping shoulders of the drunk and homeless. Foot on the pedal cutting over Main Street, a clump of turn-of-the-century buildings before turning left. The sun blocked for a few seconds as the car speeds underneath and between the Gothic steel girders of the railway bridge, then up and over the water to the French side of town. A few discomfiting seconds hovering within the limbo of her past before dropping down into the present. I am back, the young woman I used to be once again consigned to history.

Businesses and street names here are distinctly Francophone. Provencher Avenue, St. Boniface Cathedral, St. Boniface Hospital, and St. Boniface College, all in a tidy cluster. A suburb built for French speakers. I am not one of them. Like mother. Scottish roots but opting to live her final days this side of the river. Years spent struggling to keep up in our aspiring neighbourhood, hardly matters here. The privilege of the outsider. With everyone speaking French she can choose to socialise, or not.

The nuns are kind, unafraid to touch her parchment face, to hold her withered hand. In an accent like a truck driver's, pathetically grateful, she will croak out a French phrase or two, "Merci, ma sœur." Gratitude at last.

Cranking the wheel into a sharp turn to park, I slam on the brakes.

The last stop. Catching my breath, taking stock. A few cars down, Tom's black pick-up truck stands high above the smooth sedans. Tom, the son she dubbed a hellraiser, the one who cares for her. Me, the good daughter, long gone and only ever here to do my duty. I dread this place, the complexity of old guilt and new shame, the need to pretend and show willing. I want to stay in the car, or walk the streets. She does not even know who I am.

Instead, I straighten my shoulders, press my blades against the seat before opening the car door. The air outside is summer hot and the light harsh, the sheared angles of the building straight ahead sharper still underneath this brazen sun. I pull my bag from the back seat and draw out a tissue to wipe the damp from my forehead. With it comes the tint of make-up. Little by little the woman I am in London is peeled away, from the moment I left Frank on the curb at Heathrow to this brittle point. Stiff from the long flight and the drive from the airport, I stagger like a drunk for the first few steps before walking tall again. There is nowhere to go except forward.

Nursing homes are where people congregate to die. Walking through those failsafe doors, the second set opening only after the first has closed behind me, I could already detect the dust of dried flesh. I yank out another tissue to blow it away. Walking along the corridor towards my mother's room I am grateful that in this hospital, at least, there is never the oppressive fug of urine, the vinegar of life leaking into every chair and mattress. How do they manage it? If they can plug the seepage here, why can't everyone do it?

"Bonjour," a nun at the front desk, familiar from my former tours of duty, lifts her head and smiles. Though not in traditional habit, there are the telltale signs of an unblemished life in her soft complexion and curly hair the colour of tin. On the lapel of her black sweater she has pinned a small gold cross. Not quite managing a smile, I nod in return.

In front of my mother's room I stop to take a deep breath, like before plunging into deep water, or preparing to swing an axe. Both might kill me if I'm not careful.

Tom is sitting by the side of my mother's bed, his hands folded in his lap like a prayer and his handsome head bent down into his chest. His snoring is light, leaves rustling between the trees. My mother is also asleep, every breath hard labour, cramming air into the increasingly confined space of her lungs. Against the sweet tune of my brother's sleep, hers is the rumble of a bass drum.

She is flat on her back in the bed, her arms and hands extending straight out over the neatly folded covers. I take a step back. Why didn't Tom warn me that she was so ill? I stand perfectly still for a moment before moving into the room slowly. My eyes never leave her face. I don't think to kiss her. In her wasted state her teeth are bared. Her skin is blue veined and translucent, each joint in her exposed hand like a bent twig and the wedding rings on her left hand are loose, rubbing up against the knuckle. Those cheekbones, upon which her beauty once hung, are now the raw structure of a diminishing life. Picasso's blue period, the emaciated frame of the guitar player. And there, from out of nowhere, is my nightmare—the hounding of that inflated membrane, all the way from London hightailing it on the wind to drive me down. I lift a hand to

170

pull it closer, the better to get rid of it, but it is too quick for me, vanishing as quickly as it appeared, beyond my reach.

Tom has prepared for my arrival, an empty chair already in place the other side of the bed, marking my absence. The rebuke isn't his, only my guilt tripping me up. I tiptoe over so as not to wake him and sit down slowly, using my hand on the back of the chair to balance my descent. I cannot take my eyes off my mother, as if she might rise up out of this state to taunt me. In truth, she is beyond waking, her death rattle a bell clanging in the near distance.

Finally, with a hot rush of dread, I drag my eyes away from her. Searching for the box? This is her room. I look towards the small bookshelf, heavy with pictures of Tom and me, mostly from the dark ages of our childhood. My face placid in the face of my father's pointing camera, Tom grinning in every frame, on the verge of mugging it up. There are a few books and magazines that my brother has supplied, a gardening encyclopaedia with illustrations and a few old issues of MacLean's. I remember her turning the pages, entertained by the pictures rather than the content, no longer comprehending. The room is small but tidy and Tom has hung a few pictures on the walls, a print of The Hay Wain and another of Thompson's birch trees, their trunks stretching up into the sky over the lake. On the wall in our living room as children, the Constable particularly stationed like an icon over the couch. The Thompson print maintained a less reverential position in a corner to the side of the bay window, cast in perpetual shadow. Here, the blind on the double window is pulled most of the way down, only a few shafts of light breaking through to lift the gloom. I resist the urge to snap it open.

Tom is still dozing in his chair, though he grunts a few times as if he might wake, disappointing me each time by sinking down into himself even further, his head like an apple bobbing on the surface of his chest. I am torn between wanting to wake him and wishing him the consolation of sleep. Tom would have driven all night, as he always does to visit my mother. Alone in the room with her, sleep is his only refuge. There is nothing to entertain him here. He is not a reader, rather a man of action, his escape during times of stress reflected in the rugged landscape in which he lives, deep in the Rocky Mountains. He prefers to scale cliffs, or shoot down in powder. Visiting his mother is penance for a life raced through at top speed, the only mechanism he has to draw him up short. Even his children don't bring him to a standstill; they live too far away for that. But my mother, in her old age, draws him back to this room and into the dark realm of her unsorted papers and matters of estate to pin him down to a seat by her bed with heart-breaking regularity.

There is not much to do in an old person's room, particularly when the lights are out in the one you are visiting. Only the noise of the hallway for distraction, an incessant buzzer like an emergency vehicle flashing into life every thirty seconds, one more patient desperate for attention. Rubber soles squeak against the linoleum, doors open and close and there is the bright chirp of quick conversation in passing, occasionally the lightning crack of spontaneous laughter.

I shuffle in my seat and reach down into my bag to pull out my notepad. I am jet-lagged, needing to occupy myself and do not want to continue staring at my mother, her skeletal frame already turning to ash. I need only to raise my hand to catch a fistful of dust. Instead I pick up my pen, holding it uselessly over the empty page. The sheer boredom of it all. My mother is no longer a person hanging onto life. Rather, her frame is so reduced that she is on the march for a way out. I understand. A deathbed watch should be maintained in homage to the life that is passing away, regardless of who it is.

I close my notebook. Rather than focus on my mother and her disquieting efforts to escape, I take comfort in watching Tom. With his chin firmly settled into his chest, his mouth is

172

now hanging open. About to drool; I can tease him about this later. Along with Frank, Tom is the person I love best in the world. He is my elder, but only by a few years, enough for him to feel a sense of superiority and protective largesse towards me, a habit I find both endearing and irritating in equal measure. As children we had our roles to play, my mother taking ownership of me as her "good" child, while Tom was banished into the realm of "bad behaviour", which I recognise now was the only way he could please my mother, to play the part she had assigned him.

I am an unlikely sister to a man so athletically handsome. Awake he is even-jawed, my mother's cheekbones giving his expression a lift and a symmetry that sometimes cause people to misjudge his intelligence. This has never been a problem with me.

He likes to think he protected me after my father died, despite my reminding him that he was often nowhere to be seen. Stranded alone in the miserable neediness of my mother's web, I could have done with him then. Tom, though, was raising hell with his friends in grimy apartments all over town, smoking dope and listening to the mournful tones of the city's local hero, Neil Young. He can still recite every lyric the man wrote and quote whole sections of his biography. He can even do a passable imitation, often after a few drinks launching into an unearthly octave and stretching his vocal chords beyond endurance, crooning to the tune of *Helpless* about a town in north Ontario. I will either laugh or moan, depending on my mood, aware that I am in for a night of reminiscence of a youthful landscape I don't recognise and peopled with characters Tom knew in those halcyon days of his late adolescence. During that same period I was in the house with my mother, my head buried in books and my ambition finely tuned to the prospect of university, my only way out.

My portrait of him is unfair, but I am drawn to this version through the wormhole of our shared history. In fact, by his

173

early twenties Tom was in law school, and must have struggled hard to get there. Most nights he worked in a restaurant downtown. Tips, he told me years later, were his sole means of support. Still, the spin within our household was that he was irresponsible. He was rarely home: between the hours he put in slinging steaks at The Keg and those he spent in the library studying, there were not many left in change. And there was also his social life to attend to. He was lively and energetic and, unlike me, he made friends easily.

Despite this busy life, he took time out to teach me to drive, forcing me behind the wheel of my mother's clapped out Pinto. He wasn't going to risk his brand new car on me, a black streak of motorised testosterone I never admitted to enjoying. As a teenager, as a point of honour, I withheld all my interest in his concerns. I was the good kid, and he was the hell-raiser. In my adolescent arrogance I believed my disapproval would encourage his improvement. That ridiculous car of his, a wreath of flame painted on its sides, was his only luxury, and it was a necessity. How else could he have managed to keep himself afloat, pressed as he was between work and study? And still he took time out for me.

This seat is too hard and I shuffle up and down and back and forth in a vain attempt to make myself comfortable. All those noble gestures and I was a lousy kid sister, my nose turned up in an ugly expression of contempt for his brash young macho ways. He took it all without any more retaliation than the occasional teasing, hardly the blast of fury that I deserved. He taught me to drive, the preserve of the good father, with the unspoken acknowledgement that someday I would need to leave town. He already knew that driving a car is a mark of freedom, wheels to carry us away.

My mother's breath changes abruptly, caught like a spur at the back of her throat. Tom snorts into life, instantly awake.

"Shit!" Shakes his head and rubs his face with both hands, gurgling in unison with my mother. "What's happening?"

174

Another clutch for air and we both shoot up, either side of the bed.

"Her breath changed, like she missed a beat."

"Ugghh" He sits back down. "She keeps doing that. Scares the life out of me."

"You didn't tell me she was so ill."

"I didn't know. Got here this morning. Jesus, Lisa, don't start already." But he grins, picks himself up again out of the chair and walks to my side of the room. "Hello. Very good to see you."

"And you," standing up to hug him. He is a bigger man than Frank, a football player rather than a cricketer with some of the rougher edges of an ageing hockey player; aching knees, lightning speed, and the ability to see out of the back of his head.

"No computer?"

"Only a notebook." Holding it up for view.

Tom lifts his eyebrows. "Old school." He walks back to his side of the bed but doesn't sit down this time. Instead, crossing his arms he leans against the window frame. "How are you feeling? We should get something to eat, at least."

"Can we leave her here?"

"The nurses have my number. She's been like this for a couple of days."

"This could go on a long time, then?"

"'Fraid so." Tom's smile is grim, in for the long haul, though I'm not sure I am. As ever, I am prepared to leave Tom to take the rap.

"What do we do? Take turns overnight? Does someone need to be here all the time?" I put my hand to my throat, forcing it into a deeper register. I don't want to remain with my mother alone for too long.

"No need to panic. Like I said, the nurses have my number." He is watching me carefully, squinting, adjusting his focus. I must look a mess, so many hours on a plane and then arriving here without even a pit stop to change or shower. My mouth is dry, as if I've been licking envelopes, and my eyes are scratchy, itchy in the corners. I rub them hard with the clenched knuckles of my first fingers, the image of a little girl about to cry. Never, I swear, never in a million years.

"Maybe we should get you to the hotel?" Tom's brows are pinched, in concern or exhaustion, I'm not sure which. "I've booked us both rooms just over the bridge."

"Let's go. I can shower and we can eat later." I drop my notebook back into my bag before slinging it over my shoulder. "Both cars?"

"I'll meet you in the hotel car park—I've got some stuff for you in the back of the truck."

"The box?"

Tom nods, heading for the door. "The box," he says, leading the way into the corridor. "I've got the box."

Neither of us looks back at our mother, quiet now and fast asleep in the bed.

SIXTEEN

Up and over the bridge, Tom swung his truck like an anchor into safer territory heading straight for the hotel's underground parking lot, a dusty tomb if there ever was one. I bumped downwards along the circular concourse, edging my car away from the wall to avoid scratching my bumper. Why submit to such a low level existence when there were rows of empty spaces above ground? But this is the prairie way, the habit of a lifetime ensuring your vehicle, so often the casualty of weather, is kept safe from harm: the beat of the summer sun, or the corrosive effect of a winter climate harsher than any on earth. Down below the temperature is ambient, gently cool in summer, warm in winter.

Pulling into a spot beside Tom, I pinched the top of my nose. The walls were a concrete grey and the floor like parched earth, the smell of soot in the air. There were other tomb raiders down here, an old Lincoln Continental and a more recent Volvo, both cars an expression of pride and success. Tom was already peeling back the shiny black canvas at the rear of his truck. Pulling out an overnight case—my brother always travels light—he placed it on the ground, displacing a little puff of dirt. Without a word he walked to the side of the truck, stretched a little further into the cargo section, yanked at a cardboard box that was tucked behind the spare wheel bed, tied securely with a bungee rope and looped through a handle at the back of the cab. He flipped the cord loose and the hook clanged like a gun-shot against the metal floor of the truck.

I jumped back, colliding against the side of my car, a thin layer of subterranean ash now scraped clean onto me. I grunted in disgust, pounding at the offending stain with the palms of my hands. Dust billowed around me in small, dark, clouds.

"Here," Tom handed me the box, lighter than expected. Nearly dropped it. Half empty too, the contents tipping from one side to the other, shifting the balance. The box wasn't large, ten centimetres deep maybe and about a metre square, a skate box, "CCM" emblazoned on the side. My skates. A young girl's dream of dancing on ice, another Barbara Ann Scott spinning my way out of this world into the next. On the top of the box my mother's handwriting, my name scrawled in large letters with an exclamation mark at the end.

"No mistaking it's mine, then?"

"Nope. Or hers, depending on how you look at it. What happened to the skates?"

"Who knows?" Hanging on a hook in the garage. At four-teen tripping up in competition on a half flip, twisting my ankle. Never skated again. "She probably gave them away. You're going to have to hold this for a minute while I grab my cases out of the boot."

"Here we say 'trunk'."

I ignored him, clinging onto the woman I am, buying time too.

Opened the "trunk" of my car and hauled out my suitcase. Compared to Tom's, it was a brute of a bag, with just a little space left for what I might wish to bring home when this was over. "Let's go!" fitting the backpack onto my shoulders and raising the handle of my suitcase. Bleeping my car into lock, I spun the case around in a crack, heading towards the exit sign at the other end of the parking lot. Tom was still holding the box, which was fine with me. For a split second he was nonplussed, not quite knowing how to balance it and his own luggage without dropping one or the other in the adjustment.

"Whoah!" he yelled after me. "Hold up there, will you."

I paused by the door, the epitome of patience. Tom shook his head. He loves me, I know, but sometimes I am only tolerated. "What the hell have I done?" The box under his arm now, the wheels of his little case clattered against the concrete floor as he ran towards me. We might have been children again.

"Nothing, Tom. Nothing."

"It's the box, isn't it?" For a man so athletic, he was panting pretty hard.

"Maybe."

"Quit sulking. I told you, there was one for me too."

"I bet it didn't have an exclamation point at the end of your name."

"Well, no, and it was full of drawings and stuff, report cards. The good ones anyway. Oh, and my graduation picture of all things."

"Which one?"

"Law degree, of course. I don't think she really believed I graduated from high school."

"Nobody did." Through the door now and waiting by the elevator.

Tom was indignant. "I must have done something right, you know, to get into law school." Defensive after all these years, still causing him pain.

I softened my tone, "I know, Tom." And I did, the therapist in me coming to the rescue. "I'm sorry."

"Okay." The box still tucked protectively underneath his arm.

"Do you want me to take that?"

The elevator landed and the doors slid open. "I can take it up to the room for you." He led this time, holding his finger on

179

the button while I shifted and pushed my case over the raised lip at the bottom.

"Thanks." The doors closed. We were now in the silent space between floors, our images gleaming back through the tinted mirrors along each side. Rather than face ourselves, we looked at one another. Tom's expression was flat, pulling away from me.

"Tom?"

"Yeah?"

"You looked in the box?" The elevator dinged. Saved by the bell, the doors slid open before he could answer. "I would, you know. If it were me. I would have looked in the box." Chasing after him, pushing my way into the hotel's reception area.

He stopped just before the check-in desk to let me catch up. "I know *you* would have."

Tom and I look sufficiently unalike that people sometimes assume we are married. Tom makes a face at anyone who suggests such a thing, like the poor receptionist at the desk now. "God, no!" he joked.

"He's my brother," defending myself.

The woman nodded, though her smile was a little stretched. She tapped away at her computer. "You have adjoining rooms. Does that work for you?

"Fine." We said in unison.

She handed us our keys, small packets of paper and plastic. "Have a good day," not sounding at all like she meant it.

We had stayed in this hotel before, my brother swinging us both a deal on the basis of his business account. After all, he owns a hotel or two, they just happen to be at the base of a mountain, catering to skiers in winter and families travelling through the Rockies in summer. He is part owner of a ski resort, which he claims has left him in hock to a fortune, rather than making him rich. But often he picks up my tab, as if I am the poor relation, and I generously give him the gift of my acceptance. There is no doubting his success now.

The porter took our suitcases, hanging my backpack on a hook from the top bar of the trolley, while Tom held onto the box. We travelled with our luggage up to the fifth floor in silence, another mirrored sarcophagus. I slipped my card into the lock and Tom followed me in, placing the skate box onto the bed while the suitcases were unloaded.

"I can take mine from here, thanks." Tom slid his small case off the trolley and handed the porter a tip, the pink flutter of a ten dollar bill pressed into the young man's hand. Tom and I were alone in the room. I sat down on the far side of the big bed, my back to the box. Slapped a cushion over it for good measure.

"You look beat," brotherly observation, rather than concern.

"I am. A shower'll help. Then maybe we can eat?"

"We can have dinner here, if you want. The food's pretty good."

"Tonight you could serve me gruel and I probably wouldn't notice. I have a mouth like the bottom of a pail at the moment."

Tom winced, "Nice image," heading towards the door. "I'll come back in half an hour. I've got some calls to make anyway. Don't forget to brush your teeth." He paused. "God, what an image! Sometimes, Lisa …" his voice trailed off as he left the room. I heard a vague click as he moved from mine into his, the door thudding softly behind him.

I was alone.

I turned and looked towards the bed, a corner of the box protruding beyond the cushion, the space of a lifetime between us. Too worn out to do anything more than stare at it, I could have lifted it out, ripped the tape off the lid, but I didn't. Was it my imagination or had it been replaced recently, a thick layer of hockey tape instead of the tinted yellow stain of ageing scotch tape, my mother's favourite? I pushed the pillow to one side. From just below the corner of a long strip of adhesive there was a tear where the cardboard had been rubbed, or more likely torn off. If Tom had taken a peek, he had been pretty careful to maintain the same tracks as my mother when resealing the box.

I picked it up and shook it, like a child's present under the tree. The weight didn't surprise me this time and the contents clunked from one side to the other. I turned the package upside down and they dropped, again, the entire width of the box. Why a skate box for so few contents? I had expected more. Whatever was in here, I knew it wasn't the hoarding of child-hood photographs, or my old report cards. My mother had separated this portion of my life from all the rest and placed it in a carton far too big for itself. Had she imagined there might be more to add?

I wouldn't open it this evening, I was too tired. This was a morning task, when I could hold onto something of myself, remember who I was.

The room was spacious, with a desk at one end and the bed directly opposite. Between the desk and the window there was a small, two-seater couch and a coffee table. I quickly snatched up the box and dropped it on the floor by the couch, on the far side by the window and out of view unless I was hunting for it. A step closer to the window, it was still light outside and I could see across the river towards the cathe-dral and my mother's nursing home. The cathedral was a hollowed out tomb all its own. Burnt in a fire years ago, the new structure had been built inside the frame of the old one. I remembered the fire, like the gates of hell, flames striking high into the sky. Safe on my side of the river, I needed only to watch from a distance.

Time was passing and I hadn't yet taken my shower.

Jet lag makes me sluggish. Time compresses and moves very slowly. Pausing between each movement, I have seen this in others, a statuesque stillness that freeze-frames every action. No thought involved. Standing at the window. Pause. Moving to the bathroom. Pause. Turning on the shower. Pause. Waiting for the water to warm up. Pause. Shampooing my hair. Drying my hair. Brushing my teeth. Pause.

I shook out a skirt from my suitcase and twisted it at the waist to do up the clasp. I'd lost weight and the belt was a little loose. A fresh shirt and another pair of shoes, with a higher heel to give me lift. A touch of make-up and I was ready to go out again. Instead of waiting for Tom, I went into the hallway and knocked on his door. He called out "Coming!" Phone clapped to one ear, he signalled for me to come in.

I sat down on his couch, a doppelgänger of my own. The whole room was a copy of mine next door, the entire hotel a house of mirrors, elevators, and hallways, images reflected back no matter which way I turned. "Make it next Thursday," Tom's tone was solid business, giving orders to whoever was on the other end of the phone. "If they haven't finished by then, we dock ten per cent every day for five days, twenty per cent after that …" Taking it all in, my brother in professional mode, making deals and settling accounts. Not a man to be pushed around. Clever but stern with others. Gentle with me. Easily bruised by those he loves, unsettled by their failure to see his strengths. His ex-wife. My mother. Me.

"Let's go," Tom slipped the phone back into its case and shoved it into his pocket. "I called the hospital and she's settled for the night." No need to name her.

Picking myself off the couch, a little easier now than it had been earlier, I followed him into the empty hallway. How did Tom manage it, I wondered, one step ahead of me while still watching my back? I jockeyed up next to him like a pony and cribbed him in the ribs with my elbow.

"Yeow!" he yelped in mock pain. "Cut that out and behave like an adult."

He didn't poke me back. He never did, only stayed the course and kept walking forwards.

I was in bed by ten o'clock, knocked out after a steak and a whisky that would have tipped over a wrestler. Tom gripped my arm all the way up to the room, as if leading a woman astray rather than guiding her back to safety. If I was hungover in the morning, I could blame him. He had bought me the drink, insisting I take something to help me relax. He left me just inside the door, pointing to the bed like a sergeant-major. Did he think I might get lost on the way?

Stripping off my clothes, I landed heavily on the bed. Slept well, too, at least for the first few hours until the jet lag roused me at four in the morning. Despite the whisky, I did not have a headache, though I was thirsty and dug around in the minibar to find a bottle of water.

There was no getting back to sleep. Turned on the television and watched the news repeat itself a few times before finally switching it off. Restless, thoughts dispersing like fragments into the ether, nothing fitting and nothing making sense, small shifts of dread and anxiety floating by on the edge of a nightmare. My stomach was tight and the corner of my right eye twitched periodically, something I hadn't experienced since childhood. I pushed a finger hard against the bone, but it fluttered regardless. Five-thirty and I gave up the fight. The hotel supplied large, complimentary bathrobes. I wrapped myself in one like a blanket, brushed my teeth, and ordered a pot of coffee from room service. At least I could work.

It was while bending down to fetch my computer out of my backpack that I spotted the box. I wouldn't be able to avoid it much longer.

I pulled out the computer and placed it like a talisman in the centre of the desk. Took out my notebook and pen, placing them neatly beside it. Even sat at the desk and turned the machine on, the light from the screen providing a warm glow in the shadowy, early morning room. I opened my scribble pad to study my notes and created a new document in my computer file. *Introduction*, I wrote, and nothing further, the cursor blinking in reproach.

When the coffee arrived I made a place for it on the table in front of the couch and passed the waiter a five-dollar bill as a tip. Life, I thought, is getting very expensive, remembering when a dollar was enough. The computer on the desk winked a few times before turning black. I poured out a cup and added some cream. It tasted good, smooth around the edges. Fortified, I leaned over the side of the couch and heaved up the box, the contents sliding down with a soft thump as I tipped it onto its side to pull it over the chair arm and drop it onto the seat beside me. The parcel tape wasn't so difficult to undo, it came off in neat strips with a rip in the air like Velcro. I winced, the sharp sting of a bandage stripped from a wound.

Folding back the lid was like peering into the depths of a mighty well. There was nothing that I could see until a small pile of papers appeared to float to the surface. On top was a sealed envelope with an address written in my own, very neat and youthful handwriting. There was an unfranked stamp in the top right hand corner. Inside was a letter. I took a deep breath and closed my eyes against the sun stealing in too brightly through a slit in the curtains. I was lightheaded, queasy in the narrow space of the couch.

A letter. Never sent. Never received. My single attempt to reach out.

I shoved the coffee tray a few inches back and placed the letter on the table in front of it. The need to stay focused, my life in this moment reduced to just a few bits of paper, conserved by my mother for the sake of … what? To remind me? To make amends? I doubted it, but she had kept the letter, letting me know so many years later that it had never been sent, that it lay like a small coffin at the bottom of a cardboard box with all the other testimonials to that time in my life.

There were two brown envelopes paper-clipped together. I picked them up, turning the pair over a few times before separating them. Nothing written on the outside of either, nothing to say what they might contain. I put one envelope back inside the box and flipped up the tails of a metal clasp on the other. The certificate slipped out from behind its cardboard backing as if of its own accord. It was a crisp, beautiful document with an official coat of arms at the top and a notarised seal at the bottom. So clean and smooth I doubted that it had been taken out more than a couple of times. I had never seen it before. I laid it out flat on my lap and placed my right hand lightly over the top, passing it back and forth as if to give myself comfort, or to rub the contents away. I would have taken either.

A lump in my throat; I was close to crying. At the same time I was steely-eyed, oddly powerful in my lush, white bathrobe. My mother now on her deathbed, all memory wiped away, I was alone with my secret. Another time, another place. The sudden clacking of suitcase wheels in the hallway as someone moved towards the elevator echoed through from another dimension. It was as if I had placed my ear to the wall, listening to the sound of another's breathing as it resonated through the curious architecture of time and space, like the whispering gallery at St. Paul's, or the ancient building in Bologna where I had once been taken during an Italian sightseeing tour. I had stood with my face to the dark corner and listened as the man I was travelling with dared to whisper "I love you" from an implausibly long distance. I had shuddered then as I did now, my heart breaking at the impossibility of hope. After that weekend I had refused to see him again.

I lifted a terry towel arm, rubbing it hard across my face. Coffee and too much whisky the night before, but the coffee was helpful, too, both soothing and enlivening, little shots of caffeine driving me forward, small currents of warmth reminding me that I was here, that Tom was next door. If I phoned home, Frank would answer. My world was still intact. I looked over at the open computer: a touch of a button and she would light up. I wanted to follow her, the seductive mistress, take refuge in her arms.

Instead, I put the certificate back into its sleeve and placed it on top of the unsent letter.

I stood up, needing to move and shake myself out a little. I went into the bathroom and extracted a tissue from the metal box on the wall. On second thoughts, I yanked out the whole thing and walked with it back into the living area, talking to myself, muttering why the hell do hotels do this? Why can't they just leave out a box of tissues? I put it down next to the coffee tray and snatched out a double load, blew my nose, and shoved the wad into the pocket of my dressing gown. Was I catching a cold? I pulled the collar of the sumptuous gown higher around my neck and redid the tie at my waist, tightening it up. Before sitting down again, I opened the curtains. Six-thirty in the morning and there was no getting away from the summer sun now. I needed the light anyhow, to banish the dark mood of the room. I flipped off the artificial lights before stomping back over to the couch.

There was another brown envelope to go.

Inside was a legal document, several pages long and at the end of which was the tender scratch of my signature, the reluctant pressure of a young woman giving up so much more than she could imagine. Beside it was the witness signature, a name I did not recognise and a person I could not remember being there, and perhaps he hadn't been. Only my mother and I had really witnessed this legal handover, and she may well have begged a signature from someone later. Four days after signing the papers I was on the plane to London, my physical discomfort harbouring the truth of what I had just let go.

There were a few more papers still in the box, my birth certificate and my old Canadian social security card. Had I really left those behind?

Nothing more. Such a big box for so little tally.

It was as if all the air in the room was suddenly withdrawn, the pressure in my ears immense. There was only the deep pulse of my heart, pounding, pounding. I grabbed my pen. Turning quick inky circles over the top of the box to eradicate my name, I stabbed holes in it too. Hard, angry thrusts like a kitchen knife so there was nothing left of me that might be recognisable. Stricken with rage, I roared up, tossing the box hard on the floor. With my left foot I punched the sides down and then stood on it to flatten it entirely. Sobbing, and holding onto the back of the chair, I lifted the box up at the corner like a dead rat and opened the door to put it outside for the maid to collect. On second thought, I pounded down the hall to the elevator and dumped it there. All that tortuous space around so few papers.

Back in the room, I sat down on the couch. I had agreed to meet Tom for breakfast, that much of our after-dinner conversation I remembered from the night before. I rammed my hands hard against my forehead and pushed against the seat, my legs stretched out beneath the coffee table and my head tilted back as if stemming a nose bleed.

What was I meant to do now, with these dead and buried bones from my history?

I sat bolt upright again and leaned across for the first brown envelope. I took out the birth certificate for perhaps the third time in its life. It was striking. Without one, no one travels far in the world and I wondered how the revised version would read. But this was the original document, to prove that I had once had a child. A little girl, seven pounds three ounces, her father "unknown".

But I had known, and my mother had guessed, compounding her shame. On this certificate and under the mother's occupation, someone had written "student", the biggest clue of all. The new version of this certificate would, of course, name my

188

daughter's adoptive parents. Somewhere in the world floated my child, in my mind forever embryonic. Now, over thirty years old, she had never received her "mother's" letter because my mother had held it back. Even this small gesture she could not give me, handing over those pound notes at the airport in guilty compensation.

I didn't replace the birth certificate this time, only left it on top of the sad little pile on the table.

I needed to wash myself clean, last night's whisky now surfacing in the metallic taste in my mouth and the soft shade of a headache. I dug out a pill from my toiletry bag in the bathroom and popped it into my mouth, swigging a gulp of water back like a cold beer. I hated taking off the bathrobe. The water was scalding and with every little chill I ratcheted it up a notch. I came out only when I heard Tom thumping on my door. Soaking wet, I put the robe back on and padded quickly across the room, dripping all the way.

"I thought you'd died in here or something. Couldn't you hear me?"

"I was in the shower."

"So I see."

"I won't be long, promise." I scrabbled around to find some clothes and vanished back into the bathroom.

When I came out Tom was standing up, holding the birth certificate in both of his palms like an offering. He looked terrified, but defiant, too. His face was flushed, a dreadful collision of guilt and outrage. He was crying. Soft, quiet tears of the kind I couldn't quite manage.

"Tom?"

"What is this?" he held the paper out a little further towards me.

"Didn't you already look in the box?"

"Christ, no! I've already said, why would I do that? It was yours."

"Because I would have."

"I know *you* would have!" harsh, mustering a crippled laugh.

We stared at one another.

"Where was I?" he finally asked. "Where the hell was I?"

"You were here." I shrugged my shoulders. My chest was tight. Was this what it was like to die?

"How could I not know?" Slumping onto the couch.

"No one did," perched now at the end of the bed, facing him. "She made me go away ... to Ottawa. Do you remember? I was away for a couple of months and she came out for the last few weeks. Until the baby was born."

"Then you left for London?"

"Yes."

"I was so angry with you," his voice unutterably sad. He rubbed his face, a masculine swipe of his hands up and down, up and down, as if to smooth it all away.

"I'm sorry. There was nothing you could do. I couldn't come back afterwards ... It would have been too awful."

"Why? And what happened to the baby?"

"She was adopted. Immediately. "

"What do you mean, 'immediately'?"

"I never saw her after the delivery room. They thought it was best that way ... or Mom did anyway. The parents were waiting outside the room. These days you'd call it a surrogate birth, I suppose. That's what it amounted to ... I gave birth ... I held her for about five minutes and then ... and then she was gone. Mom took her away ... I never saw her again."

"Jesus!"

"I did want to keep her, you know ... I ... I didn't *want* to give her away." The shock of what I had just said rammed home and I pitched forward in a terrible sob, or a yell, an anguished shout. Tom spun out of his seat and caught me as I lurched forward, before I could hit the floor.

SEVENTEEN

Steady. Steady. Tom led me to the couch. We sat either end, facing one another. Too much space between us, yet too close for comfort. I stood up and moved back to my previous perch at the end of the bed, the birth certificate flat on the table between us. Tom ordered a pot of coffee and we sipped it quietly together in the room. Silence between us wasn't typical and we were suddenly shy, peering at one another over our cups, quick little glances checking up on the other. Occasionally, Tom smiled. Was it me, or himself, he hoped to reassure?

My thinking had fragmented into a disjointed series of words and fractured phrases, nothing holding together. This was not the result of last night's alcohol, or the mark of a restless night, but the splintering, heart-wrenching tiredness of grief. For the first time I truly empathised with my clients' struggles: Sam in his anguish, Dorothy in her disturbing account of maternal absence, her curiously swinging presentation and resistance in the room. Her bare knees. I took comfort from my work as a therapist, reminding myself that I had come a long way from the young woman who had given birth. The young woman who, almost without thinking, had lost her child.

How could I have put up so little fight? Instead, had acquiesced. A good daughter. Followed my mother's lead in every terrible decision. Let go of my child into the arms of a woman I didn't even know. Bolting to London in desperation afterwards, another case of mistaken identity. Rather, it would have taken the courage I did not have to stand up to her, to hold on to the child and raise her, probably alone.

There was a jolt in my chest and I gasped, raising my hands up flat as if to protect myself.

Tom leaned forward, ready to leap to my defence. He was watching me with all the careful scrutiny of the wary, his lips slightly pursed and his eyes drawn together to a point of sharp concern. His eyes were dark. Had I not know him better, I might have thought he was angry.

I twisted my head—right—left—nothing. Breathing again, hands safe in my lap.

We couldn't sit in silence all morning. We needed to do something.

Tom was the first to lift off, putting his cup down and suggesting we go down to breakfast. I stood up and looked out the window. Barely nine in the morning, the street below still buzzing with people on their way to work, even in this city where office life starts early. So many mornings as a university student, facing the cold at seven o'clock to begin classes at seven-thirty or eight. Summertime now, the level of traffic is a little lighter while people holiday at the lake.

Turning back into the room. "Okay, I'm ready." A little shivery, I open the closet door to fetch a cardigan. Tom takes it from me gently, holding it out for me to put on like a coat. The left arm goes in easily, though I struggle with the right sleeve, twisting from the waist to make it fit. Tom pats me on both shoulders when it's done, the touch of an affectionate parent. I don't dare turn to face him for fear he might kiss me too. "Thanks," my voice hoarse, scratchy now after so much primitive wailing.

Walking by the crushed box on the floor at the elevator, Tom raises an eyebrow. The pen scribble and the stabbing marks, the complete collapse of the box squashed under my furious footprint. But he says nothing.

The elevator is slow in coming, the box pulsating like Poe's "Tell-Tale Heart".

"Why such a big box?" I burst out, wanting to kick it again, pound it into oblivion. Instead I spin round to face Tom. "For heaven's sake, there were only a few bits of paper in there, and my social security card. She could have put it all in a manila envelope and spared us the melodrama, don't you think?"

Tom lifts his shoulders. "Maybe she thought there was more to come?"

I want to push Tom, shove him out of the way, too. "How? Everything was done and dusted within five minutes. For God's sake!" My throat raw, I swallow regardless, drawing back bile.

The elevator arrives at last, already overcrowded. I push through anyhow, tugging at Tom's sleeve. We enter side by side, arms and shoulders pressed together in a small defensive line. Instead of the usual soft landing, the elevator clunks a little at the bottom, dropping its load. My stomach lurches and before the doors open I'm shoved forward by the people behind me. Might have been trampled but Tom grabs my arm, yanking me to the side and away from the stampede.

"You okay?" he leads me towards a seat in the lobby. Feeling woozy, I sit down on the arm of a large chair. Tom remains standing, watching over me. "I thought you were going to faint back there."

"Me, too," I look back towards the lifts. "That was a pretty aggressive crowd."

Tom frowns. "I think you were a bit giddy or something, short of oxygen for a minute. Do you want some water?"

"Jet lag maybe?" I ask, hopefully. I *am* lightheaded, floating above myself. I stretch out a hand to touch Tom, something solid and comforting, hooking a finger through a loop in his jeans. "I'm feeling a bit better. Let's just get something to eat, all right?" Resisting the urge to lean forward, to rest my head against his waist, a child's longing for comfort.

"Sure. But no rush." He pats my hand.

"I think there might be in my case. I need to eat something." Bile again, the foul taste of self-disgust.

"Okay." Tom helps me up, an old lady, stiff in the knees. Crossing the long expanse of the lobby to reach the restaurant, I hold on to him for dear life.

We were safer in the restaurant. The scraping of plates, the clank and clang of cutlery and the soft buzz of early morning conversations. At a couple of tables, people conducting early morning business meetings. Tom ordered scrambled eggs with a side order of toast for himself, and pancakes, a childhood favourite, for me. Despite my ferocious hunger, the prospect of food was grit in my mouth. I sipped some water to wash it away.

"You have to eat," Tom scooped up a forkful of egg, "Do you want me to cut it up for you?"

I knew he would, too. Slicing a small portion of pancake from the bottom I smothered it in maple syrup before putting it gingerly in my mouth, fearful of the flat taste of bark. In fact, it was sweet, the best mouthful of pancake I had ever eaten. I chewed slowly, suspicious of such goodness. How could food be this good when I felt so terrible?

Tom leaned forward, elbows on the table, "Does Frank know about any of this?"

I looked away, watching a young family manoeuvre themselves around a table too small for them, parents and three children at a table in the corner meant for four. The high chair stood perched a little outside the group, a toddler kicking his heels in protest as his father impatiently shoved him further down into the seat. The mother was fashionable but untidy, scuffling with the other two children to settle them in place. The father looked prepared for a job interview, his suit and tie too sombre for such a perfect summer's day. "Pipe down, Ben, I haven't got all day." The kid let out a scream, high pitched and terrible. "Oh, for heaven's sake!" The father extracted a leg from underneath the child's bottom. How could a toddler radiate such fury and power even at this distance? He leaned down into his wife's bag and pulled out a small toy. Junior stretched out a victorious hand, grabbed the toy and laughed.

I look away, swinging my head too quickly. Floating again, there is nowhere to look except down. Opening my mouth to speak, there is only the rush of air, empty space where my voice might have been. A gulp of water and I try again. "No … No one does. Only Mom."

Tom cocked his head, to hear me better. Was I whispering? A pause before he speaks. "It makes a lot more sense."

"What does?"

"Well …"

That family again, pulling me into the corner with them. Already making a mess at the table. Mother, frantically wiping away at a spilled drink while the waiter rushes forward with extra cloths. I sit up straighter, bracing myself.

"I just never understood why you didn't seem to like being an aunt."

Had I really been so transparent? Thought I was a good aunt, bringing them gifts, remembering their birthdays, despite the distance.

"It's okay, Lisa, I wasn't accusing you of anything." He stopped. I had hurt him. Not now, perhaps, back then, acknowledging his children through obligation rather than affection. "It was as if you were afraid of my kids, somehow. I never understood it." Putting his fork down, wiping his mouth with a napkin, "Now it makes sense, that's all."

Grief, compounded on grief, I come alive with anger. "Are you a therapist all of a sudden?"

"I'm a lawyer, or was. It's just rational thinking, cause and effect … even motive I suppose."

I say nothing, stabbing at another bit of pancake.

Tom's children, three boys in quick succession, little emperors dropped into the family one after another. I lost Tom for about ten years while he attended to this expanding family and the demands of a wife a little too blonde to be true. A lawyer's wife, she was the perfect domestic partner. Like my patient, Sam, and his wife, the unwritten contract between them. He would be successful and bring home the money, while she would be a discreet and attentive spouse. Tom's wife, Bonnie, claimed she'd given up an interior decorating career to have children. Since the divorce twelve years ago when he left the law to develop his business interests—a decision Bonnie refused to tolerate—she has lived on the gift of Tom's considerable alimony. As far as I know, she still only decorates her own rooms, incessantly.

Thinking about Tom's kids and his wife now, I hated the brittle resentment it evoked, the familiar internal tirade against what passes for family life. I was too tired to be so annoyed, so why was it rearing up now? The sour taste of petty impatience; I poured more syrup onto my plate. Working through my pancakes, having dug out the bottom two, I was now on the top layer. At least while irritated I was not so burdened with grief.

"I've never known how to be with kids." The table was a confessional, my resistance the grille between us. "I wouldn't have made a very good mother."

"Who knows? Maybe you were too scared to find out."

"You're being a therapist again!" But the energy was forced, Sisyphus pushing at his infernal rock.

"Maybe, but that doesn't mean I'm wrong … who was the father?" a priest, now, delivering my penance.

"A man."

Tom snorted. "No kidding!" He shovelled the last of his scrambled eggs into his mouth, following it up with a gulp of coffee. "It wouldn't be like you, Lisa, not to know who the father is. So, why the 'unknown'?"

196

"Didn't want him to find out. Mom didn't either—claimed it would complicate things."

"Did she know who it was?" Tom tipped forward in his chair, pulling it with him to make way for the family passing in a cumbersome clutch behind him. A funeral march, grave and irregular, the toddler pounding his little toy against his mother's hip to gain her attention. She dragged him along behind her like an afterthought before bending down and yanking the toy out of his hand. The child let out an almighty, indignant, scream.

An image of my colleague, Martha, holding her expanding belly with such tenderness as she walked away from me. Did she understand the tyranny that lay behind parenthood? A claw in my chest, life scraped away. Nine months of pregnancy to build up momentum, to gather your forces and prepare. There's no turning back once you've passed the legal limit and abortion is no longer an option. And it never was for me. Between my naiveté and my secret longing not to comply with my mother's plan, I was always going to give birth, regardless. Thought I was safe when I was only passive, hoping my mother would change her mind and let me keep my child. Hoped that when she finally saw the baby …

Leaving on that plane for London was the first independent step I had ever taken, four days too late to achieve redemption. A woman on the run, opting for safety. Taking refuge in a new life forged out of desperation rather than ambition. For years afterwards developing my skills in advertising, promoting the myth of the perfect life. Life lived on the surface—not so difficult once you know how.

"Mom guessed who the father was, but never said." Words like glue in my mouth, sticking to the roof. "Talked around it a lot, like 'Sometimes it's best to do things on your own, without complications …'."

"Were there complications?"

197

"Well, for a start ... he was married." Forcing the words out, one by one, pellets of information that had been withheld for decades. A man I hadn't let myself think of in years.

"You were only twenty years old!"

"A professor. They were all sleeping with students in those days!" As if that explained everything.

"Not all of them, Lisa." Tom adjusted his fork and knife on the plate, placing them just so.

"Well, this one certainly was, and not just with me as it turned out. He had quite a reputation at the time. Like a fool, I believed I was special."

I searched the restaurant. Was he still in the city? Over thirty years ago, he could now be dead. A middle-aged man talking with a young woman at a table by the window. Was that his daughter he was meeting for breakfast? She was pretty rather than beautiful, hanging on to his every word. He banged the table with the flat of his hand and the girl jumped, before laughing out loud. The man smirked, while at the same time stretching out a hand to stroke her bare arm. I watched her blush, a soft reddish glow moving upwards, giving her feelings away.

"How did you find out?"

"Find out what?" Turning back at Tom.

"That he was sleeping with other people?"

I looked around again, any form of distraction would do. "Do you really want to know all this?"

"Of course I do! You're the one who's always saying it's good to talk about things. Now's your chance."

"It's just ... I haven't talked about it before." Twitching in the corner of my eye again. I thought of my therapy room, gaps appearing in my patients' narratives, their experiences stretching far beyond time and any solace that words could provide. Instead, there might only *be* their trauma, rising like my dream after years of concealment. No one really wants to come face to face with his own tragedy. I was no exception.

That little pile of papers on the coffee table in my room told me there was no going back. I looked at a point just above Tom's head, at a picture on the far wall, the blood-red of a grain elevator rising high over the prairie landscape. My voice had an unnatural timbre, like Dorothy's voice when I first met her in my office, brackish with disuse. I struggled to hold on to the words, to form sentences.

"Three months gone before I realised ... so naive! Mom trotted me off to the doctor's. Maybe I didn't want to know. I'd never slept with anyone before—thought he was my one great love." Shaking my head to displace the shame. "The doctor was kind, told me straight I had decisions to make."

I stopped, remembering my mother's anxiety when I finally told her the result, her fury expressed in a thousand tiny, hypochondriacal complaints, including fierce headaches and stomach complaints. I slavishly catered to all of them, apologising for my behaviour through all of my actions, fetching her endless cups of tea and cooking her favourite meals. But I would not tell her who the father was. In the end she acted as if it was her idea not to tell him, and I let her have the credit, my revenge for having kept the secret of our affair for so many months, for never telling another soul, and certainly not his wife. My pregnancy, my child, I kept it away from him.

Tom waited for me to continue.

"I hadn't seen him for a few weeks over Christmas, so went to the university to leave a note under his door. Just wanted him to ring me, that's all. Couldn't call him at home, he'd warned me about that." Words like bullets, firing them off in rounds. I knew my target now. "He was my English professor, one of them anyway. Twentieth century American literature, my favourite. He was big on Hemingway. Suppose he fancied himself a kind of priapic hero. Even had a beard like Hemingway, and a round face like in the Karsh photo. Didn't drink as much, but likely tried. Not quite the same girth, so probably passed out instead." I paused to let the image sink in. "The only fights he ever got into were likely with his long-suffering wife. Hopefully she won. Never wrote the great Canadian novel either." A break to catch my breath. "Anyway, I trekked down to the university and he was in his office. With someone else. It was obvious they'd been kissing, or groping, or some other damn thing ..." I looked at the ceiling and swallowed. "At least he had the decency to look embarrassed. I just turned and walked away. I didn't give him the note and I never attended his class again." Shivering, I pulled my cardigan closer and closed the buttons.

"What was his name?"

The restaurant was nearly empty now. The man and the younger woman had left their table without my noticing. Back to the office, or up to his room? The waiters were clearing the tables, spreading out clean tablecloths and preparing for the lunch trade.

"Lisa?" Tom called me back. "Lisa, what was his name?"

"I can't remember. Jesus!" I really couldn't. Had pushed this man so far out of my life and mind that, for the moment, I couldn't easily retrieve him. Could see him, remember him from the vantage point of time and distance, but his name was completely gone. "Honestly. Just give me a minute. It'll come back, I know." My voice thin again, edgy. A glass of water on the table and I took a gulp, wincing as I swallowed it down. My hand was shaking. Tom reached over and took the glass away, placing it down softly in front of me, then picked up my pancake dish and put it on top of his own empty plate and signalled for a waiter to clear the debris.

I rummaged around in my brain for the man's name, my child's father, and could not find him anywhere. Instead, I changed tack. "You really didn't look in the box?"

"No. I told you."

"But whenever I mentioned it you seemed to go blank, as if you were hiding something."

Tom pulled out a pen to sign the bill. "You were making such a big deal about it and I figured it was just a bunch of stuff like the pictures and report cards in mine. I was thinking more about Mom, I guess. I'm sorry. I did not look in the box!"

"Okay. I believe you."

"We should go." Tom scrunched up his napkin and put it on the table. I did the same. Back at the elevator he held the doors open for me. "Are you okay to visit Mom this morning?"

"Yes, of course. We don't have to stay there all day, do we?"

"Maybe not. We can see how she is." There were only the two of us riding up this time. I looked at the floor rather than let myself bounce back and forth with Tom in the glare of all those tinted mirrors.

"Give me ten minutes," I told him once outside the room, pushing the key card up and down into the slot. The door refused to open. What, would I have to kick it down? Tom crossed the line back to my door and took hold of the key. He pushed it into the slot and pulled it out again, the light flashing green. He turned the knob and the door swung open.

Only ten in the morning and already I had crossed a lifetime. Once in the room with the door closed behind me, there was still more time to travel. I didn't bother to sit down. Leaned over the desk and flipped open my computer, typed "*English Department University of Manitoba*" into Google Search. Trawling through various pages. Click. Click, the arrow shooting back and forth. And then there it was, his name in bold, shouting at me.

Henry Plankton.

Hideously immature, had I really taken seriously a man with the name "Henry Plankton"? Bullied to death as a kid, I reasoned, rising up out of a mean little childhood to seduce young women to the tune of great American literature. Pathetic, his name still up in lights on the faculty page.

Tom thumped on the door. "Lisa, you ready?"

"Henry Plankton," I said, opening the door.

201

"What?"

"His name. Henry Plankton. I looked him up." The more I said it, the more ridiculous it sounded. I pointed at the computer. "Fish food."

Tom peered at the screen, squinting without his glasses. He burst out laughing.

"I know. I wish it were something else, but there it is. Henry Plankton." Laughing myself now, hysterical and shaking. Uncontained and uncontainable, collapsing onto the bed because I could no longer stand up. Ribs aching, eyes burning, throat raw with the raking of so much heartache and laughter, sheer disbelief. Rolled over on the bed, ramming my face into the soft centre of a pillow to drown out the sound. Like that terrible name, the howling just kept rising, the froth of death in the corner of my mouth. My body evacuating, I rushed to the toilet, pancakes and syrup, all the sweetness of life dumped in an unholy blast of puke into the toilet.

Tom instantly beside me, no longer laughing, holding my head in his hands, wiping my brow, whispering, "No wonder you tried to forget him."

"Oh god." Put my hands up over my eyes so I would not have to look down. "This is just horrible."

"It's terrible for a lot of reasons, Lisa, but probably not because the guy has a funny name." He sat down on the edge of the bathtub.

"I know. I just haven't thought about any of this stuff in years, not even in therapy. I just wanted it all to go away." Pulling up from my knees, flushing the toilet.

"And you're the therapist!"

I wipe my face with a damp cloth. Rinse it again with hot water and place it across my eyes. "I remember why the box was so big." Didn't want to remember, wanted instead to break and smash the memory just as I had the box. Fragments of a former life I couldn't put back together, no matter how hard I tried. Eyes firmly shut, more scalding water.

"Do you?"

I drew the cloth away and squeezed, folded it neatly and draped it over the towel rack as if this was important somehow, to make the room tidy. Laid a hand lightly against Tom's shoulder and he moved down an inch along the edge of the tub to make room for me. Close again for safety but looking straight ahead through the door into the bedroom, the coffee table and papers, the open computer. "Yes. There was a letter, but I put in a soft toy too. A rabbit. Peter Rabbit. It would have fitted the box perfectly."

A week away from my due date, heavy and awkward with what was to come, walking through the Hudson's Bay Company in Ottawa, trailing other young women through the children's department as if I were one of them. Picked the rabbit off the shelf, held it in my hands and hugged it for a few hungry seconds against my chest. Imagining motherhood. Didn't stop to think. Didn't put the rabbit down, but took it instead in a blind rush to the checkout counter. Spilled my money onto the counter, a child myself emptying her piggy bank. A thief, stealing a moment alone with my child.

Then, back at the home in which I was staying, gift-wrapped my rabbit in white tissue paper and placed it beside the letter on the bureau with instructions to deliver both to my baby's new parents. My mother had promised.

Beside me now, Tom's body jerks. He straightens his back and swivels to face me, "She gave one of my kids a rabbit once. For Easter … I'm pretty sure it was Peter Rabbit." He is thinking out loud, pulling the dots together. "It was! Peter Rabbit."

"She gave it away?" My voice thin, hardly audible. I might not even have spoken out loud. Tom's son, her first grandchild. My child. Given away.

"I guess she did." Tom stands up, leaving me behind. Another surge of nausea and I am bent at the waist again over the toilet bowl, dropping hard onto my knees. Choking, choking, but there is nothing but air. A dry heave. Tom spins around, one long step and we cling to one another, both of us crying, sobs like clotted blood in our throats, neither of us can breathe.

When we are finished we walk to the bed and sit down, calm after the storm, speechless. For a moment we are children, holding hands. Like the joke clock on my wall, time in reverse. Nothing is as it seems.

EIGHTEEN

My mother's room was hot, even with the blinds closed. It simmered with the heat of Tom's anger and I was dazed, like a blind person touching the surface of things—the walls, the door frame, the back of the chair—finding my way through the maze of forgotten territory.

On tiptoes, we took our seats either side of the bed. Rather than one another, we stared at my mother, willing her to rise up and face us. The seduction of hope over experience. Through the bellows of her open mouth she circulated tiny chunks of air. Sandpaper back and forth, in and out, barely grazing her lungs. Once her eyes popped open startling us both, yet nothing registered within that glassy, demonic stare. Her eyelids fluttered and closed, fluttered and closed and then dropped completely. We did not exist.

A refreshing breeze swept through the room as a nurse entered. Tom and I both raised our heads and laughed, grateful for the diversion. The nurse looked from Tom to me and then back again, smiled and carried on. She'd seen it all before. Gently she lifted my mother's head to fluff the pillow before tucking in a sheet corner. From her pocket she extracted a pair of blue rubber gloves. "How is she?" without taking her eyes off my mother.

"Good," Tom answered, "Nothing's changed. She opened her eyes, but it didn't mean anything."

Nurse Paquin opened a small cupboard and took out a basin. "She should be comfortable. Give us a minute, okay?" A second nurse entered the room. I'd never seen her before. She smiled apologetically.

Tom and I sat in the hallway watching and listening to the clang of the ward, the incessant buzzer and the rattle of lunch trolleys, loose wheels and cutlery, the steam of mashed potatoes, meat with gravy. They rolled by our mother's room, no more nourishment here.

I bent down to dig in my bag for my computer. A sigh of frustration and Tom perked up. "What?"

"I left my computer behind. Not even a book with me."

"Me, neither."

"Oh well …"

The nurses came out, Nurse Paquin with a bundle of sheets in her hand, the other clutching a plastic bag, my mother's diaper.

From dust to dust.

Returning to the room then, facing one another over her shrinking, prostrate body. Nothing for us to do but wait, to the dreadful accompaniment of my mother's last, desperate gasps. "What's your secret, Tom?" I cut over the sound, drowning it out.

"Is that a trick question?

"No! You know mine. Now I want to know yours."

"So it makes us even?"

My mother held her breath for a few empty seconds before pulling in a big one, refusing to let go. Holding my breath, too, a lightning flash of adrenaline, the hairs on the back of my neck standing up. Both of us on our feet, rising to the occasion. The moment passed as quickly as it had arrived. The tension in our bodies released, we were back in our seats as if it nothing had happened.

As children at school close to the airport, planes had thundered and roared so loud overhead we had been forced to hold sentences in mid air until they passed. Tom and I did this now, too, continuing where we had left off. "I just want to know, that's all. Do you have a secret?"

Tom, hands like ballasts flat against his thighs, he stared at the floor between his knees. Lifted one hand and, with his first finger, rubbed a path along the inside rim of his shirt collar as if to loosen it. In that moment, imagining Tom as my patient tipping reluctantly into himself, resisting. Nothing but dust where there might have been gold. Ashamed and suffering, not aware until this moment what he has always known to be true, his unthought known. "I love my mother," gravel, churned from the bottom.

I don't hear the words so much as feel them, grinding like an auger through six feet of ice. An explosion of betrayal. How could he! In the eerie vacuum that follows, there is nothing in the room but the washboard scratch of our mother's breath as she refuses to let go, demanding everything. My child. My brother. Me. Her mouth is open, a greenish crust forming around her lips. Tom reaches over and lifts a small pot of moisturising cream from the bedside table. Using his little finger, he swabs a bit over the parched area.

I cannot stand it and leave the room, aiming for the drinks machine by the cafeteria. Two bottles of water; it would be churlish not to bring Tom one. With little spouts, they might be baby bottles.

Instead of returning immediately, I sit at the far end of a long empty table. The cafeteria is empty, only a coffee machine humming on the counter and a little bowl to accept the change. A system based on trust. Through glass doors I see others sitting outside, enjoying the sunshine. One old woman smokes. Hooked through the nose to a life support system, she puffs on, regardless, her own last gasp. Underneath a cupola of trees a few patients play cards, wheelchairs pulled up tight against a fold-up table. Beyond them another ancient woman in a wheelchair. Eyes vacant with age, while a younger woman sits beside her feeding her sips from a child's cup with a red tipped spout.

Neither Tom nor I suckled at the breast, my mother's generation quick to embrace the freedom of formula and powdered milk. My baby, too. On the aeroplane to London, the ache of my breasts afterwards, needing to pump them just a little to release the tension. A baby on board wailing for comfort in the next aisle, her mother cooing into the soft folds of the blanket the infant was wrapped in. As she discreetly opened her blouse to give her the breast, my body erupted in agony. Rushed to the washroom, using my hands on the tops of the seats to keep my balance, rocking my hip against each one along the way. Waiting, waiting for the cubicle to empty, holding my tummy first and then my breasts, not caring by then who might see me. I hold back from screaming. At the same moment the plane hits an air current and we drop like an anchor a few feet before steadying. I am lifted off the floor, slammed against the curved aperture of the window opposite. The pain in my back is now official and I yelp. A stewardess rushes forward, helping me up and finally someone emerges from the toilet to let me in. I shoot through the door like a bullet, slamming it hard behind me. In that slide of the lock, the world is shut out. I drain the milk from my breasts into the hard metal bowl of the sink. Pulling the plug, I watch it spin down the waste pipe into oblivion.

I remain in the cubicle a few more minutes, straighten my clothes, and brush my hair. For the first time in my life I put on lipstick from the small packet of make-up I had purchased with my mother's money in duty free. This is the new world order. Opening the door to the queue outside, I walk unaided back to my seat.

Now, I watch the old woman in the garden puffing her cigarette. Each drag is a heartfelt, defiant gesture, smoke expunged in great tumbling gusts. She is isolated from the others, banished into a small area surrounded by bushes. Her pleasure is hers alone, until another ageing refugee slinks in beside her, extracting from her pocket a pack of Export Plain, the magnum force of Canadian cigarettes. The old man and the woman don't even look at one another, compounding the isolation. This all plays out for me in silence behind the glass door. Between putting out one and lighting another, I see the woman rock her head back to cough. I imagine the gurgle of sludge in her lungs, the acrid taste of phlegm and old nicotine. I turn away, back towards the coffee machine where a middle-aged man is dropping money into the change pot. He does not see me, immediately turning back towards where he came from, his tray loaded up with cups and a plate of biscuits.

I don't want to move. There is nothing for me in that room upstairs. Nor for Tom. Yet, Tom loves his mother. Despite her rejection, despite her refusing to know him, to see his goodness and his intent, still he loves his mother. My pulse races with indignation. How could he!

I know love and hate; I have seen it in my patients. Sam, reckoning with his mother, and Dorothy's wild mood swings—I see her knees, like my baby's, round and bare, far too exposed in the moment of birth. Feet and toes, knees and little elbows. Fingers already folding into tiny fists, nails that scratch. I lay my head on the table, longing for sleep.

I am startled awake by the nightmare and knock over one of my water bottles. I make a lunge for it as it rolls away across the table, groping for my dream at the same time, no longer an ethereal mass, now the haunting of a child, a baby fully formed and furious, smothered in the gunk of afterbirth. The umbilical is loose, swinging like a rope between us. I try to grab it though the baby squeals, heading off in a spiral away from me.

A balloon, it vanishes into the distance, yet the squeal remains, heart-wrenching or raging, I'm not sure which. Clapping my hands over my head I am furious, shouting for it to stay away, even as I long for it to return.

Nightmare nonsense, none of it real. I stand up, kicking my legs awake. I guzzle half a bottle of water, gulp after painful gulp, and buy another one at the machine on the way back to my mother's room. Stiff in the back, stiff in the knees, I take the stairs two at a time using the bottles as exercise weights. Panting, I enter my mother's room.

The first thing I see is Tom, elbows on his knees, head in his hands. "She's gone," he says, looking up. "A couple of minutes ago. I left the room to talk to the nurse and when I came back she was gone. Just like that."

I look at my mother. There is no difference that I can see. Put my bottles down and touch her, the top of her left hand outside the covers. Still warm. The room, though, is completely quiet, no longer the rasping drag of her breath to break the interminable silence between us. What had I imagined her death would be like? I feel nothing. More than I can take in a single day. Not yet noon, the day has already spanned my entirety, from birth to death and back again. She would have expected more. Grief, at the very least, but there isn't enough left in me for that. I am already grieving for what she has taken away, for what she gave away that was never rightfully hers.

The phone in my bag buzzes. I reach over and pull it out. Frank. I punch the reject button. I can't speak to him now, not yet. I see that he has rung earlier too. I hadn't even noticed, one more notch in my refusal to let him in.

Soon, I think, soon.

"Frank." I explain.

Tom nods. "Lots to tell him."

"Not now. Later." I walk to the other side of the bed and, facing Tom's back, I lean against the window, half sitting on the radiator cover. "What do we do now?"

"The nuns let us sit here for a while and then the undertaker comes. We sort out the funeral." He turns to face me, away from my mother. "When does Frank arrive?"

"Day after tomorrow."

"We'll wait for him, then."

"I take it you mean the funeral, rather than sorting out the details."

"Of course I do."

"Just checking."

I retrieve my phone from my bag and flip it into camera mode. Pointing it towards my mother, I focus on her face.

"What are you doing?" Tom shouts, pulling me away, spinning me towards him.

"Taking a picture ... what's wrong with that?"

"It's ghoulish! What the hell for?" I hadn't known Tom's voice could reach such a pitch.

"Maybe to prove she's dead. I don't know ... just thought I'd take a picture." The phone back in my bag. "There. I won't do it again."

"I'm going to talk to the nurses. Anyway, I need some air." Only my mother's corpse stops him from slamming the door.

The room is dark, the shadowy colours of a deathbed watch. I walk around the bed, a repetitive horseshoe back and forth, never taking my eyes off her. Looking over my shoulder towards the door, but no one is coming. I take another picture, insurance that this important moment won't be lost like the other into the well of my history. This picture is proof. There is no spirit rising that I can feel, nothing glorious or even very moving. She is just gone and that's it, a life summed up in the moment of death. Everyone passes away.

I sit down. When I leave here today I will never come back, never see my mother again. Hers will be a closed coffin. The ravages of a long-winded death have taken their toll and no one wants to see a starving corpse.

Tom comes back into the room, a sheet of paper with names and telephone numbers in his hand listing the various undertakers in town. He is calmer now, determined, "Let's figure out how we're going to do this, okay?"

Brother and sister, over her corpse, we make a plan to celebrate our mother's life.

NINETEEN

The smell of death was everywhere: on my hands, my clothes, in my hair.

Tom strode across the parking lot towards his truck like it was the open range, his cattle loose beyond the gate. He had friends in town and an ex-wife. He didn't say where he was going and I didn't ask. We both needed time on our own. I watched the truck move down the road, turning left at the corner away from the hotel, a blast of Emmylou from his sound system floating mournfully over the distance between us. I pushed a lock of hair behind my ear, shoved the gear-stick into reverse and pointed the car in the opposite direction. I needed to freshen up.

In my room, I ignored the message light on my hotel phone. Frank, doing his best, reaching out. Soon. Soon.

My shower was quick, time enough to slough off the scent of death. I slipped on a dress and a change of shoes, open-toed pumps to ensure my elevation, fresh make-up and lipstick, another purchase from duty free. I stood tall in front of the full-length mirror, one final check to ensure I was fully armed. Every muscle was taut, my jawline set like an axe. I was on a mission—nothing could stop me now. Stuffed my computer into my bag—there could be more time to kill—and headed out the door.

It takes nearly half an hour to get there: south along Main Street before turning right and heading for Confusion Corner, then a straight line along Pembina Highway. This is a route I know well. I am tempted to keep heading south and the American border, another bid for escape. Three days of easy driving and I could be in Texas. Instead, I grip the wheel and cut left down the slipway towards the campus. Old and new, buildings steeped in provincial history. Strange how so little has changed, though the campus is quieter than during term time and there is only a short row of cars in the staff parking area. I aim for the far end, putting distance between us, mine the only car in the public lot.

Hallways normally busy echo with every step. Names on the doors have changed, unfamiliar. Looking this way and that; I ask a lone security guard for directions. He jabs a thumb behind him, towards the end of a long corridor. I squint for a few blind seconds down the darkened tunnel, checking for snipers. Resisting the urge to run, remind myself that I am a grown woman, a professional, and an ocean away from the girl I was then. Drawing myself up, I advance forward. Nothing can stop me now. Heels clacking on the tough, industrial tiling, the scrape of grit beneath my soles. My bag hangs heavy over my left shoulder and I adjust it a few inches to lighten the load.

At the darkest end of the hallway I stop and take account. His name is on the door. A little way open, barely a crack. I see a man bent at his desk. Bald at the top with a rim around the edge. Like a monk.

I knock, pushing the door a little further into the room.

A face I don't recognise looks up. Lines drawn straight down both cheeks to his chin, without a beard. He removes his glasses. Eyes rheumy and heavy lidded, as if keeping them open is not worth the effort. Shrunken shoulders, rounded

214

over into a thinning chest. Even while sitting I can see this is not a tall man, one dainty shoe exposed as he swivels his chair on its wheels to face me. But his smile is loaded, charming still. I pull back a step, wanting to slam the door closed.

"Professor Plankton?"

"Mmm."

"My name is Lisa Harden," edging closer into the room. Not his old office, smaller now that he is emeritus. Another desk in here; he is forced to share.

"Hello," the smile on active duty. "How can I help you?"

The first question I always ask a new patient. How can I help you?

"Are you a former student? I'm sorry if I ..."

"Yes, yes I am."

"Come in, come in." Standing now, enthusiastic, pulling out a chair from behind the second desk. "I always like to see my former students. So many of you, of course, over the years ..."

I am rendered speechless with the lack of recognition. Not even my name to conjure up a memory. Remind myself that I am a psychotherapist with a list of publications to back me up. This is a man who does little but talk. I stand tall in my shoes and stretch my lips into a smile. They crack for the want of moisture and I am tempted to pull out my lipstick. My fingers creep into the top pocket of my bag to hunt out the tube. Reassured, I tap it closed and lick my lips instead.

Professor Plankton nods his head towards the chair, paternal and friendly.

Two steps past the little man and I sit down. He takes his seat again across from me.

He doesn't know how tall I can be in a chair, but he senses something and the mottled surface of his forehead creases further to a point of confusion, his drooping eyelids lifting for the flash of a second to reveal a reluctant curiosity. It is all he can manage.

I settle into my seat of authority, saying nothing.

"You were my student … when was that, exactly?" Studying my face now, on the lookout for something familiar.

The longer I am silent the more uncomfortable he becomes, shifting in his seat, looking for a way out. Surely I'm not the only sprite from his past to pitch up in his office, though I may be the only one to know the stature and measure of a wingback chair, who understands the value of silence to unnerve even the most confident. He is such a little man, he hasn't got a hope.

His rheumy eyes swim for a moment, looking for a place to land. I lean a little to the left, my elbow on the arm of the desk chair I have turned into a throne and I know my expression is flat, waiting for him.

And he knows it, though he doesn't have a single clue what it is that I am waiting for. Still, I have time, several hours in fact before I have to be anywhere.

Gradually, I see a flash of recognition begin to dawn in the glassy surface of his eyes, a glimmer, a little shimmer of light, beyond his reach. In a flash it is gone. He twitches his shoulders, rubs his hands together and frowns again in a forlorn effort at retrieval.

I am silent. All those years with patients waiting for their deeper life to surface. Sam. Dorothy. Her bare knees, the image suddenly there before me. A sharp pang and a quick intake of breath, I lift my right hand to my chest, the other gripped to the bottom of my seat.

Professor Plankton may be foolish, but he is not a fool and he grabs at the advantage. "Lisa Harden," his shoulders relax, even rise a little out of their rounded slump. He was so much younger then. "You were a good student," he smiles.

"I was. For a while I was even your star student." Both hands now lodged in the safety of my lap, I regain the lead.

"I remember …" he rises up a few inches in his chair to meet me eye to eye, but I lift myself even higher.

"Do you?" Coming to leave my note all those years ago, his door closed against what everyone knew and no one chose to

216

see. On that occasion, a redhead. I had thought she was my friend, both of us holding our precious secret, believing we were special. She loved Fitzgerald, like me in thrall to the tragedies of Zelda and Dorothy Parker, trading books over coffee in the cafeteria between classes. Did he remember her? The redhead? Undignified groping the other side of that closed door. Were there so many of us, stacked like a row of dolls along the narrowing corridor of his academic career? We were chosen, no doubt, for the quality of our adoration.

I shuffle in my seat to shift my stiffening legs. My heels click together in a double tap. Those lidded eyes open again, a gratifying sliver of fear. No wonder he keeps them closed, to shut out the light.

For the first time I notice a wedding ring, a simple band of gold on his left hand with which he fiddles, round and round, anxiety compounded with every turn. Was he wearing it way back then? The therapist in me takes in the whole, even as I focus on the detail. He knows. I can see it in the small shiver of those narrow, slumping shoulders and the tilt of his head, veering however he can away from me. I have years of practice at second-guessing, intuiting the facts behind the experience, and I gun for him now.

"A student?" I nod my head towards his wedding ring. He stops in mid turn, caught in the headlights. Easy game. If I were merciful I would shoot him now, right between those milky, aged eyes. Instead, I want him to suffer.

"Once upon a time," he mutters, barely audible. No, not the redhead. The woman whose picture he has on his desk is dark haired, formidable, looking straight at the camera. Watching him.

She didn't run away to London.

"Children, professor? Do you have children?" My blood is pumping, preparing to swoop.

His body gives a little quiver, one that perhaps only a therapist can see, from top to toe. He is disconcerted, moving through all the dusty corners of his past in a desperate effort to find me. He knows I'm there, but where exactly? I shift in my seat but my eyes remain locked onto him. He can't move an inch without my feeling the tug.

Then, in the wrinkled span of Professor Plankton's face, she emerges.

I blink, squashing the ghost from view. When I open my eyes the faces mesh together in perfect harmony, as if I am wearing night vision glasses. There is clarity, even in the dark. The scent of danger is so fierce that I want to reach back into the unknown to reclaim my ignorance. I swing my head away towards the door. Outside there is the cheerful rattle of a few stray summer students passing down the hall. Their voices fade away like the rhythmic clack of a train I wish I could follow.

The professor watches me, confused. I see only her, beauty and unrelenting anger reflected perfectly out of the shambles of this old man's face. The kick of a spur in my chest and I nearly squeal out loud. I float above the room and in the distance I hear him respond, indecipherable from this lofty height. It doesn't matter anyhow.

Dorothy knows what I have not recognised, as I know what the professor does not.

I am such a fool that she is leaving me for America, where she will no longer have to witness my sublime ignorance, and I want nothing more than to leave this room now. If he does not already know, or cannot guess, I will not tell him.

My revenge.

A child.

He did not even remember my name.

Dorothy and her abandoning mother. Her adoptive mother deserting her and her therapist, too, in her ignorance. Failing to recognise who I am. Who she is.

I stand up, knocking over the chair and both the professor and I grab for it. Our hands meet. His skin is smooth, paper thin. Cold. Both of us blanch at the touch, so much space and ignorance between us.

I open the door and exit into the hallway.

"I always like to see my former students …" he trails away behind me hopeless and sad, beyond any chance of redemption.

There is someone in the washroom fixing her hair. I manage enough self-control before squashing myself into one of the cubicles. I hold back to vomit until she is gone, clutching my stomach and hanging my head back as if stemming a nose-bleed. The moment she leaves I retch up nothing, hardly a fragment.

A day of retching. I need to talk to Frank.

I make my way out into the parking lot, rest with my back against the car and look across the expanse of empty concrete towards the row of vehicles at the far end. Is one of them Pro-fessor Plankton's? I never want to see him again. Just in case, move to the other side, trailing a hand along the molten metal surface of the car to keep myself upright. Across the road an empty field, sawed off into strips for planting. It lies fallow, bereft, it seems to me, of any kind of life.

I grab at a memory, like a child reaching for safety. Remem-ber how I learned at an early age to plunge into cold water, rather than drip feed myself into the lake. Do it quickly before the agony of anticipation outstrips the sharp shock of momen-tary pain. I rummage through my bag to find the cellphone, so on edge that the tips of my fingers are numb and I fumble scrolling down the list to Frank's number, getting it wrong at least twice. I resist the urge to throw the phone away. I drop my bag on the ground—empty weight now—and focus, poking a blunt finger down onto the mobile's screen until I hear the bleep and see the number register at the bottom. He answers, "Where on earth have you been? I've been trying to call you all hours." In my mind's eye I see him sitting forward in his chair, ready to throttle me.

"Frank, I'm so sorry. Please. Can you come now?" Holding the phone up to my ear with both hands, otherwise it might slip away. Very little feeling in my fingers, only a slight tingling effect of life gradually returning.

The silence at the other end bounces between satellites and over the ocean several times before coming home to land. There are sweat patches beneath my arms and the car at my back radiates heat. Still, I don't move.

"I'm on the next plane, though not before you tell me something of what's been going on. Your mother for a start, how is she?"

I don't want to tell him, as if holding back the fact of her death will mean I don't have to tell him anything at all. But I also know it's too late for that, the truth has a way of spilling out. I see it all the time in my patients, in Dorothy and in Sam, the quality of their rage and their disappointment in me. I am not who I think I am.

Life in my fingers again and phone to my ear, I pull away from the car and head towards the open field. The line to London is still open and Frank's voice follows me, pressing for answers. I don't look back, cutting my way through a small thicket of trees to stand in the centre of a strip of parched earth. The soil has been tilled, small lumps of dirt, the brittle detritus of last year's harvest roiled up onto the surface. Holding tightly onto the mobile with one hand, I bend down and gather up a clump of earth with the other. But in that action I tumble, almost rolling into a somersault on that hard dry ground. I am covered in dust and the prickle of old crop. I am nothing— a middle-aged woman lying fallow.

Then I cry, sobbing into the phone, incomprehensible. Frank is calm, repeating over and over again, "It's all right, Lisa. It's all right."

Though I know that it's not, and never can be. Eventually, I find enough words to round up a degree of truth. In an empty field beneath a burning prairie sky, I tell him only that my mother is dead.

TWENTY

Frank was arriving on the five-thirty flight. I needed to see him and dreaded seeing him. I decided to leave the hotel and go for an early morning walk in Assiniboine Park. Parked on Portage Avenue and set out across the bridge, pausing to watch the beavers work along the riverbank. One branch after another, log after log building their winter lodge.

Believing I was alone, I jumped at the sound of pounding feet heading in my direction. A woman running towards me stopped halfway along the bridge. Hand to her throat, she took her pulse. Without thinking I copied her, head tilted and fingers pressed just below my jawbone. I was still alive. My wounds were still sore from my tumble in the dirt the day before. Both knees were scraped raw like a child's and I had painful, if nearly imperceptible, scratches running the length of my left arm. The bruise on my forehead was covered over with a gentle patina of "natural" make-up. My legs were stiff, as if I'd been running like this woman, stretching myself beyond endurance.

I stayed away from the hotel all morning. At lunchtime I had food poisoning. Clam chowder from a chain restaurant the shape of a box, close to the shopping mall where I purchased a new black suit to wear to the funeral. Half an hour later I was forced to pull over onto a side street, tipping from the waist at the side of my car to give vent. Gasping at the abruptness of the attack, I shook with disbelief. Even my skin hurt. I stood up straight, checking the street. No one was coming, thank goodness. In this law-abiding town I had turned down a one-way street, facing the wrong direction.

One thing at a time.

My brother would have to pick up Frank. "Tom?" How did we manage before cellphones?

"What's wrong?" Even in my haggard state I wondered why this was his first question. He wanted to pick me up. I refused, insisting that I could make the journey in instalments. He took down Frank's flight details.

Taking the back roads where I could pull over more easily, I zigzagged between Wolseley Avenue and Portage. Ashen and weak, avoiding all those hotel mirrors, I finally made it back to my room. When I pulled the curtains closed to keep out the light, Dorothy's face loomed in the shadows. I collapsed into bed aching and feverish. I had kept nothing down for nearly three days. How many more times could I be ill without vanishing altogether?

A few hours later, Frank and Tom tiptoed into the room, one of them planting my husband's suitcase by the desk. Frank bent to kiss me, touching my forehead. "You're burning up. Do we need to call a doctor?"

All I needed was sleep, I was sure, a little time to recover after such a poisoned lunch. Tom turned the desk lamp on low and sat down in a chair while Frank vanished into the bathroom to have a shower after his long flight.

"You need to tell him," keeping my voice low, I sat up, using my elbows to give me purchase. My throat was so sore it was difficult to speak. "Tom, you have to tell him."

"What do you mean?"

"You need to tell him, please."

"You mean ... the baby?"

I nodded.

"I can't do that! Why me? Shouldn't you be telling him?" He stood up, gesturing for me to move forward before fluffing up my pillows against the back of the bed.

"Please, Tom ... I'm sick."

"Not forever."

"It feels like it today," falling back onto the stack of pillows.

"You do look like hell."

"Thanks."

Frank came out of the bathroom. He stopped and looked from one to the other of us. "You look a bit better than you did a few moments ago."

"That's not what *he* said," I pointed at Tom.

"Well, he's your brother." Frank rubbed a towel over his hair. "I take it you're not joining us for dinner ..." his voice trailed away. He was looking at the table in front of the couch where the birth certificate lay exposed on top of the small pile of papers from my mother's box. His eyebrows lifted at another mystery presenting itself and I knew he was calculating in his head, trying to work it out. Shadows shifted and moved in the soft light of the desk lamp, and the room was dank. I could smell my own sweat, hear my heart beating even over the purr of the air conditioner. Frank moved back towards the bathroom without looking in my direction. "I'll have a quick shave."

"I can't tell him, Lisa," whispering again, though the door was closed. "That's your job. You have to do it."

Clutching his arm, pinching his skin through the cloth of his sleeve. "No, please. Just give him the details, okay? I can speak to him later, when I feel better. He needs to know now."

"You've kept it from him for years," yanking his arm back, rubbing with his fingers were I'd pinched. "Why the urgency now?"

"I'm too sick to tell him myself." I slid under the covers, pulling a pillow down with me for comfort, "Please … just do it?"

Tom didn't respond and I must have fallen asleep. When next I opened my eyes I was alone in the room. Before dropping off again, I got out of bed and walked towards the table. I picked up the birth certificate and turned it over a few times, like watching a familiar movie you hope this time will end happily. With every turn it was the same, my name and hers, proof of my youthful, parental betrayal. I put it down again. Frank had seen it, a random number. I had watched it detonate in his head, a fraction of a fraction of a fragmented whole.

I dropped back onto the bed and slid into a deep and feverish sleep, my only way out into safety.

When I woke in the morning my mind was much clearer. I was fragile but intact, bruised but not broken. Frank was lying awake beside me.

"Why didn't you tell me?"

"How could I, after all these years?"

"That's my point!" Frank pushed back the covers and walked across the short expanse of the room to fetch the document. I must have wanted him to see it, why otherwise leave it there for him to find? He brought it back with him to the bed, placing it flat out on the covers between us.

"Angeline?"

"A good idea at the time." A perfect name, or a young woman's idea of a perfect name. As if it would protect her. Angeline: ethereal, beyond reach. I shut my eyes against the merging images of Dorothy and Professor Plankton, a complete corruption of what I had imagined for my daughter. Why else had I given her up, except for a better life? Angeline.

Pressed the flat of my hand against my forehead, testing for pain. This morning was my mother's funeral, brought forward a day once we knew Frank was coming. What else could we do in this town, so much empty space and reduced to hotel living?

"I will tell you everything, or at least what I remember. Let me get through today first." Another postponement.

Frank picked up the certificate and dropped it on the floor beside the bed. He sighed, a note of despair before reaching out for me, and I let him. He studied the breadth of my wounded arm and touched my forehead where the bruise was now visible. I rose up to meet him, the least I could do, and I was swept away with him, grateful for his persistence and the shelter he offered. He was my last refuge, and he only wanted answers—to know me, to know his wife—and in the passion of a sorrowful morning, I could at least provide him with this one.

A few hours later and we were at the funeral, the sun beating down like punishment. We kept her obituary out of the paper, limiting attendance at the funeral to a few old friends Tom notified personally, and a nurse from the hospital. Dressed in my black mourning suit, I shivered in the ambient temperature of the funeral home. I regretted my high heels. Intending to stand tall, instead I struggled for balance, holding onto the sleeve of my husband's suit jacket throughout the short ceremony. I watched as my mother's casket travelled along the track and through the curtain into the furnace where she was reduced to ash. All that was left of her was a handful of carbon poured into a pot. Tom wanted to take the ashes home, I presumed to spread beneath the pine trees out back.

Outside the funeral home, despite the heat, I continued to tremble at the recurring images of Dorothy, Angeline as she was now, and Professor Plankton. With every eruption of the nightmare I focused harder on my mother, her death an unlikely anchor in such an unstable universe.

Afterwards we gathered at the hotel in a small room off the main dining room. Bemused waitresses, more accustomed to the robust nature of business lunches, passed around miniature ham sandwiches and cake squares the size of Scrabble tiles.

As the mourners left, I shook their hands at the door. Their condolences were gracious, somewhat distant. They were, after all, mostly ancient themselves, standing in line for their own last turn up the aisle. This was not so much grief for my mother as it was for their own lives passing. I wanted to weep, one withered hand after another sliding through mine. I imagined my mother up above, grateful for even this small morsel of attention. Had my mother ever grieved for me, I wondered, far away in London, as I did now for the child I had given away at birth? Unbearable loss managed only through the aegis of anger, as Dorothy was doing with me, as I had done with my own mother.

By lunchtime it was all over and we had checked out of the hotel. Frank and I travelled with Tom back to the mountains. We drove through the dark in our getaway car with my mother's ashes stashed carefully underneath the front seat. I closed my eyes in the back and imagined the truck like a cradle, the sweet hum of a lullaby in the spin of the wheels against the tarmac. The men conversed up front, their voices kept low for my sake. What did they talk about, in one another's company for so many hours across that flat, prairie highway? I imagined sport, and then business, the value of caution in all things.

With every kilometre that rolled behind us I tried to push away my terror, the spectre of Dorothy floating to the surface of Professor Plankton's expression, years of distance and forced absentmindedness instantly diminished by the power of that vision. Bare knees and a whimper, the angry, demanding mouths of babies everywhere. Milk spilling down a plug hole.

What I had seen in Professor Plankton was impossible, the wild fantasy of a woman who had just lost her mother, a perfectly normal response to the pressure of grief, compounded by the opening of the box. I also remembered Keith, his recognition of something in her at the door on her first visit, and his warning that she had been seen at the end of my road. How long had she been stalking me from a distance before turning up in my office? How long had she known? Despite her best efforts, I had not recognised her.

I shut my eyes and listened to the rumble of the highway, a lullaby of safety and distance.

> *Hush, little baby, now don't say a word,*
> *Mommy's going to buy you a mocking bird …*

I woke occasionally when Tom pulled in for gas, or they stopped to change drivers. I lay where I was, cramped as a foetus, hoping the night would never end.

We arrived long past midnight, Frank shaking me slightly by the shoulder to wake me. There was no light anywhere before Tom opened up the house and turned on the porch light. We each took a suitcase and Tom carefully lifted out the box containing my mother's urn and carried it inside the house. I pointed to the mantelpiece, a huge structure at the end of his oversized living room. He grimaced and shook his head. The box in his hands, he headed down the hall towards his bed-room. There had been far too many boxes lately; this one was even about the same size as the other. Perhaps he thought it wouldn't be safe with me.

Frank and I settled into Tom's guest room. Without any-one to overlook us, we left the curtains open. I lay in bed and watched the rocky peaks outlined against the glow of a waning moon. In the morning they loomed, giant shadows before the sun was able to stretch over them high enough to find a way through.

During the next few days, and for the first time in years, I did not take my computer out of its bag. Gradually it dawned on me that writing was impossible. I was far too restless for that. If Frank and Tom believed I had finally crossed over my personal river Styx with the telling of the tale, I knew I was still only hovering on the bank. There were more difficult days ahead. I was quiet and fearful, the thrum of anxiety percolating away in me with every breath, even here in the mountains where I was often most comfortable, a world away from everything.

Tom and Frank treated me like an invalid, plumping up cushions on couches (Tom) and offering me endless cups of tea (Frank). Occasionally I barked, "Stop it!" in a voice that harked back to the old Lisa, before she opened the box. Both men looked relieved, grateful for the familiar bite of my tongue. At least they knew where they stood. For increasingly longer periods we all appeared to relax, the secrets of our private anxieties kept behind the walls of our good behaviour. We hardly mentioned my mother except to reference her recent exit. This meant that we also avoided speaking directly, among the three of us, about my lost child.

Alone with Frank I told him the story, in dribs and drabs, mostly during our daily walk. Frank was usually quiet afterwards, sometimes holding my hand in both of his. Did he think he might lose me? If I woke in the night I knew he was often lying awake, too, one hand reaching out to touch me, my hip or my waist, sometimes clutching at an empty breast. I lay still, not wanting to disturb him. I slept better, it's true, knowing he was there.

Occasionally I considered my intended book, and the regular newspaper column I had hoped to resume. They were sand running through my fingers, lost possibilities and irretrievable, but still I clung to the idea of them. I imagined my old life, solid and purposeful. Professional. In an effort to rouse up hope, I dreamed up academic titles. *Working through personal abandonment: parallel process in the therapy room*, and another on the value of sibling relationships in the therapist's life: *Contained rivalry and support: positive aspects of guilt and envy*. But mostly I was riven with terror and rage, unable to focus.

I remembered colleagues I had known, or heard of, cracking under the pressure of life and work. They were overburdened by the horror of their patients' life stories, the grief and disturbance that so many clients evoked. Some therapists left the profession, or focused on teaching. In one case a male colleague, at the pinnacle of his public success, had collapsed into psychotic terror, hospitalised in the end. I had inherited a few of his former patients, distraught at the loss of their beloved therapist "parent" under such horrible circumstances.

I kept the meeting with Professor Plankton a secret from both Frank and Tom. How else was I to hold on to sanity except to mimic indifference? Dissociation was perhaps my only hope. Each time I thought of our encounter I was reminded again of what further I did not want to confront. Plankton's face rose up from foetus to old man and back again to a child, demanding all the attention I refused to give it.

What could I do anyhow, up here in the mountains, breathtakingly beautiful and a million miles away from the grubbiness of south London and the imperious demands of a client who might actually know my secret? At times I looked over my shoulder, as if she might have followed me here, saw glimpses of her between the trees, shadows of a child leaping from one branch to the next.

At the end of two weeks we packed up to return home. Tom dropped us at the airport, kissing me goodbye on both cheeks before squashing me into a bear hug. My ribs threatened to snap into twigs; he let go only when Frank gently tugged me away.

Inside the terminal, among the images of cowboys and dinosaurs, the swirling crowds of travellers, I clung to Frank. I did not want to go home. Every step towards departure was a move closer to the nightmare. At least we were flying business class, Tom having bumped us up without telling us in advance, his parting gift, to make the ride easier. An overnight flight, a restless sleep and a six o'clock landing, not even a movie

229

to distract me. After just under a month away, we were back home by eight-thirty.

How many times have I walked back into my own home? There is something entirely different about returning after a long trip. The light seems to shine in through the windows a little brighter and the shape and shade of the rooms appear more pleasing than they did before you left, as if you're seeing the place for the first time.

This time, though, there was no comfort in the familiarity of my fortress. The narrowness of the hallway, the stacking of one floor on top of another; the restricted space that had previously meant containment now signified confinement. There was no way out.

I walked into my study, my usual refuge, bulky with articles and journals I did not want to read and a litter of papers and notes that would scan as hollow as I felt. There was nothing for me here.

Frank moved around the kitchen, making us tea. His shoulders were a little bent and the skin below his eyes folded into blue, shadowy pockets. I watched him move from the sink to the cupboard to fetch the cups, a pattern I had witnessed him execute the length and breadth of our marriage. The chime of porcelain and the clink of a spoon as he dropped two measures of tea into the pot and poured in the water. He placed a cup in front of me. Of course it was good, better than all the tea in the world.

"Frank?"

"Mmm," he took a sip. By nature a home bird, three weeks in Canada had left him parched.

"Thank you." I dug out a tissue and gave my nose a honk.

"Maybe we need to grab a nap, eh?" Frank is not beyond a little deflection himself. How many months since we had laughed together. Even in the mountains, the mood between us as heavy as the surrounding granite. Between death and revelation, Frank believed he knew the whole story. One more lie, one more economy with the truth, how could I possibly tell him? Caught between the hard grate of confidentiality and the heat of my determination to get through this intact, I was trapped into silence. I could only wait, but for what? Every nerve on edge, I dreaded resuming work, Tuesday morning particularly.

Frank watched me, even in his jet-lagged state not beyond careful scrutiny of his incalculable wife. I tried to smile, but it fell lopsided into the pool between us. I stood up, pushing past the table and moving towards the stairs up to the bedroom. I was afraid I would break under too much careful examination.

"I'll see you up there."

Halfway up the steps and already out of view, the sound of cups being cleared, a counter tidied up. Frank was doing his best.

TWENTY-ONE

I woke with a nosebleed, leaking a trail like a murder victim before noticing in the bathroom mirror that blood was smeared all down the bottom half of my face. I shouted out in horror. This was to be my first morning back at the office.

Frank bounded up the stairs. He flipped the toilet seat closed and pushed me by the shoulders to sit down, "Hold your head back!" Pulling at a wad of toilet paper he rolled two little bits of paper into nose plugs and pressed them gently up both my nostrils before wiping my face clean with a damp, warm cloth. Finished, he crouched down, knees bent and balanced on the tip of his toes. Three days back in London, he should have been over his jet lag. Instead, he was exhausted. The past few weeks in the mountains had given him nothing but worry.

The plugs in my nose were already sodden. Frank rolled up a few more and gently exchanged old for new. Funny how Frank's tenderness had never quite cut through before. I had always taken it for granted, hunted it out but not valued it, as if I was entitled. I demanded his care and attention without ever appreciating that it was a choice he made every single time he extended it. Was this my personal road to Damascus? On that toilet seat, boiling with blood spilling into everything, I finally understood something fundamental. For once I didn't retch, but I wanted to, and I wanted my old complacency back, my old energy and the familiar, implacable belief that I could cope with anything.

I must have looked an ugly old toad, plugs up my nose and breathing through my mouth. I hadn't even brushed my hair yet that morning, or cleaned my teeth. The front of my dressing gown was splattered with drops of blood.

"Lisa, what the hell is going on now?"

Pressure mounting by the second, I couldn't hold back any longer. If I didn't say something immediately, it would surely kill the marriage. Blood leaking everywhere and nowhere left to hide. "My client ... The one you said worried me?" One final deep breath and I plunged in, "She's Angeline."

"What are you talking about?" eyes narrowed, shoulders straight, he stood up again. I was forced to look up to face him.

"My baby ..." swallowing blood, gulping it back. "... Angeline." I could breathe only through my mouth, in and out, in and out. "I think ... oh god ... she's my daughter." Breath and blood caught in my throat, gurgling, "I can't be certain ... yes, I can ... she is ... I know she is."

"What are you telling me?" His body stiff, every sinew and muscle taut.

"Don't shout, please, it's just what I said. It's ... it's her."

"That's impossible." Quiet now, he thought I was crazy. I could see it in the quiver of his right eye, and the way he held his hands behind him flat against the wall, looking for purchase. Beyond a fraction of a fraction, nothing was adding up.

"Frank, I know it's her, or I think I do." Thumb and first finger pressing against my nose, holding back the tide.

"How? How can you possibly know?"

"I just ... do ... Please! Can't you trust me?"

"Of course I bloody can't!" Rearing up, one hand pounding down with a thud.

234

"I know … It sounds so crazy … how could I tell you?" Frantic now, defenceless. "She looks like her father!" Gurgling still and shrieking, desperate to convince him.

"You remember him that well?" Frank didn't often use sarcasm.

"I saw him, I saw the father." Pausing for breath. "A ghost … a mirror image. Horrible!"

Frank stared and took a deep breath, "When? When did you see him?" His voice dropped an octave. "When did you see the father?"

"Before I phoned you from Canada. I couldn't call you until I'd seen him. Please understand, and then it was just terrible. I knew—I knew then—I could see her in him, like dredging someone up from the bottom. It was her, in him. I could see it." Frank didn't even blink.

"That's why she's been coming to me—*she wants me to recognise her*!"

"You're imagining this."

"No … Keith, he saw it, without even knowing. Maybe she looks like me? Remember? He even said something when we met at the park … just after I started seeing her."

"He said nothing of the kind."

"You just don't want it to be true!" Blubbering and shouting at the same time.

"Of course I don't! That's beside the point—what Keith actually said was that she was "interesting". I remember. That's all he said."

"It was months ago. Why would you remember?"

"Because that was the beginning, when you started acting peculiar. I'm not likely to forget that, am I?"

"But …"

"There's no 'but' about it. That's all he said!"

We were both so angry, Frank now staring at the floor as if he could work it out, somehow, down there on the blank surface of the bathroom tile. With his head bent so low I could see the droop of his jowls, the loose skin around his chin. He had lost weight and it was as if his exterior coating had lost its glue, the fine and solid surface of him slipping away. Ragged, peeling. Powerless.

He looked up from his calculations. "First of all, if this is true, which I doubt, she has a purpose which also means she could be dangerous. Secondly, if it's a coincidence, it's a million to one, very unlikely. The third, and even more frightening possibility is that this is simply a product of your febrile imagination."

I ignored most of what he said, "Why would she hurt me? Is that what you're suggesting?" The flash of bare knees and her laughter, her cruel delight at my expense. A hand across my forehead to brush the pictures away.

Frank grabbed my shoulder, a desperate effort to make me understand. "I'm saying I don't think it's true, but if it is, she could be dangerous."

"What if she just wants me to *know*?"

"Then why didn't she just *say*, instead of stalking you like this?"

I saw Dorothy then, Keith's vision of her standing at the end of our road staring up at the house and leaning into the wind, pointed like an arrow towards our front door. Wanting in. I said nothing. Somewhere down the road a door slammed. A child shrieked.

"Have you spoken to Max about this?"

My nose was dry now. I yanked the plugs out and flicked them into the bin. I was safe. "No, not yet."

"You need to speak to Max. Aren't there ethical issues here, at least?"

"Ethical issues?" My turn to be astonished. "Ethical issues!"

"Well, aren't there?"

"Of course there are. There are all kinds of 'issues' here. For heaven's sake!"

"You need a lawyer."

"A lawyer?"

"The police even. If this is true, you don't know what could happen. I'm asking you again, why didn't she play it straight? Go through the usual channels of tracking down her birth parents? Thousands of adopted kids do it every year, why the subterfuge?"

He was overreacting. What could either the police or a lawyer do? "She *is* a lawyer!" I shouted, as if that changed anything at all. "Anyway, I've never put my name down. I've never *wanted* to find her! Maybe that's why she's so angry." I stood up, "I'm sick every time I think about it."

Frank looked down again, calculating. "You're getting carried away, letting your imagination run wild. Your mother has just died, you've been looking at papers reminding you of events you've avoided thinking about for years. You *want* this client to be your daughter!"

"Don't be ridiculous!"

"Have you been listening to yourself, Lisa? For Christ's sake, you've been acting oddly for weeks and weeks, months even, and it's just been getting worse." His whole body lifted, still searching for purchase. "When is your appointment with Joanna?"

"Tomorrow." I shuddered, "Good timing, eh?"

"Not soon enough!"

I sat down on the edge of the bed, facing Frank through the bathroom door where he was now slumped on the edge of the tub. He looked so haggard, shaking with rage and confusion, wracking his brain to make sense of it all. "Is there anything else I need to know?"

"I'm sure there is … I just don't know what." Dorothy tapping her thigh, watching. Watching me. Tipping her body towards the house, daring me to see her. How could I explain this to Frank: fearful of seeing her again, terrified of never seeing her again.

"Call Max. Arrange to see him today." It was an order. He lifted himself up and walked over to sit beside me on the bed, every step an effort. He raised my right hand and held it between both of his, determination overriding what was once a mark of affection. I knew how cold mine was from the heat radiating through his, anger like a steam engine. I wanted to pull away, instead I sat very still. I had more to gain from this moment than I did to lose. I couldn't risk never seeing Dorothy again. My daughter. Or maybe I was just so frail now I had nothing left with which to fight. I had reached the end.

Frank continued, his voice strained from exercising so much restraint. "You need help with this. I'm not a therapist and even I know this is a crisis. If you carry this all on your own, you'll end up on your own. You need me, you need Max, and you certainly need Joanna. You can't continue as you have done recently. You'll go crazy." He breathed in and stiffened his shoulders, as if preparing to lift a huge set of weights, "In fact, I think you're a little crazy already."

I walked towards my office. After the nosebleed I was drained, bloodless. Frank had insisted I put off returning to work, but I was determined, creeping out of the flat without saying good-bye. I didn't want to risk another scene.

The first thing I noticed was the new rubber at the bottom of the stairs. Keith had tidied up. All the way up the steps there was new flooring and the hallway had also been painted, a non-committal cream.

My room was stuffy. I opened the window to let in some air and plumped up the cushions on the couch. I was brisk, try-ing to warm up to the old me, good at my job, prepared and expectant, professional. I placed the box of tissues neatly on the table beside the couch and adjusted my clock so it would be facing me just so. I gave my wing chair a test ride, making believe it was still a good fit. All this energy warding off the inevitable. When the doorbell rang I walked down the stairs with a purposeful tread holding firmly onto the banister, shiny now after its summer polish.

Sam's smile dropped in confusion when I opened the door. He peered over the threshold, as if checking it was really me. He hesitated before crossing over. I was conscious of the looseness of my skirt around my waist, the sting in my eyes where sleep deprivation was sucking me dry. Yet I didn't waver. I opened the door wider and raised a hand towards the stairs for him to lead the way.

"Did you have a good break?" taking his seat on the couch. He stared at my obvious confusion. I didn't know how to answer him. "Your break, did you have a good one?"

I looked away, out the window over the roofs of south London. There was the honk and roar of Lavender Hill traffic. In the distance another mother shouted. Was she warning her child, or admonishing her? For a moment I did not know where I was.

I turned back towards Sam and blinked. He was a blur, soft focused and very far away. Whom had I expected to be sitting there? Dorothy? He leaned forward, elbows on his knees. Viewing me through the uncluttered lens of his sobriety, I knew immediately that I was found wanting.

"Are you all right?" Sam was frightened. Never having been truly cared for, he did not know how to extend it towards me. This was unprecedented and he did not know what to do. Nor did I.

"I'm not feeling well." Flush with heat and shivering, too, gathering words into formation impossible. A door opened and closed downstairs and for a moment I heard Keith's sonic drill. For once I was not irritated so much as comforted. I was not alone in the building. I was breathless, dizzy even while sitting down. I dropped my head forward, hoping for stability.

Sam stood up, leaving the room in a hurry. His steps drummed hard on the stairs. A few moments later he bounded back up again, a glass of water in his hand and pushed it towards me.

"Here, maybe this'll help."

My throat hurt when I swallowed.

"Is there anyone you want me to ring?" He bent forward, grey eyes narrowing with concern.

"No, thank you, Sam. Thank you for the water. I'm just going to sit for a moment." Breathing more easily now, heartbeat slowing down. Was this how a mother looked at her child in her old age, when the roles were reversed, or during times of distress? Did her heart break at what she was asking of him? This was not the correct order of things: Sam was my patient. As was Dorothy. Even in my agitated state, I understood that Sam was reaching the end of his time with me. What of my other patients? Lucy, for instance, in her perpetual adolescence? She still needed nurturing, as did so many others. They should not have to look after me, any more than Sam.

He shuffled his feet, unsure what to do next.

I tried to stand, but fell back onto the chair. "Sorry, Sam … Can you let yourself out? I'll ring you soon … to rearrange."

"Of course. Are you sure?" his body poised, resisting the urge to flee.

"There's someone downstairs …" a form of absolution. "They'll help if I need anything."

Never having touched one another before, he patted my shoulder as he left, a child extending comfort to his therapeutic mother. For a moment I thought he might bend to kiss me and I lifted my cheek a little just in case. Instead there was only the whoosh of a slight breeze as he sailed out the door away from me.

For a long while I sat frozen in my chair. Gradually thawing out, my legs and feet tingled and my hands were dead white from gripping so tightly. My mind cleared, opening up into a sudden expanse of clarity. I rang Max first of all to arrange an emergency appointment, then contacted all my remaining patients for the day, apologising that I could not see them. I was relieved when it was an answer machine, though anxious that they would not get the message. I hoped no one would arrive to an empty office. I stopped by Keith's surgery just in case.

"I'm sorry about your mother," he came out into his reception area. I didn't often see him in his dentist greens, a facemask hanging around his neck. At least he wasn't wearing rubber gloves. I explained that I wasn't feeling well, that I had left messages for everyone but in case someone showed up …

"I'll explain, don't worry." His pupils were diamond hard, as if peering at me through one of his dental magnifiers. "You don't look very well, either. Can I get you something?"

I edged out the door, before he could drill any further, "Thank you, Keith," more grateful than he knew.

I took a series of buses to get to Max. I needed to stay above ground, at least for today. I reached Islington a little early, stopped in a cafe to kill time, ordered a coffee to justify my use of a table. I couldn't read, not even a newspaper. *Stop all the clocks*, runs the Auden poem. My life! I wanted to shout. I want my life back! I had not even been able to negotiate a single hour with a patient, and one with whom I believed I worked well and about whom I had intended to write. How then could I possibly meet Dorothy? I wanted to see her, dreaded it too. I held my cup with both hands, only to warm them.

During moments of anxiety as a child I had imagined skating to sooth myself. Gliding over the ice, spiralling like a dancer on the points of my skate before finessing an impossible triple axel. A lone star, shooting off light from my blades as they cut deep through the ice. My arms in the air, my body in motion, smooth, smooth, spinning safe and free, nothing on earth to hold me to the cold, hard ground.

Well, I was on the cold, hard ground now.

241

I left the cafe and walked towards Max's house. Reluctant, yet determined, I pinched the top of my nose before ringing his doorbell. I did not want another nosebleed. The buzzer sounded and I pushed my way through the door and trudged up the stairs to his therapy room, relieved to hear the silence in the house. The twins were at school, his wife at work. Max and I could sort this out alone.

Instead of waiting for me to sit down, he rose when I came in the door. "Lisa?"

"Weren't you expecting me?"

"Yes … But you look … well … you don't look very well." He gestured towards the couch. "Your skirt, Lisa, you need to fix it at the back," a note of anxiety in his voice.

My skirt was so loose it had twisted round almost entirely and the hemline somehow caught up in the waistband, exposing much of the back of my legs, though not my bottom, thank goodness. I tugged at a bit of material and the skirt broke free, dropping down again into shape. "There, fixed."

Max hadn't yet sat down. In fact, he had taken another step away from his seat towards the door.

"Why are you leaving? I need to speak to you?"

He was now next to the door. Instead of exiting he chose only to close it. Eyes fixed on mine, headlights on high beam, he walked back to his seat. "All right. Go ahead."

"You have to hear me out, Max. Don't look at me like that! I'm trying to tell you something. Something important."

He said nothing though he did take up his notebook, which I took to be a good sign. It didn't cross my mind, then, that he might need to register this session for other reasons. A wave of nausea and I crossed my arms over my stomach, "I've always tried to do the right thing."

Max nodded.

"You know that, don't you? I've always tried."

"I'm your supervisor, Lisa. This isn't Judgement Day."

"It may be for me. Something's happened and I need to tell you about it. I need your help." I did not want to cry. I did not want to scream. A popular tenet of therapy is that the truth will set you free. Or is that just psychobabble nonsense? Of course it is. The truth often causes terrible pain and disruption. Insight can only take you so far, the rest you have to do yourself. I was trapped, and the only way out into safety was to speak to Max, to hatch a plan and put out the fire.

"My client, Dorothy …" Max turned his head slightly to the left, as if to hear me better. Was I speaking too softly now? "She is … I think she is … my daughter."

Max's eyes widened and he floated for a moment above his seat. The whole room was cast adrift and the beautiful bird in the picture above his head lifted its wings and took flight out the window and was gone. I held on for dear life, bent at the waist as I had seen so many of my patients do over the years, terrified at what might be released.

"… How? How do you know this?"

"You don't believe me either?"

"No. Or, I don't believe she's your daughter, though you may believe she is."

"Do you think I'm crazy?"

"I don't know. I may know better after I've heard you out."

What I had told Frank in bits and pieces, I now had to reconfigure for Max. I could hardly find the words, let alone establish a comprehensible narrative. "I had a baby … a long time ago." Max nodded, gesturing with his pen that I continue. "I gave her up for adoption immediately afterwards. I never saw her again." Rummaging in my pocket I dug out an old tissue and wiped my nose. My forehead, too, was damp and I saw Max's nose twitch as if I was emanating some terrible smell. I brushed a hand over my hair and it was mangled, caught up in a storm. I broke from my story for a moment to try and smooth it out, caught in my fingers like knotted wire. At least my nose wasn't bleeding.

243

"The details match," I said at last, "My daughter and Dorothy … they were both born in Ottawa. It was a private adoption. My mother arranged it. Dorothy told me she was adopted, a private adoption, too. She's known all along … don't you see? That's why she's come to me. Because the adoption was private, maybe she had access to my name? Maybe she found some papers. Kids dig around in their parents' things all the time. Who knows what she found. I don't bloody know! Max, I know she's my daughter!"

"You've not mentioned this before." His voice was calm but he was enraged, a red tide rising above his shirt collar. I shuffled back a few inches on the couch.

"I didn't know. I knew something was wrong … just … not what it was." A painful swallow before continuing, "I haven't been holding anything back. I really didn't know." Why couldn't he just believe me?

"It doesn't matter whether she's your daughter or not." He spoke at last.

"What do you mean?"

"You believe she is. And either she really is your daughter, or within your response to her you've tipped over the line."

"What are you telling me?" Was I shrieking?

Max's eyes hardened, on the edge of breaking loose himself. "Do I have to remind you that I thought you needed help months ago? You've been very erratic recently, obsessed with this patient for months. At the very least, you need a break. This needs to stop. Stop now."

"You mean … stop seeing patients?"

"I do."

"Not just Dorothy?"

"You need to end carefully with Dorothy. As you do with all your other patients."

"For how long?"

Max shook his head. "I don't know."

"Can I tell them I'll be back at least?" He wanted me to give my patients away, give Dorothy away! Someone was howling. I looked around the room to be sure we were alone. Max was in his chair, so far away and small. I reached out a hand to find him, but there was only air, and the sound of howling. The bird above his head now completely vanished.

Max stood up. I thought he might come to me. Instead he walked with measured steps, as if not to frighten me, towards the corner where there was a telephone. I had never heard it ring, not once in all the years I had been seeing Max. He used it only in emergencies, he had once told me, the ringer switched off. After riffling through some notes, he picked up the receiver and dialled a number.

Martha was the first person I saw when Frank walked me into our kitchen a few hours later after leaving Max. Wheels were now clearly in motion. I had feared men in white coats, but it was Frank Max had called. The three of us in his office, both men had insisted that I close down immediately.

"Is there someone you can ask to help you ring your clients? A colleague?"

Martha. I didn't have her number, though Keith would have it. She might even be in her office. Frank had tracked her down. Now in our kitchen and huge with child, I thought she might roll off her seat and onto the floor.

"Two months still to go," empathic as ever, reading my mind. Her expression, though, was fixed into horror, as if seeing a ghost.

"Rough day," I pushed a lock of matted hair behind my ear and sat down.

Frank busied himself making tea, "Martha is going to ring all your clients," keeping his voice low. "You need to give her the first names, Max says, and all the phone numbers."

I shook my head. "No!"

245

Martha leaned across the table as far as her stomach would let her, reaching out for my hand. I plucked it away. She was a giant hen clucking over my discomfort and I was not about to let her have the satisfaction. I would not give my patients away, not to her, not to anybody.

"Lisa, you haven't got a choice," her voice, too soft for comfort.

"Listen to her." Frank's tone was much sterner. "You haven't got a choice. Do you hear?"

"I'm not giving up my practice!"

"Shh—just for the time being. Not for good." Was Martha trying to reassure me? Who would believe anyone who sounded so sweet?

"There's one person, at least, I need to see." Why was I having to beg to see my own patients?

"No, you don't." Frank put cups of tea in front of both Martha and me and then sat down himself. "Max was very clear. You need to close down for at least a little while." They were both trying to soften the blow, unlike Max who had spoken in terms of an unlimited time away.

"I want to tell them … please."

Frank and Martha looked at one another.

"I'm sorry, Lisa," And she did look sorry. Sorry *for* me. I was withered, already gone.

"This is my profession!" I stood up. All those articles, all those talks. So many clients over the years. This was me! I had cracked it and now they were looking at me as if I was cracking up. I stomped into my office, turned on the computer and printed up a list of patients Martha would need to call, but not before deleting a single name. And Sam's, of course, he already knew there would be some kind of break. I would ring him later.

I handed Martha two sheets of A4, names and addresses in two tidy columns. Frank stood to the side of the table like God the Father, taking account. I avoided his eyes, looking directly at Martha. He knew I could not show him the list for reasons of confidentiality. It would have been useless anyway as I'd never mentioned her adult name. He wouldn't know whom to look for.

Martha, though, didn't blanch, simply folded it up and tucked it into her bag. A kiss on both cheeks and she was gone, my precious load packed away in her handbag. Out of my hands, I had no idea whether or not I would ever get it back.

TWENTY-TWO

Not so crazy that I couldn't make a plan. Frank had a prescription filled from the GP and so I slept. When I woke I was calm, slipping out of the room without waking him. The night before I had left my clothes by the washing machine where they wouldn't be noticed, along with a pair of shoes hidden behind a box of detergent. To be on the safe side, I left a note for Frank on the kitchen table telling him only that I was going for an early morning walk. He might be anxious, but he wouldn't suspect. I had given Martha my list.

I let myself into the building quietly, quietly, creeping back into my old life. Maybe my last time here. The drill blessedly silent, I took everything in; the sound of the lock turning, the patch on the stairs, the smooth surface of the banister as I pulled myself up towards the office past Martha's door and the elusive Daniel's. These were already memories too painful and I shoved them aside.

Standing just inside my office, hands behind my back pressed against the door, I looked over what had once given me so much confidence; the couch and the book case, my high winged chair, the desk just behind. Forgetting almost to breathe, I drew a line up through myself, a band of steel to hold me solid. I clung to routine. A morning like any other morning. Not like any other morning.

In the kitchen a cup of coffee, lingering to enjoy the ritual. How many times had I made a cup of coffee before beginning work, how many times? Walking back to my office, I placed the steaming cup on the table beside my computer—opened the machine slowly, pain mingling with pleasure, the poignancy of times past.

Nothing more. I stared at the mostly blank screen knowing I might never write another word, at least not about what I had intended, self-help and vignettes of my clinical work. All the stuffing of my life over recent years, the fabric, now completely tattered, perhaps beyond repair.

When the doorbell rang at seven o'clock sharp I walked down the stairs, measuring every step. There would be no falling over now.

With the morning sun behind her, Dorothy glowed through the glaze of the pebbled glass. She was smiling, dressed in a neat pencil skirt with a white shirt and carrying a tidy black briefcase. Her hair was loose, falling gracefully against her shoulders. My heart pounding, pounding, I followed her up the stairs. Passing by Martha's door an additional pang of anxiety, but she would not be in for another hour at least, by which time this would all be over.

"Never *assume* anything," Dorothy had warned me during our last meeting. Now, I watched her move to the couch and shuffle the box of tissues over a few inches on the table before sitting down. She flattened out her skirt just short of her bare knees, now brown from the summer sun. This was a confident young woman, not the shuddering victim I remembered from our first meeting.

I touched the belt around my waist, making certain nothing had twisted around. I needed to be contained for this meeting, awake and alive. I sat down opposite my patient, smoothing out my own skirt. It fell in a soft fold just over my knees. They were bare, too, on this hot summer morning, though not so brown as hers. I felt the back of my seat bracing and solid, in my peripheral vision wing tips either side of the chair. If I was looking for Professor Plankton, he was not here now. Dorothy was beautiful, ethereal, only her briefcase pinning her down to earth.

My daughter watched me, pushing herself forward a few inches, hands on her knees. "I nearly didn't come today."

"Why did you?"

Tipping her head this way and that, "I've been fine while you've been away. Great, in fact."

"No need for therapy, then, is that what you're saying?"

"I'm leaving in a few weeks anyway. New York, remember?"

Chest on fire, throat seared in pain, "I remember." Could she hear the rasp in my voice? The sudden brackishness?

Sitting back in her seat: "You know … you don't look so well …" Curiosity, overladen with fear, short sharp tap to the side of her thigh. I touch my hair, smooth now as I had taken such care this morning. Remind myself—stay awake, stay alive. "You're … afraid I will leave you?"

"No!"

"You sound pretty insistent." Pushing through the fire …

"I'm leaving *you*. I just said."

"I know. That's important, isn't it? To do the leaving."

"What do you mean?" her voice cracking at the edges, high pitched, wavering—and me, resisting the urge to clutch at my chest.

"You've been left. Twice. Your biological mother and then your … adoptive mother. Both gone. Better to leave yourself, now, than … than wait for me to leave?"

"You don't know what you're talking about?"

"Yes, I do!" Electricity passing between us, burning the house down.

251

Fists thumping her thighs now, three times with both hands, pulling herself back. I wait, pressing down in my wing tipped chair. No time to take flight. My job now to hold on to her distress, as a mother would, absorbing her child's anguish, providing comfort and safety. But there is no safety here, not for either of us.

"This is my last appointment?" a wailing child.

I can hardly speak, my voice caught on a hook in my throat. I push through regardless—push and push. "You need to leave. You need to leave *me*," words ripped ragged into the room.

"You want me to go?"

"No, Dorothy, the very opposite."

"Then why?!"

"New York beckons." My smile lopsided, out of kilter.

"That's not it. I don't go for weeks, for three weeks. Why stop now?"

"A few minutes ago you were all for leaving."

"But ... that was my choice. This seems to be yours."

"It's got twisted around, hasn't it? You wanted to do the leaving but now, somehow, it's me leaving you."

Dorothy's eyes flashing, looking for a way out. "I don't want to go. But I do. Both."

My daughter. My child. My patient. "How did you know?" I blurt at last, for my benefit rather than hers, too late to catch myself. Too late.

"Papers ... family papers. My father admitted it all: I'm a lawyer, I followed the trail, and here you were," voice dropping, eyes glazing over.

I lean forward, a hand stretched out, catching myself just short of touching her small, bare knees. Her eyes widen, shimmering in terror. I pull back quickly, too quickly knocking my elbow hard against the chair, shaking the wings. Another moment to steady myself.

"I didn't think this would mean so much," her voice quiet now. "I thought I could just come and then go again. It wouldn't make any difference, really. I would just give it a try … to say I did."

"Nothing is really as we expect?"

"I … I just wanted to see who you were. What you were like."

"Not this way. It's not the way. Not as a patient."

"I didn't know." The clock ticking, only a few minutes left. Time passing, passing. Not enough words, so little time to say it. Head in her hands now, "I'm sorry. I'm sorry I've been so horrible."

"Would there have been any other way to behave with me? I … I was pretty blind most of the time."

"All of the time, really." Looking up, one final tap to her thigh, "I only wanted you to understand!"

"We need to end now, Dorothy. Our time's up," legs buckling as I try to stand. "Time's up," falling back onto the seat.

She seemed not to notice, walked straight to the door and opened it. I took a deep breath, tried again to stand. Legs shaking but upright, followed her down the stairs. At the door she turned and leaned forward, kissing me suddenly. I held her, inhaling her hair, her skin, feeling the softness of her skin. Then I let her go. From the open doorway I watch as she makes her way down the street into a life without me. Again.

Frank arrived a few minutes later, chasing me down. I was still at the door, eyes cast over the empty distance.

I rang the doorbell. Joanna's tread, still familiar after all this time as she walked down the hall to meet me. I signalled to Frank waiting in the car, ensuring that I attend this appointment. He needn't have worried. I was in the corner now with nowhere else to turn. The door opened. She was so small, her head reaching only a little above my shoulder. I followed her back down the hall. She had moved since we'd last worked together and this was new territory. Her office was a little wider and deeper than the last one, but here I had a view of the garden, some of it parched after such a hot spell.

I sat down and Joanna took the seat opposite. Not a winged chair like mine, instead a modest wooden frame with an extra cushion to secure her back. She was older now, her hair still looped into a knot at the back of her neck, grey flecks here and there and deeper lines around her eyes where age had carved its way through. She folded her hands neatly into her lap, indicating that I should begin.

"… I have something to tell you."

"Good. I've been waiting for you."

ACKNOWLEDGEMENTS

Like any author, I could not have written this book without the support of others. I would like to thank particularly: Donald Freed, Patricia Rae Freed, Tilly Lavenas, Victoria Jones, Richard Bath, Rosie and Tristan Allsop, Jennifer Adams, Laura Jenner, and Sofie Bager-Charleson. The Loo Loos team cheered me on for more than ten years, and I also owe a special thanks to my fellow writers who were with me when I first got on that bus six years ago in Italy and have waited so patiently for me to finally disembark. A special thank you to Sophia Adams and Alex Adams, both of whom gave me the gift of distraction when I most needed it, and my brother, Paul Adams, who is so often a source of deep inspiration. Finally, my husband, Gordon Stobart, who, while being persecuted relentlessly to give feedback, consistently practised what he preaches. I am deeply grateful.

ABOUT THE AUTHOR

Marie Adams is a writer and practising psychotherapist. She is on the staff at the Metanoia Institute on the Professional Doctorate programme, and is a visiting lecturer at a number of other training institutes, including the Institute For Arts in Therapy and Education. Marie has had a long association with the BBC: for many years she was a producer on the Today Programme and, more recently, a consulting psychotherapist to news and documentary staff. Her book, *The Myth of the Untroubled Therapist*, is now a standard text on counselling and psychotherapy training courses throughout the country.